RAGE OF THE ASSASSIN

EDWARD MARSTON

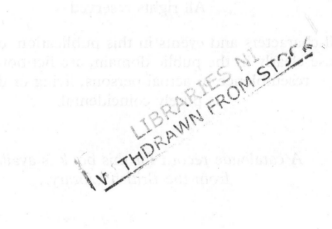

ISIS
LARGE PRINT

First published in Great Britain 2020
by
Allison & Busby Limited

First Isis Edition
published 2021
by arrangement with
Allison & Busby Limited

A catalogue record for this book is available
from the British Library.

ISBN 978–1–78541–923–2

Published by
Ulverscroft Limited
Anstey, Leicestershire

Set by Words & Graphics Ltd.
Anstey, Leicestershire
Printed and bound in Great Britain by
TJ Books Ltd., Padstow, Cornwall

This book is printed on acid-free paper

CHAPTER ONE

1817

When he set out that evening, Paul Skillen had no warning of the tragedy that lay ahead. He assumed that he'd simply be performing his usual task of escorting Hannah Granville safely through an overexcited mob of admirers. It was one of the penalties that fame had inflicted upon her. Hannah was playing the part of Lady Macbeth in the production of Shakespeare's play at the Covent Garden Theatre. Night after night, a huge audience watched in wonder. Dazzled by her beauty, roused by her passion, shocked by her murderous ambition yet saddened by her descent into madness, they were completely at her mercy. Paul knew that it would be the same again that evening. When she appeared at the curtain call, a thunderous ovation would greet her.

As he arrived at the theatre, a crowd was already gathering outside the stage door and jostling for position. Though *Macbeth* was followed by a comical afterpiece, none of the rakes and fops assembled there was interested in staying to watch it. Their priority was to get close enough to the finest actress in London to gloat, ogle, scrutinise and, if at all possible, to touch their goddess. Hannah had learnt to ignore the regular litany of propositions that would come from all sides. When she left the building, she would be holding Paul's arm, relying on his virile appearance to keep the fervent admirers at bay.

On this occasion, however, it was different. Before he could make his way to the stage door and go on to Hannah's dressing room, Paul heard a familiar voice ring out above the hubbub.

"Stand aside, please!"

It was Micah Yeomans, the Bow Street Runner, supported as usual by Alfred Hale. The two Runners had an important assignment that evening.

"Make way for His Majesty!" bellowed Yeomans, using authoritative elbows to create a path for his companion.

Paul was alarmed. Hannah was well able to keep other would-be suitors at arm's length, but she could not dispatch the Prince Regent quite so easily. Flabby, dissipated and waddling along as fast as his gout would permit, he exuded an air of supreme entitlement. He was going to be first.

For once, however, royal prerogative was not respected. Someone yelled aloud as if in great pain, everyone turned in the direction of the sound, then a shot was fired behind them. Uproar ensued. The waiting pack scrambled for safety, cursing as they bumped into each other and bewailing the loss of their vantage points. The Prince Regent was hustled through the stage door by the two Runners. And Paul was left standing beside the lifeless body of a man whose

dreams of meeting Lady Macbeth had died instantly
with him.

CHAPTER
TWO

drems of meeting   had died instantly
with him.

When she heard the sharp knock on her door, Hannah fully expected that Paul had come for her. Accordingly, she nodded to her dresser and Jenny Pye went across the room to turn the key in the lock. Opening the door, she stepped back to allow Paul to enter. But he was not there. Both she and Hannah were shocked to see instead the solid frame of Micah Yeomans filling the space. He whisked off his hat.

"Pardon this intrusion, Miss Granville," he said, "but there is someone who is very anxious to make your acquaintance."

He stood aside to allow the Prince Regent to hobble into the dressing room with a beaming smile on his powdered face. A ludicrous chestnut wig sat on his head. Hannah was taken aback. She had never been quite that close to royalty before and, though she found her visitor verging on the grotesque, part of her was obscurely flattered by his attention. Before she could step out of reach, he grabbed her hand, lifted it to his lips and planted a wet kiss on it.

"I am in thrall to your magnificence, dear lady," he said.

4

"That's a compliment I shall treasure, Your Royal Highness," she replied.

"It will be the first of many, I do assure you."

"I am deeply honoured."

Though she spoke firmly and retained her poise, Hannah was ill at ease. The look in the Prince Regent's eyes was all too easy to interpret. It was the acquisitive glint of a lecher. He was not merely there to congratulate her on an incomparable performance. He was eyeing a prospective prize. Trembling inwardly, she kept asking herself the same question over and over again.

Where on earth was Paul?

In fact, he was kneeling beside the corpse. Having established that the man was indeed dead, Paul was searching his pockets as he looked for something that might indicate his identity. Clearly, he was wealthy, middle-aged and had an eye for fashion. Paul could see that the man had to pay substantial tailor's bills. The rings on each hand were highly expensive and there were other signs of indulgence. Even in death, he had a touch of nobility about him, offset, as it was, by the blood-covered scalp. Feeling inside the coat, Paul's hand closed around a purse. At the moment he brought it out, he realised that he had company.

Yeomans was standing over him in triumph.

"So that's what you've descended to, is it?" he sneered. "You kill him first, then you rob the poor devil."

"Don't be absurd."

"You're under arrest."

"On what charge?" asked Paul, getting to his feet. "I was here, as you well know, for a legitimate purpose. Before I could reach Miss Granville to escort her from the theatre, you came blundering along and ordered everyone to get out of the way. The next moment, someone tried to assassinate the Prince Regent and killed this gentleman by mistake. If you're hired to protect royalty, Micah," he went on, "you ought to do it more efficiently."

"We *were* efficient," declared Yeomans. "While Alfred Hale and I were guarding him, the Prince Regent was never in danger."

"Then why did someone fire a pistol at him?"

"Don't try to talk your way out of this, Skillen. *You* were the man with the weapon and the fellow at your feet was the intended target."

"Then where is the pistol now?" asked Paul, arms at full length. "Search me as thoroughly as you wish. You'll find no weapon. And please bear something in mind. When I'm not solving crimes that the Runners fail to solve, I work at the shooting gallery. With a pistol in my hand, I never miss, yet that's what the assassin did. In the disturbance caused by your arrival, it's my belief that he took his chance. We were first distracted by a shout from a confederate, causing every head to turn away. Aiming for His Royal Highness, the assassin instead shot the man standing closest to him. Look," he said, pointing, "you can see the wound in the back of his head. It should have been in the Prince Regent's skull."

"Nobody would *dare* to shoot at His Royal Highness when they saw me at his side."

"It isn't the first time an attempt has been made on his life. At the start of the year, someone hurled a rock that shattered the window of his coach."

"*This* is the unfortunate target," insisted Yeomans, looking down at the dead body. "There's no doubting that." Turning to Paul, he curled a lip. "But I can see that I was perhaps too hasty in laying his murder at your door."

"I accept your apology, Micah."

"It was not an apology, just a statement of fact." He extended a palm. "I'll take charge now. Give me that purse. It belongs with his other effects."

"At least let me find out who he is."

"That's our responsibility, Skillen. You've no jurisdiction here."

"I'm an interested party."

"Hand over that money. We'll take care of it." Seeing Paul's reluctance, he snapped his fingers. "Be quick about it, man!"

"He's wearing a wedding ring, so the money belongs to his wife. Make sure that the purse reaches her without a penny missing."

Yeomans swelled up with righteous indignation. "I've sworn to uphold the law," he said, beating his chest. "My integrity is beyond question. Due process will be followed, I guarantee. My first task will be to find out who he is."

"Then you'll need this," said Paul, stooping to pick up a hat from the ground. "That bloodstained hole is where the ball passed through as it burrowed into his brain."

"Why the devil should I need his hat?"

"It will tell you where to start your search. Unless I'm mistaken, this hat was made at Bayley's in Jermyn Street. It bears all their hallmarks. They'll know who bought it." He thrust it into the Runner's hands. "Do your job properly for once."

Before Yeomans could protest, Paul let himself into the theatre and went in search of Hannah. He had a strong feeling that he'd be needed.

It was ironic. In the course of her career, Hannah had been a princess, a queen and even an empress on many occasions. She had a natural aptitude for such roles. Faced with genuine royalty, however, she found herself almost speechless. As he gazed covetously at her body, the Prince Regent did something that took her completely by surprise. Extracting a snuff box from his pocket, he held it in his left hand, opened it with the other, then took out a sizeable pinch before introducing it to his nose and inhaling it with all the force he could muster. Hannah winced at the disgusting noise. Putting the box away, her visitor plucked a handkerchief from his sleeve to dust away the residue; He was about to take a step closer to Hannah when he was diverted by the sound of an argument outside the door. Next moment, it was flung open and Paul entered with Alfred Hale vainly trying to hold him back.

"Forgive this untimely interruption, Your Majesty," said Paul, "but you are in grave danger. The assassin is still at liberty and may strike again. Hale will conduct you to a place of safety until the villain is caught. I, meanwhile, will leave the theatre by another exit with Miss Granville. There's no time for delay."

Offering his arm to Hannah, he took her quickly out of the room with Jenny Pye trotting in their wake. From the way that she clung to him, Paul could tell that Hannah was both grateful and relieved. He'd arrived just in time.

"What's this about an assassin?" she asked, worriedly.

"He tried to shoot the Prince Regent."

"How do you know?"

"I was standing only feet away."

"Were you in danger?" she gasped.

"No, I was not."

"Are you sure of that, Paul?"

"I'm not important enough to be killed."

"You're the most important man in the world to me."

"When we're alone together," he said with a grin, "I'll give you every opportunity to tell me why."

CHAPTER
THREE

Work began early at the shooting gallery. Since they lived on the premises, Gully Ackford and Jem Huckvale were available to patrons who wished to have a lesson before they went to work or who simply preferred an appointment not long after dawn. Instruction in shooting, archery, boxing and fencing were all on offer. Now in his forties, Ackford, a retired soldier, was still an expert in all four disciplines and he was a gifted teacher. It was years since he'd taken the diminutive Huckvale under his wing, giving him only menial tasks at first. By dint of hard work, Huckvale had learnt quickly and was now able to take on pupils of his own. Still in his twenties, he was so quick and nimble in a boxing ring that opponents were often unable to land a blow on him.

After teaching someone the rudiments of pugilism that morning, Huckvale adjourned to the room that was both office and storeroom. Ackford was there, enjoying his breakfast.

"Come and join me, lad. You must be famished."

"Thank you, Gully," said the other, taking a seat at the table. "After an hour with Mr Nevin, I need a rest."

Ackford laughed. "If *you're* tired, he must be near exhaustion."

"He could hardly move at the end. Next time he comes here, Mr Nevin is going to pay me to stand still in the ring."

"That would be cheating. Avoiding a punch is as important as landing one."

"I keep telling him that." He looked up as he heard the outer door being unlocked. "That will be Peter, I expect."

"Don't ever get into a boxing ring with *him*. Even *I* would think twice about doing that. And the same goes for Paul."

The door opened and Peter Skillen walked into the room.

"My ears are burning," he said. "Is someone talking about me?"

"I mentioned both you and your brother," admitted Ackford, "but only to praise your skills. Where is Paul, anyway? He should be here by now."

"He sent word that he'd be late today, Gully. There was trouble at the theatre last night. It appears that my brother came close to witnessing the assassination of the Prince Regent, if that's what it really was. Paul is having doubts about it now."

"Why?"

"The letter he sent by hand didn't go into details. All I know is this."

He told them about the incident outside the stage door and how his brother had been able to save

Hannah from the attentions of an unwanted royal admirer.

"Charlotte and I saw the first night of the production and, as usual, Hannah was sublime. Beauty like hers, however, always inflames a certain species of gentleman. In this case, mind you, I'd have thought that her devotees might be diminished in number."

"Why is that?" asked Huckvale.

"Lady Macbeth — the role taken by Hannah — is a monster. When the King of Scotland is a guest at their castle, she urges her husband to kill him in order to be crowned in his place. After the murder, Macbeth is afflicted by guilt and fear, but his wife is cold and callous, ordering him to steady his nerve and handling a pair of bloodstained daggers without batting an eyelid. Would such a woman have an appeal to either of you?"

"She'd terrify me," confessed Huckvale.

"I'd think twice about wanting to meet her in the flesh," said Ackford. "But, then, she's not a real person, is she? Lady Macbeth is just a part in a play."

"Hannah made her seem so *real*," said Peter. "She was spine-chilling, yet dozens still rushed to the stage door for a glimpse of her."

"They were obviously disappointed last night."

"Yes, Gully. It was a case of life imitating art. A king was murdered *inside* the theatre and a Prince Regent was almost assassinated outside it. At least, that's what my brother believed at first. I'll be interested to know what really happened."

"When will he be coming to the gallery?"

12

"That depends on how long it takes him to calm Hannah down. When she's really upset, it can be the work of a whole day. I don't envy Paul. Restoring her equanimity is in the nature of a Herculean labour."

There had been little sleep for either of them. When they'd returned the previous night to the home they shared, Hannah had been too agitated even to think of retiring to bed. It was only when sheer fatigue finally claimed her that Paul was able to carry her upstairs. No sooner had he placed her gently on the bed than she awoke and voiced her anxieties all over again. It was a pattern followed throughout the night. They were now sitting at the breakfast table and taking it in turns to yawn.

Hannah returned to the subject that had been vexing her all night.

"That's it," she announced. "I'll never play Lady Macbeth again."

"But you signed a contract, my love."

"It was the biggest mistake of my career."

"That's patent nonsense, Hannah. Your performance has been rightly hailed. London is at your feet. Audiences that applauded Mrs Siddons in the role no longer even remember her. You have made the role your own."

She tossed her head. "I do that with every part I play."

"Your performance is absolutely peerless."

"Unfortunately, it brought disaster in its wake. It's my own fault. I didn't heed the warnings. Everyone knows that the play is cursed. Last night, I found that out to my cost."

"Yet the night before, you told me that you were deliriously happy."

"I was deceived."

"Hannah . . ."

"Don't try to dissuade me, Paul. My mind is made up."

"Is it all because of one unfortunate incident?"

"Is that what you call it?" she asked with a hollow laugh. "The assassination of the Prince Regent merits a far stronger description than that. Suppose that *you* had been the target? I'd have been left in utter despair. Or suppose that the shot was fired when I emerged through the stage door. *I* might have been the victim. Have you considered that? Because of this hateful play, I could have been killed."

"You attach too much importance to superstition, my love."

"Then don't listen to *me*. Talk to countless other members of my profession who came to grief while taking part in that ill-fated Scottish play. Ghosts have appeared, injuries have been sustained, scenery has collapsed, sickness has affected the whole cast. And there are dozens of other examples I could give you."

"Yet when you were offered the part, you seized it with alacrity."

"I'm the first to confess my folly."

"Have you so soon forgotten your other success in the play?" he asked. "You not only brought Lady

14

Macbeth to life in Paris, you did so in French. No other English actress could ever do that."

"Then they are spared the misery that I had to endure."

"You were feted, Hannah. Paris adored you."

"One of the men adored me rather too much," she recalled with a grimace. "But for the intervention of yourself and a courageous French gentleman, I'd have been abducted and brutally abused. The curse of that play struck once again."

Conscious that they were having a conversation that they'd already had at least three or four times, Paul sought to break the impasse. Hannah was beyond the reach of reason. It was no use pointing out that she'd be damaging her future prospects if she pulled out of the production at short notice. Managers were not impressed by examples of pique and unreliability. Since Hannah was adamant, there was only one course of action left to him.

"Very well," he said, changing tack. "I accept and endorse your decision. If the play offends you so much, spare no more time on the ordeal of taking part in it. Besides, there are only two more performances to go. I'm sure that she can cope perfectly well with those."

Hannah started. "*She?*"

"Miss Glenn."

"Why mention her? If I withdraw, the performances will be cancelled."

"The manager can't afford to do that, Hannah. He'd have to refund a large amount of money. Even without you, the play must go on. Dorothea Glenn will be an adequate replacement."

"Nobody can replace *me*," she snarled.

"In the strictest sense, you are quite right. No actress alive can attain your high standards but, then, Miss Glenn is not in competition with her idol. She accepts that she can only give a pale version of your performance, but the play will at least *have* a Lady Macbeth. Audiences will be disappointed when they hear of your indisposition but they will not be turned away."

He paused to see what effect his words were having on Hannah. Much as he loved her, he was fully aware of her vanity and capriciousness. Paul saw it as his job to moderate her behaviour and steer her away from impulses that could have serious consequences. In raising the prospect of a replacement, he'd caught her on the raw. Hannah was very possessive. The idea of someone else taking over *her* role was anathema to her. He pressed on.

"You've often said that Miss Glenn has great promise."

"It's true," she conceded.

"Like many young actresses, she's modelled herself on you. It's not often that you befriend newcomers to the profession, but that's what you did with her."

"Dorothea is . . . a likeable young lady."

"Do you believe she will go far?"

"I'm certain of it."

"Then seize this opportunity to advance her career," suggested Paul. "Since you feel unable to take on the

16

role yourself, allow her to step out from beneath your shadow and show the audience what she has to offer." There was a long silence. In the end, Paul had to prod her out of it. "Well?"

"I'll think about it."

"The decision is already made. You wish to withdraw from the play and it's only fair to advise the manager of the emergency as soon as possible so that Miss Glenn can be rehearsed throughout the day." He got up from the table. "Unless you have anything else to say, I'll ride to Covent Garden immediately and break the news. It will cause alarm, of course — that's inevitable — but there'll be no cancellation. The audience will see a Lady Macbeth onstage this evening, albeit one without any of your intensity and brilliance."

"Wait a moment," she said.

"You wish to come with me?"

"No, I don't."

"It would make more sense if you did so, Hannah. You could explain exactly why you are unable to face the challenge of two more performances in the role. If you stayed for the rehearsal," he went on, "you'd be able to pass on some advice to Miss Glenn. She'd be eternally grateful for it, I'm sure."

Hannah fell silent. She was brooding.

When he knocked on the door of the shooting gallery, the man was surprised when it was opened by a woman. He'd never expected someone so beautiful, well dressed and relatively young to work at such an establishment but that is what Charlotte Skillen had been doing for some time. She conducted the visitor into the office and reached for the appointments book, opening it at the appropriate page.

"What sort of instruction do you require, sir?" she asked. "We have bookings for the rest of this week but there are some gaps after that."

"I've come to speak to Mr Skillen," said the man, nervously.

"Which Mr Skillen do you mean? We have two here — Peter Skillen, my husband, and Paul, his brother. The latter, I fear, is otherwise engaged at the moment."

"Then I'll speak to your husband, please. It's urgent."

"He'll be finishing a fencing lesson any moment," she said. "Sit down while you wait, Mr . . .?"

"Hooper. Seth Hooper."

"Make yourself comfortable, Mr Hooper."

Lowering himself into a chair, he remained tense and anxious. Charlotte appraised him. He was a stocky man of medium height and middle years, with bushy side whiskers holding his face in position like a pair of hirsute bookends. She could see the perspiration on his brow. His accent told her that he came from somewhere much further north. Wearing apparel that was manifestly too tight for him, he was almost squirming with embarrassment. Dealing with a well-educated woman like her was evidently a novel experience for him.

"May I know what brought you here?" she asked, politely.

"This place was well-spoken-of."

18

"We aim to please, Mr Hooper."

"They say as how you . . . solve terrible crimes."

"Both my husband and his brother have dedicated their lives to doing just that. They'll give you all the help you need. What crime has occurred?"

"I'd rather not discuss it wi' a lady."

"I'm not as delicate as I may look," she told him with a smile. "During my time here, we've handled cases of kidnap, fraud, theft, forgery, rape, robbery with violence and worse. I've learnt to take gruesome details in my stride."

"If it's all the same to you, I'd still rather talk to Mr Skillen."

"Yes, of course."

"Man to man, as it were . . ."

Right on cue, she heard footsteps descending the stairs and went out into the hall in time to see her husband bidding farewell to his pupil, a willowy youth with staring eyes. Once he'd left, she told Peter that they had a visitor who had obviously come with a serious problem he refused to divulge to her.

"Leave him to me, Charlotte," he said.

After giving her an affectionate squeeze, he went into the room and introduced himself to the stranger. Hooper was on his feet at once, shaking the outstretched hand as if drawing water from a village pump. Peter could see and feel the man's grief.

"How may I help you?" he asked.

"My friend were shot dead."

"I'm sorry to hear that, Mr Hooper."

"He went out last night and never came back. When I heard rumours of a murder, I knew it must be him. He'd never miss a meeting. It's not in his character."

"What's the name of your friend?"

"Sir Roger Mellanby."

"Ah," said Peter with interest. "I've heard good things about him. He's a Member of Parliament, isn't he?"

"Aye, and he were the only decent man in that madhouse," said Hooper with sudden fury. "That's the reason he were put down."

CHAPTER
FOUR

Hannah had changed her mind. Stung by the thought that someone might replace her as Lady Macbeth — even for a mere two performances — she decided that she would return to the company, after all. Before that, she needed a long sleep to restore her strength and spirits. Paul took her up to the bedroom and waited until she'd climbed between the sheets. Within minutes of placing her head on the pillow, she was fast asleep, allowing him to bestow a gentle kiss on her brow before creeping out of the room and closing the door silently behind him. Paul went downstairs, put on his coat and hat, then left the house. Intending to ride to the shooting gallery, he was confronted by the sight of an unexpected and decidedly unwelcome visitor. Micah Yeomans was alighting from a cab.

"Have you come to arrest me again?" taunted Paul.

"No, Skillen, I'm here to warn you."

"What am I supposed to have done now?"

"It's what you'll be tempted to do," said Yeomans, walking up to him. "And by the way, I didn't need that fancy hat of his to identify the murder victim. A friend of his came to report him missing and gave us his name."

"Who is he?"

"Sir Roger Mellanby."

"That name rings a bell."

"He was a politician."

"And who was this friend of his?"

"He's strange company for a man of quality. Mellanby was a firebrand with wild ideas about reform unusual in someone with his education. In the House of Commons, I'm told, he's known as the Radical Dandy. The so-called friend is one Seth Hooper, a brush-maker from Nottingham, a sweaty fellow who has difficulty stringing words together."

"That's the effect you have on some people, Micah."

"Don't mock me," warned the other.

"What did you tell Hooper?"

"I told him that we'd taken charge of the case and sent him on his way."

"Didn't you mention that *I* was a witness to the murder?"

"There was no need. Since I was there as well, I was able to tell him a little of what happened. Too much detail would have clouded his brain. He had the nerve to say that he wanted to be involved in the hunt for the assassin. I'd never allow any interference from him — or from you, for that matter. In fact," said Yeomans, "that's why I'm here. Keep well clear of this investigation."

"But I have a personal stake in it."

"Mellanby was clearly a rich man. A large reward will be offered for the capture of his killer. I don't want you and that confounded brother of yours getting in

22

our way, as you usually contrive to do. That's not just a warning from *me*. It's a command from His Royal Highness, the Prince Regent. Since *I* was protecting him last night, he wants me to be the person who brings this villain to justice."

"Then he'll wait until Doomsday."

"Our record of success speaks for itself."

"It's far outweighed by your repeated failures."

"Don't meddle in this case, Skillen."

"I've no choice. When a man is shot dead only feet away from me, I feel that it's my duty to hunt down his killer."

"Would you defy a royal decision?"

"In the name of justice," said Paul, "I'll do whatever is necessary. First of all, however, I need to make a confession. I was wrong to imagine that the Prince Regent was the designated target."

"I told you that," said Yeomans.

"The assassin was definitely hired to kill Sir Roger Mellanby."

"At least we agree on something."

"Because the man was proficient in his trade, one shot was all it took and he made sure that nobody saw him fire it."

"What made you realise that your first guess was wrong?"

"I thought of His Royal Highness."

"So?"

"That monstrous bulk of his presented a much bigger target than Mellanby. From that short distance, a child with a popgun couldn't have missed hitting the heir to the throne. In a matter of seconds," added Paul, "the assassin earned his money. He'd come well prepared. He knew exactly where to find his victim and could rely on his being off guard."

"Yes," said Yeomans, a sly grin on his face. "All that Mellanby was thinking about was how to get his hands on Miss Granville. That hope blinded him to everything else. Without meaning to, she helped the assassin by bewitching Mellanby. You might mention that to her."

Paul had to control a sudden urge to hit him.

Peter felt sorry for Seth Hooper. The man clearly revered the murder victim and spoke of him in hushed tones. From time to time, tears welled up in his eyes. Peter waited patiently and listened intently. Mellanby and Hooper had arrived from Nottingham on the previous day. While the former had stayed at one of the most prestigious hotels in the capital, his companion had, of necessity, sought more modest accommodation. The two men were in London to attend a meeting of the Hampden Club, an association for those committed to a campaign for social and political reform. As a delegate from Nottingham, the brush-maker would be expected to make a speech, but it was the Radical Dandy whom the other members would really come to hear. He was their acknowledged spokesman. Mellanby would not only rouse them to fever pitch with blazing oratory, he would present their petition to the Prince Regent.

"Sir Francis Burdett was asked first," explained Hooper, "but he refused. Sir Roger stepped forward at once. Nothing frightened him. He believed in our cause and did all he could to help us."

"He sounds like an extraordinary man," said Peter.

"There were nobody quite like him."

"So it appears."

"He were a saint, Mr Skillen."

Peter had doubts about that. Men who flocked to the stage door of a theatre in order to drool over a beautiful actress were rarely candidates for canonisation. The social and intellectual gap between the two friends was manifestly enormous. While Mellanby had been basking in a performance of a Shakespeare play, Hooper had been sitting in an attic room in a tavern, struggling to write his speech. Sadly, it would never be delivered now. The much-anticipated visit to London had been a disaster.

Hooper ended with a heartfelt plea for help.

"I beg you to find the killer, Mr Skillen."

"An official investigation will already have been launched."

"I know," said the other. "I spoke to a Bow Street Runner named Mr Yeomans, but he turned me away with harsh words. Catching Sir Roger's killer was *his* job, he told me, and I were to go back home to Nottingham and wait for news."

"Yes," said Peter, "that's typical of Micah Yeomans. He hates interference."

"I asked people from the Hampden Club where else I could go. Yours was the first name on their lips."

"Don't forget my brother. We operate as a team."

"I've no money to pay you at the moment," confessed Hooper, "but I'm sure that I can raise it when I take the hat round."

"I won't ask for a fee at this point. Paul and I choose to be paid by results. If we fail, you owe us nothing. If we succeed — and we usually do — we can decide on a fair return for our labours."

"Whatever it costs, I'll find the money somehow. The question is this — will you take on the search for the killer?"

"I can't make that decision, Mr Hooper. I find the case intriguing, but my brother will have a much stronger claim."

"Why is that?"

"Paul was actually there last night," said Peter, choosing his words with care. "My brother acts as a bodyguard to one of the actresses in the play. His task is to conduct her safely through the phalanx of admirers."

"I still don't understand what Sir Roger were doing there."

"Didn't he tell you that he was going to the theatre?"

"No," said Hooper. "He told me that he was having dinner with a friend in Mayfair. There were no mention made of Covent Garden. I wonder what made him change his mind and go to see a play instead?"

Peter didn't wish to disillusion him. It was clear that Mellanby had intended to watch *Macbeth* all along and had fobbed Hooper off with a blatant lie. When he was on the loose in London, the politician enjoyed himself. His behaviour there, Peter guessed, was almost certainly at variance with the image of himself that he'd carefully created in his home town. It sounded to him as if the man worshipped by Hooper might well be a voluptuary when liberated from his domestic concerns in the Midlands. Evidently, Mellanby led a complex life. The notion of uncovering it only served to heighten Peter's interest in the case.

"The Runners have greater resources," he said, "and they'll have the chief magistrate urging them to secure a speedy arrest and conviction. To give him credit, Yeomans will work hard to find the killer but his overconfidence is a weakness. Because he's so sure of himself, he's thrown away a priceless asset."

"Has he?" asked Hooper. "What is it?"

"It's more a question of *who* it is. Look in the mirror and you'll see him clearly. Yes, Mr Hooper," he went on as the visitor gaped, "*you* are that asset. What Yeomans discarded so rashly is a bonus that my brother and I will seize upon. Since you worked hand in glove with him, you can give us crucial details about Sir Roger's private life as well as about his political activities."

"We've been close these past six years, Mr Skillen."

"Then you have a fund of information on which we can draw."

"That's what I told Mr Yeomans."

"Forget him. The Runners are our rivals. Our methods differ from theirs and they usually bear fruit. However, I must issue a warning."

"What is it?"

"This could be a long and difficult case."

Hooper frowned. "That means it could be very expensive."

"Have no fear on that score," said Peter. "If Yeomans and his men track down the assassin, it won't cost you anything. If, on the other hand, my brother and I solve the crime, we'd stand to gain what could well be a large amount of reward money. The bill we'd present to you will be a very small one."

"Thank you so much," said Hooper, eyes moistening. "That takes a great weight off my mind. I was afraid that you'd turn me down."

"We'd never turn down an opportunity to humiliate the Runners. It adds spice to our work. Yet we mustn't underestimate them. If I know Micah Yeomans, he'll already be devising a plan to hamper our investigation."

The Peacock Inn was far more than simply a welcoming hostelry that served excellent ale and delicious pies. It was also the base from which the Bow Street Runners routinely operated. Yeomans had an office at his disposal but he preferred to work in the Peacock where the landlord was a good friend, the atmosphere was friendly and the barmaids were excessively pretty. Other patrons never dared to sit at the table in the corner. It was reserved exclusively for the Runners. At that moment, Yeomans was in his usual chair, munching his way through the remains of his meal. He was a big, hulking, middle-aged man with an unsightly face that struck fear into the hearts of the criminal fraternity. Seated beside him was Alfred Hale, shorter, a trifle younger and of slighter build. He needed a long sip of ale before he had the courage to criticise his superior.

"You may have made a mistake, Micah," he said, quietly.

"I *never* make mistakes," growled the other.

"I'm talking about that man, Hooper. You were too quick to send him on his way. He could have been useful to us."

"What do you mean?"

"He *knew* Sir Roger Mellanby."

"So?"

"He might have given us information about him."

"The only information we need, to know is that he was shot dead outside the stage door of the Theatre Royal. We were actually there. Hooper wasn't."

"Yet he came to London with Sir Roger."

"They may have travelled in the same coach but not as companions. The man was a brush-maker, for heaven's sake. Can you imagine an aristocrat like Sir Roger befriending a nonentity like that? Of course not," said Yeomans with disdain. "While the Radical Dandy was *inside* the coach, Hooper would have been on top of it, clinging on for dear life."

"I still think we might have learnt something from him."

"Yes — we learnt that he had bad breath, sweated like a pancake and could hardly get any words out of his mouth. Oh, one other thing — there was a button missing off his waistcoat."

"There was no need to treat him so roughly, Micah."

"He was in my way."

"You were cruel."

"I was realistic," said Yeomans. "Why waste precious time on a fool like Hooper when there are so many important people to speak to? Now that I've finished my pie, we can go off to meet one of them — Captain Golightly. You saw that letter we found on Mellanby. The captain was a *real* friend of his. We'll get far more information out of him than we will from that bumbling brush-maker."

"What about Paul Skillen?"

"I've taken care of him."

"He was there last night," Hale reminded him. "That means he'll want to solve the murder before we do."

"He won't get a chance, Alfred. I've warned him that the Prince Regent is very angry with him. Before His Majesty could get close to her, Skillen grabbed Miss Granville and took her out of reach."

"I know. They brushed past me as they fled."

"I told Skillen that he's expressly forbidden to poke his nose into this investigation. Since that order has the power of the Crown behind it," said Yeomans, grandly, "Paul Skillen will have to obey it."

After the shock of hearing that a man he admired had been shot dead, Seth Hooper had been in despair. Curt rejection by the Runners had added to his distress. When he'd been directed to the shooting gallery, he didn't know if anyone would take on the case or, if they did, whether there was any possibility of success. To the brush-maker's relief, Peter Skillen had been kind and sympathetic. During the time they spent together, Hooper slowly came out of his dejection. He even dared to entertain hope. As the two men were chatting, they heard the main door being unlocked. Peter excused himself and went out into the hall. Hooper, meanwhile, looked around the room with interest. He was impressed by the array of swords, pistols and archery equipment stored there. Everything was neatly displayed and obviously kept in good condition.

When the door opened again, he saw whom he believed to be Peter coming back into the room. There was something rather odd about him. It took Hooper a few seconds to realise that he was wearing rather more flamboyant attire now.

He was startled. "However did you find time to change?"

"I didn't."

"Minutes ago, you were wearing something quite different."

"That was my brother, Peter," explained the other. "I'm *Paul* Skillen. Peter obviously forgot to tell you that we're identical twins."

"It's . . . uncanny," said Hooper, staring in amazement.

"You'll grow accustomed to it."

"Do you know who I am?"

"Peter has just explained and yes, it's true that I was at the theatre last night. In fact, I was quite close to Sir Roger when he was shot dead. In the general panic, the killer and his accomplice got away."

Hooper blinked. "There were *two* of them?"

"I'm certain of it. I'll tell you exactly what happened, if you wish."

"Yes, please!"

"First, I must assure you that we will do all that's possible to find out who was responsible for Sir Roger's death. This was no random attack. Someone hired that assassin. I want to find out why."

"I'm so grateful, Mr Skillen — to you and your brother."

"It won't be easy. Be warned about that. To start with, we'll have constant trouble from the Runners. They can be very possessive."

"I found that out."

"Also, we have a more fearsome enemy to worry about."

"Oh — who is that?"

"The Prince Regent. He's given specific orders that I'm not to be involved in an investigation into the murder."

"Why did he do that?"

"Call it revenge," said Paul with a wry smile. "I frustrated his ambitions with regard to a certain young lady, and I fancy that I'll have to do it again before too long. With regard to the murder, not even a member of the royal family is going to stop me trying to solve it. For the Runners," he went on, "it's just a routine assignment; for me, however, it's much more than that. I see it as a kind of mission."

CHAPTER
FIVE

Captain Hector Golightly was a tall, sturdy, straight-backed individual with greying hair and moustache. A born soldier, he made sure that his house in Mayfair was run with military precision. Walls were adorned with paintings of famous battles in which British soldiers had been victorious. Golightly had served with distinction in two of the encounters on display. He was working in his study when told that he had visitors. Annoyed at the interruption, he nevertheless agreed to see them. A minute later, Micah Yeomans and Alfred Hale were conducted into the room. They found him standing in front of the fireplace with an air of unchallengeable authority. When Yeomans introduced himself and his companion, Golightly stiffened.

"Why the devil are Bow Street Runners bothering me?" he demanded. "I'm one of the most law-abiding men in London."

"We've not come to arrest you, Captain," said Hale.

"No," added Yeomans, "we're the bearers of bad news, I fear. It's my sad duty to inform you that Sir Roger Mellanby died last night."

"That's impossible," said Golightly, stamping a foot. "He was in rude health when I last saw him. The fellow has another thirty years in him."

"He did not die by natural means, Captain."

"What do you mean?"

"Sir Roger was shot dead."

"Never!" exclaimed Golightly. "I refuse to believe it."

"We were there at the time," said Hale. "We were acting as bodyguards to the Prince Regent while he watched a play at the Theatre Royal in Covent Garden. After the performance, His Majesty expressed a wish to go to the stage door."

"And that's where the murder took place," said Yeomans. "As we joined the crowd there, a pistol was fired and everyone ran away in panic, leaving the body of the man we now know as Sir Roger Mellanby dead on the ground."

Golightly slowly adjusted to the grim news. His body was slack, his face ashen and his manner abruptly changed. All the authority seemed to have been drained out of him. In the course of a long career in the army, he'd seen many men perish on the battlefield. Yet none of the deaths he'd witnessed had left him with the searing pain he now felt.

"Has an arrest been made?" he asked at length.

"I fear not," replied Yeomans. "It was dark and the killer got away in the commotion. We had to wait until this morning to find out who the victim was. The friend who identified him told us the name of the hotel where Sir Roger had stayed. During our search there of his

34

luggage, we found a letter sent by you and inviting him to dine here this evening."

"It's true. We'd planned to attend a meeting together this afternoon. Once that was done, he'd have joined me and some like-minded friends here. He's dead?" he asked, shaking his head in disbelief. "This cannot be. We were like brothers. I valued his company above that of almost everyone else."

"You won't enjoy it any more," murmured Hale.

"The villain must be caught," insisted Golightly, recovering his composure. "Whatever it takes, he must be hunted down with all celerity. Hanging is too good for him. If it were left to me, I'd have his rotten carcass torn apart by two horses, and his head displayed on a spike outside the Tower."

"We must follow legal procedure, Captain," said Yeomans.

"What steps have been taken?"

"My men are out searching for the killer at this very moment."

"Are you confident of success?"

"We have an army of informers we can call on. They have ears all over London. Sooner or later, we'll get the name we want."

"A large reward will help to smoke him out," said Hale.

"I'll be happy to provide the money," volunteered Golightly.

"Surely that should be left to Sir Roger's family?"

"Speed is of the essence here, man. I'll brook no delay."

"I agree," said Yeomans. "Waiting for the family to respond might take two or three days. Prompt action is needed."

"I want reward notices printed immediately and put up today. As for the amount on offer, I want you to give me a figure you think fit — then double it. In the hunt for this monster," declared Golightly, "no expense must be spared."

Paul Skillen was also acutely aware of the importance of acting quickly. With the help of his sister-in-law, he'd extracted the relevant information needed. As Seth Hooper answered all the questions fired at him, Charlotte had written down the answers until a small biography of Sir Roger Mellanby emerged. Inevitably, there were gaps. While he was able to describe his hero's political achievements in detail, the brush-maker was less forthcoming about his family life. Though he was proud to be called a friend of the murder victim, he had never once been invited into the man's home. When she and Peter were left alone, it was something on which Charlotte commented.

"Mr Hooper never even got as far as the servants' entrance."

"Mellanby obviously kept his private and public life rigidly apart," said Paul. "I'm certain that his wife knew nothing about his predilection for the theatre. By the same token, his London acquaintances were probably kept ignorant of the respectable existence he led in Nottingham when Parliament was in recess."

36

"Why did a man like that join the fight for electoral reform?"

"He sincerely believed in it, Charlotte. There's no other explanation. It won him a lot of friends, but it also earned him many enemies. Most of them, I daresay, were satisfied with simply pouring scorn on his views. Others may have felt that he was becoming too dangerous and had to be silenced."

"Where do we look for suspects — amongst politicians?"

"Oh, no," said Paul. "We must cast our net far wider than Westminster."

"What do you mean?"

"His murder may have nothing to do with his role as a Member of Parliament. The person who ordered his death might be a jealous husband, perhaps a thwarted businessman, an unpaid creditor, a discarded friend or someone who has nursed a grudge against him that festered until it demanded expression."

"Where will you begin your search for him?"

Paul smiled. "Why do you think it has to be a man?"

"It was a natural assumption."

"Well, it's not one that I'm making. As far as I'm concerned," he said, "it could equally well be a woman."

The difference was remarkable. Seth Hooper's journey to London had been long, bruising and hazardous. Seated on top of a swaying stagecoach, he was exposed to rain, wind, the jostling of other passengers and the multiple shortcomings of roads that were no more than mud-caked tracks. On his return to Nottingham, by contrast, he was one of four passengers travelling inside a mail coach that was cleaner, more restful and much faster. Apart from the driver, there was also a guard outside, dressed in the Post Office livery of maroon and gold, and armed with two pistols and a blunderbuss. Hooper couldn't believe that he deserved such comparative luxury. He was an interloper. Comfort made him feel uncomfortable.

Peter Skillen, however, was completely at ease.

"This was a wise choice," he said. "It's over a hundred miles to Nottingham. This coach should get us there in less than sixteen hours."

"The stagecoach that brought me to London took a lot longer than that."

"The person to thank for this mode of transport is John Palmer."

"Why is that?" asked Hooper.

"He helped to design a vehicle like this. Palmer used to be involved with a theatre in Bath and was always complaining how long it took to move actors and scenery to and fro. To speed up journeys, Palmer hired post-chaises. When he suggested to the government that the Post Office should make use of smaller, lighter, swifter coaches, he was asked for a demonstration of a vehicle very much like this. It was a great success. As a result," said Peter, "it set the standard."

"I've never had such a fast ride, Mr Skillen."

"Sit back and enjoy it."

"I'm in no mood to enjoy anything," said Hooper, solemnly.

38

"That's understandable."

Almost immediately, one wheel of the coach went into a deep pothole and the passengers were thrown violently sideways. It was a timely reminder that, in return for more speed, they would have to get used to such sudden lurches on a treacherous road surface. Their journey, Peter mused, was a metaphor for the task they'd set themselves. In the course of their investigation, there would be an endless series of bumps, wobbles, jarring jolts and uncontrollable swaying. Yet he remained confident that — like the mail coach — they would eventually reach their destination.

The Clarendon Hotel, one of the most fashionable in the capital, was a former town house in Bedford Place. Because of his association with it, Paul Skillen approached the building with mixed feelings. During the days when he'd been a frequent gambler, he had once lost hundreds of pounds in a card game at the hotel. Paying off the debt had been a very painful exercise. The thought of it made him shudder. By way of consolation, an image of Hannah Granville came into his mind. She had brought stability into his life. She'd also rescued him from an existence that revolved around drink, debauchery and nights at the gaming table. Paul was a new man now.

When he entered the lobby, he was reminded of a more pleasant memory of the Clarendon. Recognising him at once, the manager surged forward to shake him vigorously by the hand. He beamed at Paul.

"Welcome back, Mr Skillen. You've neglected us for too long."

"It's good to see you again, Mr Treen. Your hotel looks as splendid as ever."

"We strive to maintain its sparkle. Most of our guests revel in our hospitality but, very occasionally, there are those who abuse it."

Paul knew what he meant. During an earlier visit, there had been a drunken fight in the lobby between two men who ignored all pleas to stop. In an effort to calm them down, Treen had shouted himself hoarse. It was only when Paul had stepped into the hotel that the unseemly brawl was stopped. Summing up the situation instantly, Paul had stepped in, used brute force to separate the combatants, then taken each of them by the scruff of the neck before throwing them out into the street. He'd earned a round of applause from relieved onlookers as well as the undying thanks of the manager. Treen was a short, slight, pale-faced man in his fifties whose hands fluttered expressively like a pair of giant butterflies.

"To what do we owe the pleasure of this visit?" he asked.

"I need to ask a favour of you, Mr Treen."

"It's granted before it's even put into words."

"It concerns a recent guest of yours — Sir Roger Mellanby." The manager's face fell. "A sad case, I know. You have my sympathy."

"My sympathy goes to his family. It will come as a dreadful shock to them."

"I wonder if I might have access to his room?"

"Why? What interest can it hold for you?"

"I'm curious, that's all," said Paul, not wishing to divulge the fact that he'd actually been present when Mellanby was shot. "I will only need a minute."

"The room is completely empty, Mr Skillen. Some Bow Street Runners searched it earlier and took his luggage away with them."

"Did you watch them while they did so?"

"I most certainly did. We always safeguard our guests' property. That's why I insisted on taking an inventory of everything Sir Roger had brought with him. It's not that I don't trust the Runners but . . . one cannot be too careful."

"A glance at that inventory will save me the trouble of looking at the room," said Paul. "It's not only personal interest that's brought me here. I'm acting on behalf of someone who travelled from Nottingham with Sir Roger Mellanby and who is even now on his way to convey the sad tidings to his family."

"He's stayed here on many occasions and there has never been a whiff of trouble. Sir Roger has been a perfect guest — except for one small blemish."

"Oh — and what was that?"

"He spurned the greatest treat we have to offer."

Paul grinned. "You're talking about the dining room."

"Jacquiers is the finest chef in the whole of London," insisted Treen. "Before he came to this country, he was in royal service. French cuisine is incomparable and Jacquiers is the absolute master of it."

"I agree. I've always enjoyed superb food here."

"So why did Sir Roger plan to eat elsewhere both last night and this evening?"

"He had his reasons, I daresay."

"They died with him, alas. However," said Treen, taking him by the elbow, "you asked to see that inventory. Let's go to my office . . ."

A long sleep had revived Hannah Granville. Since she liked to get to the theatre hours before a performance was due, she took a cab late that afternoon. The journey gave her time to reflect on what had happened the previous day. A murder had taken place outside the stage door. Immediately afterwards, the Prince Regent had suddenly arrived in her dressing room to pay homage and plant a moist kiss on her hand. He'd made it plain that he desired much closer contact than that and — had Paul not spirited her away — some kind of invitation might well have been offered. Repulsive as she'd found the man, she was unsure whether it would be wise to refuse a royal summons. Whatever happened, she resolved to be on guard and to avoid situations from which even Paul might be unable to rescue her.

Arriving at the theatre, she was relieved to discover that there was no missive from the palace and no lavish gifts awaiting her in the dressing room. Hannah dared to hope that the Prince Regent had already forgotten her and gone off in pursuit of other possible conquests. Moments later, Jenny Pye came into the room to help begin the long process of turning her into Lady Macbeth again.

"After what happened last night," Jenny began, "I feared that you might not wish to come back this evening."

"I could never let an audience down," said Hannah, piously. "Besides, nothing would have prevented me from fulfilling my contractual obligations."

Jenny turned away to hide her smile. As well as being her dresser, she was Hannah's trusted friend and advisor. No woman was closer or knew her better. She remembered only too well that, during rehearsals for a new work at Drury Lane Theatre, Hannah had developed such a loathing for the man who wrote it that she threatened to tear her contract to bits. Because she had no compunction about letting him down, her antics had reduced the manager to a gibbering wreck. Her headstrong behaviour had been carefully erased from Hannah's mind but it was an indelible memory to her dresser.

"The house is full again tonight," said Jenny.

"It always is when I grace its boards."

"Dorothea Glenn told me that she wished she could be in the audience one night so that she could watch your performance."

"Then she needs to be reminded that she is an actress. Her place is onstage. She cannot only enjoy my performance there, she's in a position to enhance it. I like the girl very much," said Hannah, "but she still has much to learn."

"Dorothea is fortunate. There's no better teacher than you."

"It's one of my many virtues."

Jenny sighed.

Peter Skillen was highly conscious of his companion's unease. Seated in a mail coach with three immaculate gentlemen, Seth Hooper was squirming. He had neither the confidence nor the education to take part in a conversation with the others so he sat there in silence and cursed his social inferiority. The coach stopped every ten or fifteen miles in order that the horses could be changed. It was at the third stop that Hooper finally found his voice again. He and Peter were in the courtyard of a coaching inn, stretching their legs and getting some fresh air.

"I were shaken," Hooper confided. "When they told me where Sir Roger had been killed, I simply had to go straight to the place where it happened. Honest, I were that shocked."

"Was there a pool of blood?"

"No, Mr Skillen, it weren't the area outside the stage door that upset me. It were Covent Garden itself. I'd never seen the like. I've been to markets before but not like this one. It were full of beggars and thieves and wild-eyed men, not to mention women wi' no shame. I'm a married man, sir," he went on, "and I go to church every Sunday wi' my wife on my arm. I blushed at some of the things those powdered harlots offered me — in broad daylight, too. It were indecent, Mr Skillen. If this is what London is really like, I'm glad I don't live here."

"Parts of the city *have* become the haunts of pleasure-seekers," admitted Peter, "but there are many respectable districts. I'm sorry that your first visit to the nation's capital was so disappointing."

"There were so much noise and bustle and that awful stink is still in my nostrils. Forgive me for speaking out, sir. I've no wish to offend."

"You're the person who's been offended, Mr Hooper, and you have my sympathy. In our own small way, my brother and I try to police the city. It's like trying to drain a sea of crime with only one bucket between us."

"That's why I'm so grateful you're taking on this case."

"Sir Roger's family deserve to know what happened," said Peter, "and I'll be able to pass on the details that my brother gave me. I won't be the first to break the dreadful news, however. They'll have dispatched a courier by now. By riding hard and changing horses regularly, he'll get there ahead of us. Besides, it will be dark by the time our coach finally arrives."

"You'll need somewhere to stay," said Hooper, shuffling his feet in embarrassment. "We've only a small house but you're welcome to a bed if you need somewhere to lay your head tonight."

"Thank you," said Peter. "I'll gladly accept that kind offer."

"There's one more thing."

"What's that?"

"When I'm at the Black Horse wi' my friends, I can make a speech at the drop of a hat. Words just gush out of my mouth. It were different wi' Sir Roger. In his company, I were always tongue-tied. It'll be the same wi' his family. My voice will disappear again. When we meet them," said Hooper, "do you think that *you* could do the talking?"

Peter gave him a reassuring smile. "Leave it to me."

CHAPTER
SIX

When he heard the clang of the doorbell, Hector Golightly hoped that the Runners might have returned to his house with good news about the manhunt. He was disappointed to learn that his visitor was a complete stranger. However, he was impressed by the sight of the tall, lithe, handsome figure of Paul Skillen when the latter stepped into the drawing room. Dismissing the butler who'd admitted the newcomer, Golightly let Paul introduce himself and explain why he'd come. The older man subjected him to a penetrating gaze.

"You say that you're here in connection with the death of Sir Roger Mellanby," he observed. "Could you be more specific?"

"I was there at the time, Captain Golightly."

"Really? Are you claiming that you were part of that motley crew outside the stage door?"

"Not exactly," said Paul. "Everyone else was there to admire Miss Granville, the famous actress who plays Lady Macbeth. My job was to escort her safely through the crowd. I do that every night. If you doubt me, Miss Granville will confirm it."

"Are you employed by the lady?"

"We are . . . close friends."

"I see."

Golightly waved Paul to a chair and sat opposite him, still maintaining his intense scrutiny of his visitor's face.

"I want a detailed account of what happened," said Golightly. "I've already had one version of events from a Runner by the name of Yeomans. It was rather garbled."

"Micah Yeomans is not famed for his clarity."

"You know him?"

"We are in constant touch," said Paul with a twinkle in his eye.

He went on to give an account of what had occurred the previous night. It was both succinct yet comprehensive. Golightly was pleased because it had the lucidity and accuracy of a military report. All of the supplementary questions he went on to aim at Paul were answered honestly and satisfactorily. The captain sat back in his chair and relaxed slightly.

"Why did you come to me?"

"I was told that you were a close friend of Sir Roger's."

"It's true. We were due to attend a meeting of the Hampden Club this afternoon before coming back here for dinner. Who gave you my name?"

"It was a man named Hooper who came here from Nottingham with Sir Roger. He was due to speak at the meeting you just referred to. Instead of that, he's now travelling back home with sad tidings. Hooper had heard mention of your name by Sir Roger but had no idea where you lived."

48

"Then how did you find me?"

"I went to Stevens' Hotel in Bond Street. Since it's a haven for army officers, I felt that someone was bound to have heard of Captain Golightly. In fact, you were well known to most of the officers there."

"That was very enterprising of you, Skillen."

"It was important to locate you."

"Why is that?"

"I need your help."

"What can *I* possibly do?"

"Without realising it," said Paul, "you might have some idea who was behind the murder." Golightly shook his head. "Consider this. In order to fire the fatal shot, the assassin had to know where and when he could find his target. In short, the person who hired him had to be familiar with Sir Roger's habits. He *knew* that he would attend last night's performance in Covent Garden and that he'd feel impelled to go to the stage door for a glimpse — if not more — of Miss Granville."

"What are you telling me?"

"I'm telling you what you already know about Sir Roger's character. As soon as he arrived in London, he sought diversion. After all the effort of getting here, you'd have expected him to need a restorative meal and a long rest. Yet he disdained the cuisine of the celebrated Jacquiers at the Clarendon Hotel and went off to the theatre." He raised an eyebrow. "Do you follow my reasoning, Captain?"

"I'm beginning to, Mr Skillen."

49

"We could be looking for someone within Sir Roger's circle."

"I dispute that," said Golightly. "His friends are unswervingly loyal."

"One of them could have been overheard making an unguarded remark about Sir Roger's fondness for the theatre and his interest in a particular actress. I can't imagine that Nottingham could provide him with someone remotely like Miss Granville or, if it did, that he'd be allowed anywhere near her. It was only when he was in London," suggested Paul, "that he was — let me put this politely — unfettered by family obligations."

"Sir Roger was happily married."

"Most of those who cluster around that stage door are the same. I see them every night, remember. When they are with their wives, they are all happily married. After watching a play unaccompanied by their spouses, however, they tend to become lusty bachelors."

"I wouldn't know. Theatre is not to my taste."

"When did you last see Sir Roger?"

"It was some weeks ago."

"Since you are such a good friend, I'd have thought he'd be in touch with you the moment he arrived here. He might even have invited you to join him in a meal at the Clarendon Hotel. Instead of that —"

"There's no need to labour the point," said the other, tetchily.

"All I'm saying is that your friend had priorities."

"And so do I, Skillen. An appalling crime has taken place. My priority is simple. I want it solved quickly."

50

"That's why I'm here, Captain. With your permission, I need to ask some questions that may indirectly lead to an arrest. Do you have any objection?" After a few moments, Golightly shook his head. "Thank you. Let's begin, shall we?"

At the end of the working day, Charlotte was tidying everything up at the shooting gallery. Gully Ackford came into the room, rubbing one arm.

"I'm getting too old for this," he complained. "A couple of hours with a sword in my hand tires me out completely."

"You should let Jem give all the fencing lessons."

"He's got enough to do as it is, Charlotte. Since I'm losing Peter and Paul for a while, I'll have to take on more of the work myself. If there's too much to cope with, I'll have to bring in help."

"We'll just have to hope that this case doesn't take up too much time," she said. "I'd prefer my husband to be here, not charging off to Nottingham. However, Peter has to go where he might find evidence."

"Yes, he does."

"Paul is still in London, grappling with two very difficult jobs. One of them is to track down the assassin and the other, as we know, is equally demanding. He has to protect Hannah from the attentions of the Prince Regent. Knowing her, I think she'll feel frightened at the idea that he might come back to make impossible demands. She needs Paul as a shield.

"After the events of last night," she continued, "His Royal Highness's ardour may have cooled somewhat.

The fact that someone was shot dead outside the theatre right next to him might make him afraid to go anywhere near Covent Garden. As for the hunt for the killer, Paul is supposed to stay well away from it."

"Who told him that?" asked Ackford.

"Micah Yeomans delivered the message, but it actually came from the Prince Regent himself. He was infuriated by the speed with which Paul snatched Hannah away from under his nose. My brother-in-law is being restrained by royal command."

Ackford laughed. "Nothing can restrain Paul," he said. "It will only have made him more determined to bring the assassin to justice. That will not only give him great satisfaction, there's the question of a reward. He'd love to get his hands on that. It's bound to be substantial."

Since he featured in them so regularly, Harry Scattergood always kept a close eye on any reward notices that were put up. When he saw the latest one pasted to a wall, he gasped at the amount of money on offer. Scattergood was a slender, wiry, quick-witted man in his forties who was surprisingly nimble for his age. His unrivalled success as a thief enabled him to dress well, eat heartily and enjoy the kind of dissolute life that appealed to him. He was always alert to the possibility of a new source of money. Looking at the reward notice, he believed that he'd just found one.

After noting the details, he went off laughing to himself.

* * *

Speaking with a mingled affection and regret, Golightly talked at length about his friendship with Mellanby, emphasising the latter's determination to give a voice to those people denied one. Paul kept feeding him questions until he eventually ran out.

"Thank you for being so honest, Captain Golightly," he said.

"There's no reason to be anything else. Sir Roger had his flaws — which of us does not? — but he was, at heart, a people's champion. Though he stood for Parliament as a Whig, he was really one of Nature's revolutionaries."

"And what of *you*?" asked Paul.

"I don't follow."

"Why have you espoused the same causes? A career in the army rarely imbues a man with sympathy for the lower orders, still less for revolution. What makes you so different?"

"I can give you the answer in two words."

"What are they?"

"Orator Hunt."

"Ah, yes," said Paul, "I've heard Henry Hunt speak. He held a crowd of thousands utterly spellbound. He was talking about the Corn Laws, except that he called them Starvation Laws because that's what they amount to."

"I couldn't agree more. They were passed by a mean-spirited Parliament of landowners who couldn't bear the idea that the price of bread would go down at the end of the war. To maintain their high profits, they

53

banned the import of wheat. The result is that, all over this country, people are dying of hunger because they can't afford to buy bread at exorbitant prices. Lord Liverpool and his iniquitous Tory government do nothing whatsoever to relieve their distress. On the contrary," said Golightly, wagging a finger, "they intensify it by bringing in repressive laws and — worst of all — by suspending the Habeas Corpus Act."

"It's shameful."

"Sir Roger was much more eloquent on the subject than I am."

"That eloquence may have cost him his life."

"I fear that may be true, Skillen. Hampden Clubs were established in major cities so that people had a forum for debate. The Tories are already claiming that they exist solely to foment rebellion. That's an arrant lie. Freedom of speech must be allowed, surely. It's a basic right. That was always Sir Roger's battle cry."

"It obviously inspired a lot of people."

"I know. I'm one of them."

"Look at it from the point of view of the government," said Paul. "If they felt that he was becoming too effective as a rabble-rouser, who would give the order to have him dealt with?"

"It would be Sidmouth — the Home Secretary."

It was well after midnight when they finally arrived in Nottingham. As the four passengers took it in turns to alight from the coach, they were stiff, aching in every bone and grateful that the journey was finally over. They waited for their luggage to be passed down from the roof of the vehicle. Peter had planned to stay at the coaching inn where they'd just arrived but he didn't wish to refuse Hooper's invitation. The more time he spent with the man, he reasoned, the more he could glean about the character and political life of Sir Roger Mellanby. Again, the brush-maker would talk much more freely in his own home than he could in front of strangers in the confines of a mail coach.

The house was no more than a few hundred yards away and, as they trudged through the streets, Peter took a first look at Nottingham in silhouette. Children bawled in crowded bedrooms. Cats stalked in the shadows and dogs barked incessantly. Accustomed to the abiding stench of the capital, Peter found the air less of an assault on his nostrils. In the last census, the population had been recorded as just over thirty-four thousand, making it huge in comparison with the surrounding villages but small when measured against London's million and more citizens.

"Have you always lived here?" asked Peter.

Hooper nodded. "I were born in a cottage down by the river."

"Do you like Nottingham?"

"I love it, Mr Skillen. But I'd love it even more if we had better wages, enough food in our bellies and the right to vote. We're cruelly exploited, that's the truth of it. Sir Roger were trying to make our lives better."

"He'll be sorely missed."

"When people know what happened to him, there'll be a lot of tears shed. We've nobody to take his place."

"What's the first thing you need to do?"

"I have to spread the word as soon as possible," said Hooper. "After I've told Win, my wife, that you'll be staying the night, I must go out again to start knocking on doors. I'm sorry about that, Mr Skillen."

"Don't apologise. In your position, I'd do exactly the same."

"Will you excuse me?"

"You don't need my permission," said Peter. "If I may, I'll keep you company. I'll be interested to meet all your friends and — since I'm involved in hunting down Sir Roger's assassin — *they* might be glad to meet me."

"Oh, they will. You can bank on it."

"That's good to hear."

"You'll be welcomed as a friend," said Hooper, voice filled with emotion. "I can't tell you how grateful I am to you, Mr Skillen. When I came to that shooting gallery, I were in despair. You and your brother lifted me out of it. I know we can put our faith in you."

"We're not miracle-workers, Mr Hooper. Be aware of that. What we *can* bring to this investigation, however, is a capacity for hard work and an unflagging tenacity. We simply never give up. Also," Peter assured him, "we've had experience of chasing and catching villains. My brother is staying in London because that, in all likelihood, is where the assassin resides. For my part, I'm eager to find his paymaster who may, I fancy, live much closer to where we are standing right now."

Harry Scattergood knew the importance of careful preparation. Born into a life of crime, he had quickly learnt the tricks of the trade from his parents. When

56

they died, he'd branched out on his own. Most of his early success came from opportunism, spotting a chance of stealing something, seizing it instantly and haring off in the certain knowledge that nobody was fast enough to catch him. As time passed, he learnt to plan his crimes with care, choosing more profitable targets and leaving nothing to chance. His latest scheme was an enticing one.

Looking the part was essential. He'd seen the patrons flooding into the Covent Garden Theatre on many occasions. In order to mingle with them, he needed the finest garments from his wardrobe. He chose a short, square-cut white vest with small lapels and a single-breasted waistcoat. Buttoned at the side, his pantaloons were tight and reached the middle of his calves. He wore tasselled Hessians on his feet. At his neck was a black stock. His blue coat had broad swallowtails and was cut away squarely at the waist with large buttons of crystal silver. When he looked at himself in the mirror, he was impressed at how elegant a figure he cut. The disguise would allow him to mix easily with the most stylish of dandies. Some items in his apparel didn't fit him perfectly, but then, the person from whom he'd stolen them had slightly different dimensions so Scattergood was prepared to forgive him.

He was in the audience bewitched by the magic of Hannah Granville that evening. As if attesting her ownership of the role of Lady Macbeth, she played the part to the hilt. Scattergood was amongst those who clapped until their hands began to ache. Ignoring the comic afterpiece, he left the theatre and went round to the stage door with a crowd of panting admirers, listening to their conversations to pick up every nugget of information he could.

"I was here last night," said one man, "when someone was shot dead."

"Heavens!" exclaimed his companion.

"It could have been me."

"What a frightening thought!"

"I wouldn't say that. If I could choose the manner of my death, what better way to quit this world than at the feet of Hannah Granville as she came out of that stage door? If that happened, I'd die in ecstasy."

Most of what Scattergood heard was inconsequential chatter but there were others who been there on the previous night. Each had his story to tell and every detail was noted by him. Care had been taken to make a repetition of the outrage almost impossible. Extra lanterns had been hung so that the area was brightly lit and two armed men were stationed outside the stage door. More than one person who tried to bribe his way into the theatre was turned roughly away. The sound of loud protests behind him made Scattergood turn round in time to see a broad-shouldered man pushing his way through the crowd. Though he recognised the newcomer as one of the Skillen brothers, Scattergood couldn't be sure which one it was. What he did know, however, was that during his long career, Peter and Paul Skillen were the only people who had ever managed to arrest him.

To the irritation of everyone there, Paul was allowed into the theatre at once and the door was closed after him. Five minutes later, he reappeared with Hannah on his arm and her dresser in tow. There was the usual concerted cry of delight followed by a groan of envy. Admirers pressed forward to get nearer to their idol but Scattergood's interest was in her companion. He stood directly in front of Paul so that the latter had a good look at his face before brushing him aside and taking Hannah on to the waiting coach. Scattergood was delighted. If one of the Skillen brothers had failed to recognise him, he had no worries. He could put his plan into operation.

CHAPTER
SEVEN

Given the limited accommodation at Hooper's house, Peter was struck by the man's kindness in inviting him to spend the night there. He noticed the efforts made on his behalf. After changing the sheets, Hooper and his wife moved out of their bedroom and into the other one, even though it was already occupied by Winifred Hooper's aged mother. While Peter slept in the relative comfort of a bed, his hosts were lying side by side on the floorboards in the adjacent room, listening to the old lady's continuous wheezing. Winifred was a short, skinny, anxious woman with an exaggerated respect for those of a higher social class. Whenever she spoke to him, Peter could almost hear a curtsey in her voice.

That certainly hadn't been the case with the men on whom Hooper had earlier called with his visitor from London. Having come together to seek reform, they were people who deferred to nobody, freeborn Englishmen secure in the belief that they had as much right as anyone else to take part in the process of electing the government that had such power over them and their families. Peter admired their gruff honesty, their determination and their courage in pursuing radical political reform. They were stunned by the news of the murder of Sir Roger Mellanby and embraced Peter readily when they learnt why he'd come to Nottingham. Many of them had theories about who had been responsible for the death of their talisman. Peter committed the suggested names to memory. While he was glad of their willingness to confide in him, he could feel the burden of expectation slowly but inexorably building. Welcomed as a saviour, he knew that he now had to justify the immense faith placed in him. It was a forbidding task.

Breakfast the next morning comprised a simple but nourishing meal and a string of apologies from Winifred about the shortcomings of their hospitality.

"If an apology is due, Mrs Hooper," said Peter, "it should come from me for imposing upon you without warning. I have no complaints. I slept well, ate well and am indebted to you and your husband."

"You're always welcome here, Mr Skillen," said Hooper.

"Thank you."

"If you're ready, we'd best be off."

"Then let's be on our way."

Hooper had borrowed a horse and trap from a friend of his so that they could drive out to Mellanby Hall. It was only when he climbed up into the vehicle that Peter realised just how little he knew about the family he was setting off to visit. Hooper had spoken in glowing terms about his hero but said little about his wife and children. On the journey there, Peter gathered more information about Mellanby's two sons, one of whom, Edmund, was married and lived some distance away from the family home. There was also a daughter who lived with her husband near Ravenshead.

"What of Sir Roger's wife?" asked Peter.

"Lady Mellanby is not in the best of health," explained Hooper, "so we may not even be able to speak to her. The news will have been a big blow to her. David, the younger son, will be there and so will Mr Oxley, I daresay."

"Who is Mr Oxley?"

"He's a lawyer and Sir Roger's best friend. He was his agent during any election and looked after his affairs whenever Sir Roger was away for any length of time. Mr Oxley is almost like one of the family. When the news of . . . what happened in London reached Mellanby Hall yesterday, Mr Oxley would have been summoned immediately."

"What manner of man is he?"

There was a moment's hesitation before the answer came.

"Oh, he's very . . . able."

"I hear a note of reservation in your voice," said Peter.

"No, no," said Hooper, quickly, "I've no criticism to make of Mr Oxley. He's loyal and hard-working. His job is — or *was*, anyway — to take the load off Sir Roger and he did that very well."

He went on to list the man's attributes, but Peter was not fooled. He sensed that Hooper didn't like or trust Oxley. He wondered why.

Mellanby Hall was less than five miles from Nottingham. Set in a large estate, it played tricks on them, peeping out from behind bushes like a naughty child then disappearing briefly before coming fleetingly into view elsewhere. The endless glimpses were more than enough to whet Peter's appetite. When the house finally rose up before them, he was struck by its size and solidity. Built two centuries earlier, it was rigidly symmetrical, its four corner towers flanking three recessed and gabled bays. Its facade of grey stone was rather forbidding. Peter could see that Hooper was approaching the place with some trepidation. The latter turned to him.

"You'll not forget your promise, Mr Skillen, will you?"

"Of course not," replied Peter. "I'll do the talking."

"Truth is . . . I've not ever been able to speak proper to Mr Oxley."

"Why is that?"

"I don't know."

As soon as they pulled up on the forecourt, a manservant came out to hold the bridle while they got out of the trap. When the visitors walked towards the house, Hooper stayed half a pace behind Peter. The butler was waiting at the open door, face darkened by grief.

"This is a house in mourning," he said, solemnly. "As a result, this is not a fit time to welcome stray visitors."

"We are not stray visitors," said Peter with polite firmness.

He was about to explain why they were there when he saw, over the butler's shoulder, a tall, slim figure entering the hall at the far end and coming towards them. Peter guessed at once that it must be David Mellanby, the younger son. When he saw what the man was wearing, he realised that Hooper had failed to provide a telling detail about him. David Mellanby was a clergyman.

Micah Yeomans and Alfred Hale were back at their usual table in the Peacock Inn that morning. When one of their colleagues came in, they looked up with interest.

"Well?" asked Yeomans. "Do you have a name?"

"Yes and no," said the other.

"Talk sense, man."

"Yes, I have a name. In fact, I have more than one. But, no, I don't think that any of them is the name you want."

"Let us be the judge of that, Chevy," said Hale. "What have you discovered?"

Chevy Ruddock cleared his throat. He was a big, ungainly man in his twenties who took great pride in his work with the Runners. Tireless and ever-willing, he'd been rounding up some of the many paid informers on whom they relied to betray their criminal associates. Beads of sweat ran down Ruddock's face. He'd clearly exerted himself.

"Come on," prompted Yeomans. "Who was the assassin?"

"Two people gave me the same name," said Ruddock.

"What was it?"

"Ezra Gammon."

Hale snorted. "That's impossible."

"Next time you see these two barefaced liars," said Yeomans, rancorously, "kick their arses from one end of Piccadilly to the other."

"Why is that?" asked Ruddock.

"Ezra Gammon is somewhere in the middle of the Pacific Ocean on his way to Australia. I know that because I had the pleasure of arresting him. You've obviously forgotten that the rogue was transported. Since he's lying in chains below deck, how could he possibly shoot someone dead in Covent Garden?"

"Ah," said Ruddock. "I had a feeling they were misleading me."

"Then you should have knocked their heads together."

"Yes, sir."

"Gammon aside, what other villains were suggested?"

Ruddock took a notebook from his pocket and opened it to the appropriate page. He read out four names in succession, each one producing derisive sneers from the others. Yeomans grabbed the notebook from him and tore out the page from which Ruddock had been reading. He thrust the notebook back into the younger man's hands.

"Those names are worthless," he snarled.

"I did my best, Mr Yeomans."

"To extract useful information from them, you have to use pain. It's the only way to get the truth out of the lying devils. Let me show you."

Knocking Ruddock's hat from his head, he grabbed him by the hair as if to tear it from his scalp. When his victim yelped in agony, Yeomans released him.

"If you weren't so tall, Chevy," said Hale, laughing coarsely, "he'd have lifted you up from the ground and swung you in the air. Learn from his example and use force. It's the only way to make them respect us."

"Yes, Mr Hale."

"Do that and you'll make a good Runner one day."

"That's my ambition. I'll work hard to achieve it."

"Then before you continue your search," said Yeomans, "remember this. We're not just hunting the assassin. He had a confederate who was there to make us all look the wrong way so that none of us saw the shot being fired. Who was that confederate? If we can find *him*," he went on, "he'll lead us to the man we really want. The pair of them can then hang side by side on the gallows like a brace of plucked turkeys." After bending down to pick up the hat, he handed it to Ruddock. "Now get out there and start behaving like me."

When he came out of his club in Albemarle Street, the man was in a buoyant mood. He'd spent a comfortable night there and enjoyed an excellent breakfast. His hat was set at a rakish angle and his cane tapped out a pleasing rhythm on the pavement as he walked along. It was a short-lived stroll. An elegant, sleek, smirking individual stepped out of a doorway to block his path.

"I knew that you'd come sooner or later," he said.

"What the devil are you doing here?" hissed the other.

"I needed to see you."

"Our business transaction is over and done with. I told you I never wanted to see you again. You agreed to abide by that arrangement."

"Things have changed since then."

"You did as requested and were well paid."

"All I was told was that, at a given signal from you, I was to distract people by shouting aloud. You never mentioned that you were going to kill someone."

"It was no concern of yours."

"Oh, yes it was," said the other. "You made me an accessory to murder. That means my life is in as much danger as yours. What I did outside that stage door deserves far more than the paltry amount you gave me."

"You had what you were worth," insisted the other, grabbing him by the arm. "You're a useless, drunken, unemployed actor whom no theatre manager would deign to touch, let alone engage. I not only gave you a role to play — if only for a second — I also rewarded you handsomely." He released his grip. "There's an end to it. Do you understand? I never want to set eyes on you again."

"If *you* won't pay me," said the actor, rubbing his arm gingerly, "then I'll have to get the money from another source."

"What are you blabbering about?"

"Clearly, you haven't seen the reward notice. For information leading to the arrest and conviction of the person who killed Sir Roger Mellanby, a reward of seven hundred pounds and fifty will be paid."

"So?"

"All I have to do is to whisper your name and I'm a rich man."

"You wouldn't dare!" challenged the other.

"Yes, I would — if you drive me to it."

"You'd only put yourself in danger as an accessory."

"There are ways to get around that inconvenience. I'd use a friend to speak to the Runners, then let him have a small share of the proceeds. Unless, of course . . ."

Having left his club with an air of quiet triumph, the man was now extremely worried. Patently, it was no idle threat. The actor he'd used really was in a position to imperil him. He couldn't simply be shrugged off or silenced with a dire warning.

"Very well," he said at length. "How much do you want?"

"Two hundred and fifty pounds." The actor sniggered when he saw the expression of alarm on the other man's face. "I could get a lot more if I name you as the assassin. Remember that." He stepped in closer. "Is it agreed?"

After a long pause, his companion gave a reluctant nod.

"That's settled, then," said the other, grinning.

"You may have to wait a little."

"I want the money *now*."

"I can't just conjure it out of the air."

"You killed a well-known member of the aristocracy. Someone must have paid you a great deal to do that. I want a share of it."

"Give me a few days."

"No — I won't let you have a chance to disappear. I need it today."

"That's going to be difficult."

"Then I'll get the money from elsewhere," warned the actor, starting to walk away. "Farewell."

"Wait!" said the other. "I'll get it today somehow. I swear it."

The actor came back to him. "Where and when shall we meet?"

"I'll send a message to your lodging."

"How do I know that I can trust you?"

"I speak as one gentleman to another," asserted the man, looking him in the eye. "My word is my bond."

He extended a hand and, after a few moments, the actor shook it.

The Reverend. David Mellanby was an ascetic man with a soft voice and deep commitment to his chosen path in life. In becoming a parish priest, he'd willingly renounced all the privileges he'd hitherto enjoyed. When he heard why the visitors had come, he gave them a cordial welcome and invited them into the drawing room. Though Peter settled comfortably into his chair, Hooper sat stiffly on the edge of his with the look of a man who felt that he was trespassing and in imminent danger of ejection. Since Paul Skillen had actually been present at the scene of the murder, David wanted to hear every last detail passed on to his brother. He was touched that Peter and Paul had joined the search for the assassin of a man neither of them knew, even though their involvement could put them in jeopardy.

"I'm also grateful to *you*, Mr Hooper," said David. "My father often spoke of you as being wonderfully supportive to him in his work."

"Oh," said Hooper, surprised by the praise, "it were very kind of him to say so. I worshipped him."

"I would question your choice of the word 'worship'. Much as I loved my father, I reserve worship solely for our supreme Father in heaven. He is the source of all being. No human can begin to compete with him."

"Mr Hooper is a God-fearing Christian," said Peter in the man's defence. "When I slept in the bedroom he and his wife so kindly vacated, I did so under a sampler made by Mrs Hooper. It had a text from the Bible. All that he meant to say was that Sir Roger was a beacon of hope to people like himself."

"That's true," echoed Hooper.

David smiled. "Forgive me for being so pedantic."

The mood was sober and the conversation, albeit muted, was pleasant and unforced. The tone changed markedly when Barrington Oxley arrived. He was a fleshy man of sixty with a bald head fringed by white curls. He had a scholarly hunch, a sizeable paunch and a pair of dark green eyes that peered intently over the spectacles perched on the end of his nose. Peter felt the full force of the suspicion in his gaze. Oxley dismissed Hooper with a mere glance. It was left to David to introduce the visitors to his father's closest friend.

"Did I hear aright, Mr Skillen?" asked Oxley, eyebrows arched in incredulity "You have taken it upon yourself to undertake a search for Sir Roger's killer?"

"It's true," confirmed Peter.

"May I ask what possible right you have to do so?"

"*I* asked him, sir," muttered Hooper.

"Be so good as to remain silent. Mr Skillen can answer for himself."

"Oh . . . beg pardon, sir."

"Mr Hooper is correct," said Peter. "He made contact with me on behalf of the association to which he and Sir Roger belong. You'll remember that the two of them travelled together to London to speak at the Hampden Club."

"I'm well aware of Sir Roger's movements," said Oxley, sharply.

"Then you'll be equally aware of the faith he placed in Mr Hooper."

"That's irrelevant."

"I feel that we should be grateful to Mr Skillen," said David.

"The matter should be kept firmly in more official hands. When a crime takes place in London, surely it's the business of the Bow Street Runners to solve it."

"Then where are they, Mr Oxley? It was they who dispatched a courier with the dreadful news of my father's death, but there's no sign of them actually coming here to keep us abreast of developments."

"Nor will there be," explained Peter. "London is awash with crime and the Runners simply do not have enough men at their disposal to police the city with any real effect. They certainly have none to spare on a visit here. We are seasoned rivals of theirs. Where they falter, my brother and I have been in the fortunate position of taking their place and achieving success."

"I beg leave to doubt that," said Oxley with a sniff. "If you are such skilful detectives, why are you and your brother not in the capital together this very moment searching for the killer?"

"We have divided our forces. While Paul is on the trail of the assassin in London, I am hunting for his paymaster."

Oxley's cheeks reddened. "You're surely not suggesting that the plot to kill Sir Roger was hatched here in Nottinghamshire," he cried. "That's a ludicrous suggestion. Your journey here has been a complete waste of time."

"Not at all," said David. "I'm very grateful to Mr Skillen for coming all this way to give me the precise details of my father's death. It shows consideration. My brother and my sister will be equally grateful."

"I hope to meet them both in due course," said Peter. "All three of you can provide me with information about Sir Roger that could be significant in a way that you'd never imagine. And the same goes for you," he continued, turning to Oxley. "In view of the close relationship you had with Sir Roger, your assistance will be of paramount importance. I do hope that I may count on it."

Oxley spluttered.

CHAPTER
EIGHT

Paul's visit to Captain Golightly the previous day had eventually borne fruit. As a result of his persistence, he'd managed to get three names out of him of people who could be considered as Mellanby's arch enemies. Two were fellow Members of Parliament who despised him for what they saw as his unforgivable political stance, and one was a man who'd made the mistake of fighting a duel with him. Paul was still trying to analyse all the information he'd gathered from Golightly and from his prickly conversations with the trio of possible suspects. Over a late breakfast with Hannah, he told her about the duel.

"What provoked it?" she asked.

"The man believed that Sir Roger had designs on his wife."

"And did he?"

"Captain Golightly claimed that his friend was innocent of the charge. But when someone challenges you to a duel, he can't be ignored. Sir Roger, it seems, was very proficient with a sword in his hand and could have sliced the fellow to ribbons. In the event," said Paul, "he contented himself with inflicting wounds that were utterly humiliating. His accuser, Hugh Denley by name, more or less crawled away and would have had great difficulty sitting down."

"That would have left him embittered."

"When I spoke to him, Denley refused to be drawn on that point."

"Was he still angry?"

"He had good cause to be, Hannah. Losing the duel was bad enough but, when his wife realised that he'd thought her capable of encouraging another man's interest, she took umbrage and stormed out of the house."

"Who can blame her?"

"Would you have done the same in similar circumstances?"

"I'd never have been stupid enough to marry a man who couldn't hold his own in a duel. So," she said, "you now have three suspects. It's a start."

"Captain Golightly has promised to come up with some other suggestions today. Now that I've won his trust, he's ready to cooperate."

"That's good news, Paul, but you mustn't assign the entire day to him. We have our final performance this evening and I need you to accompany me to the party afterwards."

"I'll be there, my love."

"To be honest, I'm not looking forward to it."

"That's understandable," said Paul. "After your triumph on that stage, you must be sad at the prospect of parting company with Lady Macbeth."

"Far from it!" she retorted. "I've never discarded a role more willingly. It's been a bane in every sense.

Then there's the small matter of the invasion of my dressing room by no less a person than the Prince Regent, as ugly and odious a man as I've ever seen at close quarters. I felt threatened, Paul."

"You can forget him, my love."

"What if he pursues me?"

"That's highly unlikely to happen. It's common knowledge that Lady Hertford is his mistress and that the two of them are rarely apart."

"They were apart two nights ago."

"He's probably forgotten that he ventured anywhere near Covent Garden."

"*I* haven't," she said. "He frightened me. As for that grisly Scotswoman, I'll be delighted to see the back of her. Lady Macbeth is the personification of evil and it's not in my nature to enjoy such a role."

"A much more suitable one awaits you, Hannah."

"Does it?"

"Yes," he told her. "After a week's rest, you start rehearsals for a production of *Measure for Measure* in which you are set to shine brightly as Isabella. Shakespeare could not have tailored a part that reflects your character more precisely." He gave her a teasing grin. "Isabella has just entered a nunnery."

Hannah let out a yell of rage and snatched up the pepper pot, but she was far too slow. Paul had already fled from the room, his laughter echoing in the hallway.

On an errand that morning, Jem Huckvale caught sight of the reward poster relating to Sir Roger Mellanby's murder. He was astonished at the amount on offer and, when he got back to the shooting gallery, told Ackford and Charlotte what he'd seen. Both were impressed.

"I could retire in luxury on an amount like that," said Ackford.

"You'd never give this place up," argued Charlotte. "In spite of the effort involved, you love this kind of life. It fits you like a glove."

"And me," said Huckvale.

"That's true, Jem. You and Gully are two of a pair."

"We'll have to hope that Peter and Paul earn at least some of that reward money," said Ackford. "It will compensate them for the dangers both of them will face. They're up against someone who will obviously stop at nothing."

"They are not like Sir Roger Mellanby," said Charlotte. "They'd never be caught off guard as he was. When it comes to danger, they each have a sixth sense. I've learnt to put my trust in it, Gully."

"But if Peter is right that the person who ordered the murder might live near Nottingham, it will make him more difficult to find. He'll be on unknown territory there. Here, in London, he's familiar with all the dark corners and would be on home ground."

"I think the killer and his accomplice are *here*," said Huckvale.

"What about the person who hired them?"

"Your guess is as good as mine, Gully."

"He or she is here as well," declared Charlotte with confidence. "I've been thinking it through. Look at the circumstances. If someone had wanted Sir Roger killed, it would have been much easier to arrange the murder in some quiet place with nobody else around. Instead of that, the stage door of the Covent Garden Theatre was deliberately chosen as the venue. My feeling is that it was selected by the paymaster rather than the assassin."

"I see what you mean," said Huckvale.

"So do I," added Ackford, "and I wish I'd paid more attention to the actual scene of the crime. It tells us something. Most murders take place in private so that the killer can make his escape without being seen. This was, in effect, a public execution. Why?"

"I wish I knew," said Charlotte, "but you take my point, don't you? Whoever is behind this assassination chose the theatre for a purpose and could count on Sir Roger being there at a particular time. How on earth could they do that?"

"Are you saying that Peter is wasting his time going to Nottingham?"

"Not at all, Gully. Who knows? There may well he enemies there who are party to the murder and who need to be called to account. But the person leading the conspiracy — if that's what it is — lives here in the capital and is keenly aware of how Sir Roger behaves whenever he comes here. That made it possible to set a trap for him. It was surely a pure coincidence," she went on, "that the Prince Regent happened to come along at the same time."

"Without meaning to," said Ackford, "he actually helped the killer. That's what Paul told me. The moment Prinny arrived at the stage door with the Runners, all eyes turned to him. The man with the pistol couldn't believe his luck. He struck almost immediately."

"Sir Roger must have been a very important man," said Huckvale. "You can see that by the amount of reward money being offered. It's bound to arouse a lot of interest."

"It certainly will, lad. At this very moment, a queue is probably forming in Bow Street. It will consist of deep-dyed rogues ready to tell any lie to get a slice of that cash."

Harry Scattergood had made a conscious effort to move up in the world. As his income had swelled, so did his social aspirations. Having habitually lived amongst the dregs of society, he spurned the rat-infested accommodation in which he'd often been forced to hide and instead acquired a comfortable lodging in a respectable area of the city. He now ate better food, slept in cleaner sheets and wore smarter clothing. To pass himself off as a gentleman, he behaved with the necessary airs and graces, carefully rehearsed in front of a mirror. Most of the work was spent on his voice, altering its timbre, perfecting educated vowels and learning ease of speech. His appearance had also changed. Gone were the straggly hair and the pinched cheeks. A well-trimmed beard transformed his face enough to fool someone as eagle-eyed as one of the Skillen brothers. Emboldened by that success, Scattergood felt that his mask gave him total anonymity.

It was time to go in pursuit of the reward money.

Seeing his friend's palpable discomfort, Peter Skillen took pity on Hooper and suggested that he should return home and go back to work. Peter promised to report any findings to him later in the day. Relieved to escape, Hooper drove off in the trap. Peter was the only person who noticed that he'd gone. As far as Oxley was concerned, Hooper was never really there in the first place. Notwithstanding his hostility to Peter, Oxley talked freely about Sir Roger's political career and how the man's ideas had evolved over the years. David Mellanby supplied an occasional rider but, once started, Oxley was difficult to interrupt.

It fell to Edmund, the elder brother, to bring him to an abrupt halt. Flinging open the door, he strode into the drawing room with a whip in one hand and his hat in the other, his riding boots shedding mud with every step he took. His voice was harsh, his eyes aglow and his manner unfriendly. After nodding to his brother and to Oxley, he switched his gaze to Peter.

"And who might you be, pray?"

"This is Mr Skillen," replied David, "and he's taking part in the search for those involved in the murder of our father."

"Have any arrests been made yet?"

"I very much doubt it," said Peter.

"Why is there such a delay?"

"Before we can apprehend those responsible, we have to identify them."

"Then why aren't you in London doing just that?"

"Mr Skillen has this absurd idea," said Oxley, rolling his eyes, "that the person behind the outrage might live here in Nottinghamshire."

"Stuff and nonsense!" growled Edmund.

"That was my view."

"We can't rule anything out," suggested Peter, reasonably.

"Someone killed my father. Go back to London and find him."

"There's no need to shout, Edmund," said his brother. "You haven't been properly introduced to our visitor yet. Why don't you put your things down and take a seat? You've just ridden the best part of ten miles to get here."

"Where's Mother?"

"She's taken to her bed. Our dear sister is with her."

"How are they coping with the news?"

"To be frank, they're not. Mother is distraught."

"Then your place is beside her, David. Since you took the ill-conceived decision to become a shepherd, why aren't you offering succour to the most important member of your flock?"

David flushed. "I find that remark in the worst possible taste, Edmund."

"Mother needs you."

"The thing she needs even more is to hear of the arrest of the killer. That's why I'm so anxious to help Mr Skillen in his search. The villain must be caught."

"There are at least three people involved," said Peter. "The assassin had an accomplice and, almost certainly, both were hired by a third person. It's not impossible, however, that we're dealing with a wider conspiracy. That's why I came here."

Oxley clicked his tongue. "I've tried to explain to Mr Skillen that Sir Roger is viewed with the utmost respect in this part of the country. Nobody here would *dare* to harm him."

"Quite right," said Edmund.

"He may have been called rude names during an election, perhaps, but he dismissed that as mindless banter. Every time he stood, he won the support of a clear majority of electors."

"But a vast number of people," Peter reminded them, "were not eligible to vote. Sir Roger took up their cause. That must have angered those of more traditional views. Is it not possible that one or more of them objected to the way that his oratory was stirring up the local population?"

Edmund Mellanby walked across to Peter and loomed over him.

"Who *are* you, Mr Skillen?"

"I'm here in order to solve this heinous crime."

"Who sent you?"

"I came of my own volition."

"Do you have any credentials?"

"I have a record of success in such investigations."

"He's prying into the family's private affairs," complained Oxley. "He wants to know everything about Mellanby Hall except how often the bed sheets are changed. It is damnably intrusive."

"I disagree," said David. "Mr Skillen has asked some pertinent questions."

"But does he have the right to do so?" asked his brother.

"Yes, Edmund — I granted him that right."

"He did so in defiance of my advice," said Oxley. "Skillen is an intruder."

"I'm offering my *help*," insisted Peter.

"We can do without it," snapped Edmund. "Don't say anything," he went on as David tried to intervene. "*I'm* the head of the family now. I make all the decisions. When it comes to judgement of character, I prize Oxley's opinion above yours. You have this irritating habit of finding good in even the most disreputable people." His eyes shifted to Peter. "You are not wanted, sir. I'll thank you to get out of this house, never to return. Is that plain enough for you?"

"It is," said Peter, rising calmly to his feet. "I bid you all good day."

"One moment," said David, jumping up.

"Let him go," ordered his brother.

"But he has no means of transport, Edmund. His friend, Mr Hooper, took the trap that brought the pair of them here. Common decency obliges us to offer him a ride back to Nottingham."

"That's very kind of you," said Peter, "but I'm fit enough to walk and happy to do so. Now that I've had some insight into how this family operates, I've got what I came for." He distributed a smile between them. "Once more, gentlemen — goodbye."

Captain Golightly was in a far more hospitable mood. He invited Paul into his study and called for refreshments. When they'd been provided with sherry and biscuits, he made a confession to his visitor.

"I must apologise, Mr Skillen," he said.

"I see no cause for an apology."

"Friendship got the better of honesty. Out of loyalty to Sir Roger, I held back information that might have some bearing on the case."

"I'll be pleased to hear it."

"Did you speak to Hugh Denley?"

"Yes, I spent an interesting time in his company. He was unashamedly delighted to hear of Sir Roger's death but denied having anything to do with it."

"Did you believe him?"

"Not for one moment," said Paul. "Of the three people I spoke to, Denley would be my chief suspect. It was curious. Being embarrassed in a duel seemed to rankle far more than losing his wife."

"It was never a happy marriage. Sir Roger realised that and exploited the fact."

Paul was taken aback. "There *was* a dalliance with Mrs Denley?"

"I fear that there was."

"But the lady denied it hotly."

"She was seizing on the excuse to part with her husband."

"And did the relationship with Sir Roger continue afterwards?"

"Yes, it did," said Golightly. "In matters of the heart, he followed his own inclinations and . . . Kitty Denley is an uncommonly pretty woman." He sucked his teeth.

"You know the worst about him now. Forgive me for trying to shield him from the taint of scandal."

"That's a natural instinct. I don't blame you."

"Thank you."

"What state will Mrs Denley be in now?"

"I should imagine that she's in despair."

"Do you have her address, by any chance?"

"Yes, I do, but I'd counsel against your approaching her at such a time."

"Why is that, Captain?"

"She's in mourning for the death of the most important man in her life."

"That may be the best time to speak to her. At times of crisis, people often lower their guard. If Mrs Denley was that close to Sir Roger, she'll know things about him that might be of great value to me. Much as I hate the notion of intruding on her grief," said Paul, "I believe that, in this instance, it might be necessary."

Golightly needed the best part of a minute to come to a decision. Having made it, he got to his feet and crossed to his desk.

"I'll get the address for you," he said.

Peter Skillen made the best of the situation forced upon him. He used the long walk back to Nottingham as a chance to inhale clear country air and to reflect on what he'd learnt at Mellanby Hall. Two things had struck him forcibly. The first was the stark difference between the brothers. David had been kind, mild-mannered and grateful for what Peter was doing. Edmund, by contrast, was brusque, resentful and keen

84

to assert his authority. Within minutes of meeting their visitor from London, he'd sent him unceremoniously on his way and made it clear that he wouldn't be allowed into the house again. One major source of information had been closed to Peter.

The second thing was that Barrington Oxley had been so defensive. A man who knew most about Mellanby's political life was the one least ready to talk about it. While he gave fairly straight answers to some of Peter's questions, Oxley dodged most of them. Well spoken and highly educated, he was also slippery and secretive. It was almost as if he didn't want to help in the search for the assassin. What annoyed Peter was the way in which the man had treated Hooper. It was open contempt. Yet Hooper was typical of the people whose cause Sir Roger had been leading. Was Oxley actually opposed to an increase in suffrage?

Peter had walked the best part of a mile before he heard the brisk clip-clop of hooves and the rasping sound of wheels. He turned to see a curricle coming towards him with David Mellanby seated inside it. When he got close, David reined in the horse and the vehicle came to a halt. In response to a beckoning gesture, Peter climbed in beside the driver.

"I can't apologise enough for my brother's behaviour," said David, penitently. "It was shameful of Edmund to treat a guest like that."

"I was more offended on *your* behalf," said Peter. "Taking holy orders is an act of faith that should be respected. It involves making great sacrifices. Your brother was wrong to mock you."

"That was ever Edmund's way."

"I can't believe that your father approved of his attitude."

"They were often at loggerheads about it, Mr Skillen." He flicked the reins and the horse set off at a trot. "I'm sorry that your visit was in vain."

"Not at all," said Peter, "I learnt a great deal. That was largely down to you, of course. Mr Oxley was less obliging."

"He's still dazed by the shock of father's sudden death."

"To be frank, I doubt if Mr Oxley is dazed by anything. He seems to be remarkably self-possessed."

"Father relied heavily on his judgement."

"He's clearly a shrewd man but intensely private. One can't say that about your brother. He's more assertive and he relishes his role as the elder son."

David pursed his lips. "Growing up with Edmund had its problems, I must admit."

"What does he do?"

"He has an uncanny knack for buying and selling large estates," said David, "though I suspect that he may have another career in mind now."

"How do you know?"

"Father's death creates a vacancy and Edmund has always rather fancied himself as a Member of Parliament. Unlike me, he did actually go to the House of Commons to hear debates. When I've been in London, I always make straight for St Paul's Cathedral."

"Would he be likely to win a by-election?"

"He would if Mr Oxley was by his side. The family name would be a real advantage, naturally. Even voters who didn't agree with Father's views on reform nevertheless supported him. They'd stick by Edmund."

"On my brief acquaintance with him," said Peter, "I didn't get the feeling that he was in the same mould as Sir Roger."

David gave a dry laugh. "You're very perceptive, Mr Skillen," he said. "Edmund would enter Parliament for his *own* benefit, not for that of others. I'm sure that he's been saddened by the turn of events, but he'll never actually show it. And his anguish won't stop him taking full advantage of Father's death. While the rest of the family is in torment, Edmund will be poised to fulfil a long-held ambition. There'll be no holding him back now."

As soon as they were left alone together, Edmund Mellanby wanted to know how Peter had been let into the house at a time when they most needed to be left alone. He was appalled to hear about the freedom with which his younger brother had talked about the family. Oxley was scathing.

"The worst of it was," he said, "that he brought that untutored oaf, Hooper, with him. The man just sat there, fiddling with the sleeves of his coat and looking at Skillen as if he were a latter-day Messiah. Your father would never have allowed Hooper into the stables, still less into the house itself."

"What's your estimate of Skillen?"

"He's intelligent," conceded Oxley, "there's no question about that. I fear that he could be more than just a nuisance."

"Is he dangerous?" asked Edmund. "That's all I wish to know."

"He could be."

"I want him watched while he's here."

"Yes, of course. I'll see to it."

"Now that *I'm* making the decisions, this family will be given the protection it deserves. Skillen must not be allowed anywhere near Mellanby Hall again."

"I'll give orders to that effect."

"And we must devise a way to keep David away from him. My brother is such a gullible fool. He offers his friendship too easily. Skillen will try to exploit that. I leave the arrangements to you," he said. "Have him watched for the rest of the day, then send me a report of his movements." He slapped the side of his boot with the whip. "We need to send this interfering, self-appointed policeman back to London before he starts to cause trouble."

CHAPTER
NINE

The house was in a narrow road off Regent Street. It was neat, unpretentious and of moderate size. Paul was not at all sure what sort of a reception he would get. It all depended, he felt, on whether or not Kitty Denley had heard the news of the murder. If she had, it was unlikely that she'd agree to speak to a complete stranger at a time when she would be so distressed and vulnerable. Even if she were ignorant of the tragedy, Paul might be turned away but there was less chance of that happening. Because it was so important to win her confidence, he rehearsed his lines carefully beforehand. Only when he felt word perfect did he eventually ring the bell. The moment the door was half opened by a maidservant, he knew that the sad tidings had already reached the house. Her face was a study in sadness.

"I'm aware that this is a difficult time to call," he said, considerately, "but it's imperative that I speak to your mistress on a private matter. My name is Paul Skillen. Only the urgency of the situation would compel me to come here. Please convey that information to Mrs Denley."

"Yes, sir," said the girl.

After bobbing at him, she closed the door. Paul was left on the pavement so long that he feared his request had been summarily turned down. Then he became aware that he was being studied from an upstairs window. Pretending to be unaware of the surveillance, he moved two paces backwards so that he could be seen more clearly from the house. After another extended wait, he heard footsteps in the hall, then the door swung fully open.

"You're to come in, Mr Skillen," said the maidservant.

"Thank you."

She stood back so that he could step into the house then closed the door again. After leading him down a corridor, she paused outside the drawing room and tapped on the door. A frail, female voice invited her to enter. Obeying the command, she ushered Paul into the room then left. Hat in hand, he stood there and marvelled. Captain Golightly had described the woman as uncommonly pretty, but it was a gross understatement. Kitty Denley was uncompromisingly beautiful. Years younger than her husband, she had a slender figure and sculptured features that reminded him of Hannah. She examined him through large, moist blue eyes.

"Who are you, Mr Skillen?" she asked.

"I'm searching for the man who killed Sir Roger Mellanby."

She gave a shrug. "I don't believe that I know such a person."

"Then I beg your forgiveness and will intrude no longer."

After offering her an apologetic bow, he turned on his heel and walked away.

"Wait," she called.

He stopped and looked back at her. "Yes, Mrs Denley?"

"Who sent you?"

"Nobody sent me. I felt impelled to come, that's all."

"Why?"

"If you're not acquainted with Sir Roger, there's no point in my telling you. He was a friend of mine," he lied. "I had the misfortune to be standing next to him when he was shot dead." He saw her jerk involuntarily. "But I won't alarm you with details of what befell a person you never met. Good day to you."

"One moment," she said, rising gracefully to her feet and looking him in the eye. "I fancy that I . . . *may* have heard of the gentleman."

"He'd certainly heard of *you*, Mrs Denley. Whenever he mentioned your name, his face glowed with pleasure. The hope of catching a glimpse of you made the long journey to London almost enjoyable." A smile flitted across her face. "Evidently, this is not a time for reminiscences. You would rather be alone with your own thoughts. I appreciate that."

Before he could turn away again, she touched his elbow.

"Please stay. I sense that you are a man of discretion, Mr Skillen."

"I'm not here to pry. I've committed myself to the search for his assassin and wondered — just wondered, that's all — if you could furnish me with details about him that might somehow be of use in that search. Now that we're face-to-face, I realise that it's too great an imposition on you."

"What sort of details?" she asked.

"Sir Roger had enemies. I need to know who they are."

"If you're his friend, surely he told you."

"He named two Members of Parliament who'd made verbal threats," said Paul, "and he once made a passing reference to a duel he'd fought. That was how *your* name came to my ears."

"My husband misunderstood my relationship with Sir Roger."

"Did Mr Denley move in political circles?"

"No, he didn't."

"Did he number Oswald Ferriday among his friends?"

"Not as far as I know."

"What about Sir Marcus Brough?"

"I've never heard that name mentioned."

"If he had no interest in politicians, then he probably hadn't met Sir Roger before he fought a —"

"That's true," she said, interrupting him.

"How would your husband have reacted to news of his death?"

"I've no idea, Mr Skillen. We no longer live as man and wife, you see."

"That's your business, Mrs Denley, and I've neither the right nor desire to pry into it. What I really wish to know is this: did Sir Roger ever describe someone to you as . . . well, a serious danger to him?"

She pondered. "There *was* someone," she said at length.

Luck was a crucial component of Harry Scattergood's success. He'd lost count of the number of unlocked doors and half-open windows that had beckoned him in the past. Most people took care to guard their property, but he had the good fortune to come across householders who were less careful. It was almost as if they were begging to be robbed. In his pursuit of the reward money, he knew that the problem was to convince the Runners that his information was genuine. He therefore repaired to the Peacock Inn and glanced through the window.

Once again, he was in luck. Alfred Hale was there by himself. Had the Runner been with Micah Yeomans, it would have been different. Scattergood would have hesitated because it would have been more difficult to win the latter's confidence. On his own, Hale was an easier target, less suspicious and more ready to listen. Instead of peering through the window, Scattergood used it as a mirror in which he could tip his hat slightly and adjust his apparel. When he felt his disguise was perfect, he strutted boldly into the Peacock as if it had been named after him.

"I'm looking for Mr Yeomans," he announced.

"He's not here, sir," said Hale, politely. "I can speak for him. He and I work together. What might your business be with Mr Yeomans?"

"I've come about the reward concerning the murder of Sir Roger Mellanby."

"Ah, I see." Hale became sceptical. "You're not the first to do that," he went on, sizing the visitor up. "We've had fraudsters galore, each one turning up with a different pack of lies."

"Don't insult me, sir."

"I'm just warning you."

"Clearly," said Scattergood with disdain, "I need to speak to Mr Yeomans himself rather than to an underling. I suspect that he'll be a keener judge of character. What is your name, may I ask?"

"Alfred Hale."

"When is Mr Yeomans likely to be here?"

"If you can tarry for an hour or so, he'll return."

"I have business to attend to, Mr Hale. When he does arrive, you may tell him that Giles Clearwater called to see him with information that might possibly lead to the arrest of Sir Roger Mellanby's killer. It is not, I do assure you, a pack of lies. I can lay claim to an advantage that none of your fraudsters can match."

"And what is it, Mr Clearwater?"

"I was there at the time."

Hales gaped. "You were outside the stage door?"

"I was indeed," said Scattergood, grandly. "I was part of a crowd that saw the Prince Regent arrive with two bodyguards." He stared hard at Hale. "One of them, in fact, looked rather like you."

"It *was* me. Mr Yeomans and I were on royal duty."

"Shortly after you arrived, I heard someone cry out in agony. Then a fatal shot was fired. It was far too close for comfort. Like everyone else there, I took to my heels — but not before I'd seen the man holding the pistol."

"Who was he?"

"I prefer to talk to Mr Yeomans. There's far too much disbelief swirling in your eyes. I'll return when I can count on a fairer hearing. Good day, Mr Hale."

"Wait . . ."

"I'll report you to your superior in due course."

Before he could be stopped, Scattergood flounced out of the inn and left Hale with the uneasy feeling that he'd just made an embarrassing mistake.

After a visit to his bank, the assassin returned to his lodging so that he could count out the money he'd just withdrawn. He was seething with rage. The actor he'd employed had set a high price on his silence and his demand simply had to be met. When he'd finished counting, he reached for a pen and wrote a curt note to the man.

The deadly transaction had been set in motion.

It was the second time that Paul Skillen had heard the name. According to Kitty Denley, the man Sir Roger Mellanby viewed as a major threat to his life was called the Doctor. Paul knew at once that it was Henry Addington, Viscount Sidmouth, the incumbent Home Secretary. Captain Golightly had also mentioned him.

It had startled Paul at first because — even though he'd never met Sidmouth — he'd always thought well of him. There was a family connection. During the Napoleonic Wars, his brother, Peter, had worked as one of Sidmouth's agents in France and spoke often of the Home Secretary's intelligence, commitment and quiet efficiency. Could a man with such integrity really be implicated in the murder of a Member of Parliament? Paul was unconvinced.

"Are you *sure* that that was the name he mentioned, Mrs Denley?"

"Yes, Mr Skillen. I was shocked at first."

"So was I," admitted Paul. "Political life may be full of intrigue and vaulting ambition but even the most impassioned individuals would stop short of plotting someone's death. While there may be occasional duels between political enemies, I know of no examples of outright murder."

"Sir Roger felt that he was in jeopardy."

"Then why didn't he travel with a bodyguard?"

"He poured scorn on the notion," said Kitty, "and, with a sword in his hand, was well able to defend himself. My husband discovered that."

"Were any other enemies named by Sir Roger?"

"No," replied Kitty, "only the Doctor."

"He was called that because his father was a notable physician. It's hardly an appropriate nickname, is it? Doctors are supposed to *save* lives. They follow in the footsteps of Hippocrates and seek to cure. *Primum non nocere* is a phrase I learnt at school — 'First, do no harm'. If the Home Secretary *is* involved, then he's in direct contravention of medical ethics."

"I never thought of that."

Although she'd been conducting an affair with one man while married to another, Kitty Denley had a strange innocence about her. Paul could see how someone like Mellanby had been attracted to such a woman. It was not only her beauty that had captivated him. He'd also been drawn by her patent honesty and her desire to lead a very private life. Since some of it would be shared with him, he'd found her irresistible. For her part, she'd been in love for the first time and waited patiently for his occasional visits to brighten her otherwise lonely existence.

Putting her head at an angle, she stared at him with interest.

"You're a brave man, Mr Skillen."

"I'm simply one who believes in justice."

"Sir Roger often said that."

"Then he and I have a bond."

"I'm truly worried for your safety."

"There's no need," said Paul. "I've been in danger before. You might say that it's my natural habitat. Have no fears on my account."

"If you were there when it happened, it must have been frightening."

"It took me by surprise, perhaps, but I felt no alarm. I was simply left with this urge to catch the men responsible and haul them into a court of law."

"You could never do that to the Home Secretary."

"We don't know that he was definitely a party to the murder."

"That's true."

"So let's not condemn him without first getting clear evidence."

"How could you possibly do that?" she asked, hopelessly. "You'd never be allowed to get anywhere near the Doctor."

"Maybe not," said Paul with a smile, "but I do know someone who *does* have privileged access to him. In fact, I know him extremely well."

Even though he'd shared a coach with him for what seemed like endless hours, Peter Skillen had learnt very little of use from Seth Hooper. The man was too cowed by the situation to say more than a few words. It was only at one of the stops along the way that the brush-maker briefly found his voice. David Mellanby was very different. When they travelled towards Nottingham in the curricle, he was an absolute fountain of information. It spurted out of him in an endless stream. Peter learnt things about the relationships in the family that explained why Mellanby's three children saw so little of each other. It was a source of great bitterness to David that neither of his siblings had ever attended his church to hear him preach. With her first child due in a matter of months, his sister, Judith, had not even approached him with regard to the baptism. That would take place elsewhere.

"What about your father?" asked Peter. "Did he come to your church?"

"Oh, yes — but only out of necessity."

"What do you mean?"

"It was a case of *noblesse oblige*. Father had to be *seen*. There are a number of people in my congregation who voted for him. They expected him to exchange pleasantries with them on a Sunday."

"Was he not a religious man?"

"Only fitfully, I fear."

"Your brother seems to take after him."

"Edmund is far worse, believe me."

"Why do you say that?"

It was almost the last thing that Peter had the opportunity of saying because his companion launched into what was an extended sermon. As the youngest in the family, David had been the whipping boy almost from birth and there was an element of something akin to joy in his martyrdom. He simultaneously resented and wallowed in it. When he'd taken holy orders, he'd hoped that it would bring him closer to the rest of the family, but it had done just the reverse. Only his mother approved of his choice of profession. His brother teased him mercilessly and his sister more or less ignored him. Each lived in worlds from which David was deliberately excluded.

When they reached Nottingham, Peter asked him if he could be driven to the Black Horse, the public house where Seth Hooper and his friends held their meetings. David duly brought the horse to a halt outside the premises.

"I can't thank you enough," said Peter. "Being offered a lift was a godsend but your honesty about your family was the real bonus. Without Mr Oxley looking over your shoulder, you were able to speak much more freely."

"I felt such a relief at being able to do so, Mr Skillen. I love my family, of course, but I've never been well treated by them. I'd imagined that father's death would draw us closer together. That was yet another false hope. And don't pay any attention to Edmund's criticism of you," he continued. "It's all too characteristic of him. You are performing a great service for us. I'll pray for your success."

"I appreciate that."

After shaking hands with him, Peter alighted from the curricle then waved him off. He waited until the vehicle had turned a corner before going into the public house. But for the landlord, the place was almost empty. The man was wiping the bar counter with a cloth. When he saw the visitor enter, he stopped.

"I'm a friend of Seth Hooper's," said Peter.

"We all know who you are, sir, and you're welcome."

"I'm coming to the meeting this evening."

"Then you'll hear Seth speak. He's to tell us what happened in London. Seth's a grand lad. He has a way with words."

Peter hoped that his presence wouldn't inhibit Hooper. There'd been no sign of his eloquence so far. Crossing to the bar counter, he weighed up the landlord. The man was in his fifties, short, bearded, running to fat and with a face that was resolutely set in an expression of disapproval. Yet there was cordiality in his voice and, without being asked, he offered Peter a tankard of beer.

"Oh — thank you very much."

"You'll not be allowed to buy a drink here, Mr Skillen. It's free to you."

"We might have to argue about that."

The landlord was blunt. "You'll lose, believe me."

"Are all the meetings held here?" asked Peter, looking around.

"Each and every one — we're of the same mind at the Black Horse."

"Unity is important."

"That was one of Sir Roger's sayings. We'll miss him."

"How often are the meetings held?"

"Oh, it's once a week at least."

"Who's the main speaker when Sir Roger isn't here?"

"That would be Seth. He talks our language."

"And who is allowed to attend the meetings?"

"Only those who truly believe in our avowed policy," said the other. "Strangers are turned away. We want no eavesdroppers."

"So you've never had someone outside Nottingham coming by chance?"

"It only happened once, Mr Skillen — at the last meeting, as it happens. We were taken by surprise, to be honest. He'd never been in the Black Horse before, but we could hardly turn him away. Sir Roger wouldn't have let us."

"Why not?"

"It was his son, Edmund."

Alfred Hale had been cursing himself. After a string of fraudulent claims regarding the murder, a more credible witness had appeared. Yet Hale had failed to question him properly or to keep him there until Yeomans had returned. Giles Clearwater, he believed, had not simply come in pursuit of the reward money. Judging by his appearance and his lordly manner, he was already a wealthy man. Financial gain was not his motivation. He wanted the assassin caught and convicted.

By the time that Yeomans arrived, Hale was shamefaced. It didn't take him long to make his confession. Yeomans was furious.

"You let him *go*?"

"He had business in hand, Micah."

"And so do we, you numbskull. In case you've forgotten, we are in pursuit of a killer. I've just spent an hour with the chief magistrate getting the rough edge of his tongue, flayed because of our lack of progress. And what do you do when we finally have someone who was actually there at the time of the murder?"

"I have apologised," said Hale, meekly.

"You should be down on your knees in penitence."

"Anyone can make a mistake, Micah."

"*I* would never have blundered the way that you did. Even a dolt like Chevy Ruddock would have had the sense to take a statement from him."

"Mr Clearwater did say that he'd come back."

"He'd better do so," said Yeomans, eyes ablaze. "When he does, be sure to keep your trap shut." He clicked his tongue. "There are times when I despair of you, Alfred, and this is one of them. I'm bound to ask if you're getting too old for this job."

"But I'm years younger than you."

"My judgement is not in question. I still have all my faculties."

"And so do I. My mind is crystal clear."

"Then why did you make such a serious mistake? Why didn't you question this man more thoroughly to establish his honesty? You know my rule. Trust nobody until you have cast-iron proof that they are who they say they are. Mr Clearwater sounds promising, I grant you, but he hasn't been interrogated by a master of the art like me." Yeomans tapped his chest and bared his teeth, "*I'll* get the truth out of him, I warrant you."

He was at the appointed place well before time. It was in Covent Garden, close to a tavern frequented by unemployed actors like him. That was where he'd been approached by a man who offered him money in return for what had sounded like a simple service. He'd accepted the offer immediately. Then, as now, he'd been the epitome of elegance, hiding his poverty behind a fashionable carapace. With a large amount of money in the offing, his situation was about to improve. He could afford to pay a visit to his tailor again. A striking appearance was part of his stock-in-trade. It impressed managers of the city's theatres. Having money to spend, he might yet be able to resurrect his career.

When he'd received the man's letter, he'd been at once excited and fearful, exhilarated by the promise of a large fee yet worried that he might be tricked. Someone who could shoot a man in cold blood could never be wholly trusted. To settle his nerves, therefore, he'd popped into the tavern for a drink or two. He was now beside the alleyway, waiting to claim his prize. The actor even dared to believe that there could be further booty. After he'd spent his way through the first payment, he could blackmail the assassin again. But that enterprise lay in the future. His mind was focussed on what was about to happen now.

Expecting to see the man approach, he was startled to hear his voice behind him. The assassin emerged from the shadow of the alleyway.

"I'm glad that you obeyed orders," he said.

"You forget something," retaliated the actor. "*I'm* the one issuing orders."

"This is a final payment, mark you. I don't want you coming back to me in the future with more demands."

"It would never cross my mind."

"Do you swear that?"

"Willingly," said the actor, raising a hand.

"So be it. I have the agreed amount with me." He produced it from inside his coat to prove that he was keeping his end of the bargain. "I'm not going to hand it over in public. There are too many prying eyes. Step into the shadows with me."

Desperate to get his hands on the money, the actor followed him into the alleyway. He was almost trembling with excitement. The assassin handed over the banknotes with a wry smile.

"You'll never be paid so handsomely for such a fleeting performance."

"Is it all here?" asked the other.

"Count it to make sure."

The actor couldn't wait to do so, turning away slightly to get the best of what little light was available. It was a grave mistake. Preoccupied with his money, he didn't see the dagger that was swiftly drawn by his companion. With one hand over the actor's mouth, the assassin sank the blade deep into his victim's heart, holding him tight until the convulsing body lost all trace of life. After lowering him gently to the ground, the killer retrieved his money then melted into the shadows.

The rage of the assassin had been assuaged.

CHAPTER
TEN

While being driven to the theatre, Hannah Granville was at the mercy of mixed emotions. She was on her way to what would be the final performance of an acclaimed production. Transforming herself into Lady Macbeth once more, she'd be able to savour the adoration of a packed audience. It was her lifeblood. Hannah would feel yet again that thrilling surge of power. Set against that pleasure was the nagging fear that something would go drastically wrong. Only two days earlier the area outside the stage door where she was worshipped by her admirers had been the scene of a murder. Paul Skillen, the man she loved, might easily have been killed. Had she left the building earlier, Hannah herself might have been the victim. That thought was still dizzying. No amount of applause could expunge it from her mind.

And there was another source of apprehension. No less a person than the Prince Regent had been entranced by her performance. He'd come into her dressing room and ogled her with disturbing frankness. Hannah had been rocked. How could she prevent his being allowed into the theatre once more? Even Paul could not keep the future king at arm's length indefinitely. Where would His Royal Majesty's interest in her lead? The possibilities were unnerving.

Arriving at the theatre, she was met by two attendants who escorted her into the building. They conducted her to the dressing room and one of them tapped on the door. It was unlocked by Jenny Pye who gave Hannah a warm smile as she beckoned her inside. Though she'd been involved in final performances many times before, the actress was nevertheless astonished by what she saw. The room had been filled with so many baskets of flowers that it resembled a garden. Almost every surface was covered. On the remaining space was a pile of gifts, stacked high. When her gaze fell on the collection of cards and letters beside it, Hannah quivered.

"Have you looked at them?" she asked.

"No, I haven't," said her dresser.

"Please do so now."

"Is that wise?"

"It's what I wish you to do, Jenny."

"I'd be upset if I found something that might have a bad effect on your performance tonight."

"Do as you're told," snapped Hannah. Regretting her tone, she embraced the woman at once. "Forgive me, Jenny. I'm so troubled."

"I understand."

"I shouldn't ask you to do something I ought to do myself."

"I'm glad to help."

"I feel guilty. It's unfair of me."

Picking up the cards and letters, she glanced through them, recognising the handwriting of many well-wishers. Hannah was tentative to the point of timidity. Jenny looked on hopefully. When she'd been through all of the missives, Hannah was overwhelmed by a sense of relief. She then glanced at the pile of gifts.

"I did take the liberty of looking at those," said Jenny, quickly, "and there's nothing that will upset you."

"Are you quite sure?"

"I studied them very carefully. If he had meant to send a gift, I believe that the Prince Regent would have ordered something suitably lavish. Nothing in the pile fits that description. You are quite safe," said Jenny. "I guarantee that His Royal Highness will not be in the audience."

Hannah felt a heavy weight being lifted from her shoulders. She could breathe easily once more. At the same time, however, she was piqued. Having aroused the interest of the Prince Regent, she was annoyed that she'd been dismissed so quickly from his mind. It was an insult. On balance, however, she was glad at the turn of events. Having entered the theatre with foreboding, she now had the most wonderful sense of freedom. It made her resolve to give the performance of a lifetime.

Hannah wanted to get rid of Lady Macbeth for good.

Having spoken to five strangers in his search for the truth, Paul Skillen returned to the shooting gallery so that he could talk to someone he actually knew. His sister-in-law was delighted to see him and anxious to hear what he'd learnt. Close as they were, he could never have had such a conversation with Hannah. She had no interest at all in political affairs. Charlotte, however, was different. She not only kept abreast of the latest developments, she was able to hold her own in any discussion of them. Paul knew that he could rely on her to listen patiently. He told her about the potential suspects to whom he'd spoken.

"The first," he recalled, "was a man named Oswald Ferriday, a pompous toad who more or less refused to speak to me. He tried to hide his delight at Sir Roger's death but the smirk on his face gave him away. Ferriday is a Cabinet minister, so he was party to the discussions about the imposition of the Corn Laws."

"They're still causing untold misery," said Charlotte. "Mr Hooper told me that Sir Roger fought against them tooth and nail. One of his dearest wishes was to have them repealed."

"Ferriday called them an absolute necessity and sneered at those who opposed the legislation in Parliament. Needless to say, Ferriday is a wealthy landowner. He's never going to starve and doesn't care two hoots about those who certainly will."

"Did you get the impression that he might somehow be involved in what happened to Sir Roger Mellanby?"

"I'd put nothing past him, Charlotte."

"Who else did you approach?"

"It was another politician, Sir Marcus Brough. Like Ferriday, he was also a Tory but a much more reasonable one. He was prepared to talk more openly about what had happened and even had the grace to say that he was sorry to hear of Sir Roger's death."

"Did you believe him?"

"I'm not sure."

"That's unusual for you, Paul."

"I suppose that it is. Everything Sir Marcus said had the semblance of truth yet, in retrospect, his words sound rather hollow. Ferriday, on the other hand, was a blatant liar. I shudder to think that he has a say in the government of this nation."

"What's the next step?"

"I need to find out far more about both men."

"How can you do that?"

"I have an ally — a Captain Golightly. He offered to do some digging for me."

"I'm glad that you have at least one person on your side."

"He was a good friend to Sir Roger and is as keen as we are to track down those responsible for his death."

"Is he a politician?"

"No, but he has a lot of acquaintances in Parliament. Golightly has already been a great help to me. It was he who put me on to Hugh Denley."

"Who is he?"

"Denley is a man who unwisely challenged Sir Roger to a duel. It was an incident he didn't wish to be reminded about because it left him with several scars and made his wife leave him."

Paul then told her about his meeting with Denley and, later on, with the man's wife. Charlotte was upset to learn of Sir Roger's relationship with Kitty Denley and immediately thought of Seth Hooper.

"I hope that he never learns about this," she said. "Mr Hooper thought of Sir Roger as a paragon. It would come as a shattering blow to him."

"I'm not about to disillusion him, Charlotte."

"Did you think that Mr Denley was a plausible suspect?"

"Yes, and I still do. I'll keep his name very much in mind."

"You've made a promising start, Paul — as usual."

"We may have a long way to go yet," he warned.

He smiled fondly at her and reflected on the difference between Charlotte and Hannah. Before she'd married Peter, he'd courted Charlotte assiduously and was disappointed when she'd chosen his brother instead. He soon came to accept that Peter had attributes that would make him an ideal husband for her, and that Charlotte was not perhaps the right woman for him. Hannah, however, clearly was. Living with her was a continuing adventure that comprised long periods of elation offset by her sudden outbursts and wild demands. He could never have discussed an investigation calmly and sensibly with her as he'd just done with Charlotte. Hearing about other people's problems held no appeal for Hannah. She was too obsessed with her own immediate needs. It didn't prevent him from loving her but there were times — and this was one of them — when a conversation with Charlotte was a positive tonic.

"You have a gift for listening," he told her.

"I like to know what's going on, Paul."

"I always feel refreshed after talking to you."

"The feeling is mutual," she said, smiling. "By the way, have you seen the reward that's being offered?"

"Yes, I have."

"It would be nice to have a share of that."

"Why settle for a share?" he asked with a grin. "We want *all* of it."

Harry Scattergood had decided to make them wait. He didn't wish them to think that he was desperate to get his hands on the money. In deceiving Alfred Hale, he'd passed the first test. The Runner knew what Scattergood looked like because he'd seen him locked up as a result of being caught by the Skillen brothers. Hale simply didn't recognise him as the man he'd once seen behind bars. What had really convinced the Runner was Scattergood's claim to have been outside the theatre when the murder occurred. Having been there the following night, he'd picked up the information that the Prince Regent had been guarded by two Runners and assumed, correctly, that they must have been Yeomans and Hale. That had put the seal on his credibility.

Secure in his disguise, he returned to the Peacock Inn. Yeomans and Hale were there, waiting impatiently. Seeing him enter, Hale nudged his companion. Yeomans got to his feet and confronted Scattergood.

"So, you are Mr Clearwater, are you?"

"Yes, I am."

"And you claim to have been at the theatre on the night in question?"

"It's not a claim," said Scattergood, indignantly. "It's the plain, unvarnished truth. If you don't believe me, I'll speak to the chief magistrate instead."

Yeomans drew himself up. "Do you know who I am?"

"I assume that you're Mr Yeomans. You and Mr Hale were acting as bodyguards to the Prince Regent that night. I remember the two of you clearing the rest of us out of the way."

"That's true," Hale interjected.

"When the shot was fired, you hurried him in through the stage door."

"You see, Micah?"

"Be quiet," said Yeomans.

"Mr Clearwater really *was* there."

"Let me do the talking." He narrowed his eyes. "Who put you up to this?"

"What do you mean?" asked Scattergood, feigning innocence.

"Was it Paul Skillen?"

"I'm unfamiliar with that name."

"He really *was* outside the theatre."

"So were lots of other people, Mr Yeomans."

"He could have told you what happened."

"There was no need. I was as much a witness as this Paul Skillen was. Question me as closely as you wish. I've no reason to deceive you. I'm simply trying to help you catch a killer."

"I think he means it," said Hale.

"Keep your mouth shut."

"Sorry, Micah."

"Very well," said Yeomans. "Let me test you. Imagine that this room is the area outside the Covent Garden Theatre. The door behind you is the stage door. Do you understand, Mr Clearwater?"

"Yes, I do," said Scattergood. "You want to ask me where I was standing." He moved into position. "I was roughly about here when you and Mr Hale arrived. I was one of a cluster of gentlemen trying to get a good view of Miss Granville."

"So where did the shot come from?"

Scattergood pointed a finger. "It was in that corner."

"He's right," said Hale. "He *had* to be there to know that."

Yeomans was still doubtful. "I wonder . . ."

"This is getting tedious," said Scattergood with disgust. "Since you clearly don't believe me, I'll give you time to ponder what I've told you. Wiser counsel may then prevail. I, meanwhile, will be going to the theatre once again to see the ravishing Miss Granville give her final performance as Lady Macbeth. I wouldn't miss that for anything. Goodbye."

Leaving them open-mouthed, Scattergood went out with a flourish.

Peter Skillen was so perturbed at having deprived Seth Hooper and his wife of their marriage bed that he decided to spend the second night at the Black Horse. He therefore retrieved his valise from their house and showered Winifred Hooper with thanks. Apart from easing his conscience, it also meant that he simply had to descend the stairs to attend the meeting that evening. Several of those who turned up had already met him. The remainder accepted him at once on Hooper's recommendation. Peter was interested to see how much weight the brush-maker carried. When he was not quashed into silence by the Radical Dandy, he was a natural leader. Before the meeting, Peter had the opportunity to talk to some of the others in the group and it was an education for him. He soon realised that living in London had cut him off from important events taking part in the provinces. One name interested him.

"What did you call them?" he asked.

"Blanketeers," replied a thickset man with a fringe beard and gruff voice.

"Why was that?"

"Each man carried a blanket so's he could sleep under it on t'road to London. It showed he were a textile worker. Some five thousand spinners and weavers were planning to leave Manchester in groups of ten so they couldn't be accused of unlawful assembly. It was a *peaceful* march, Mr Skillen. They obeyed the law."

"What happened?"

"They were part of huge crowd as met in Manchester. Before they even left, they were set on by King's Dragoon Guards. Leaders were arrested. Rest of 'em didn't gi'e up easily. Hundreds set off bravely with a petition for the Prince Regent. They didn't get far."

"Why not?"

"They were attacked by dragoons with them sabres. Some of their wounds were serious. These were decent, law-abidin' men, Mr Skillen, yet they were treated as if they were deadly enemies."

"What did the petition say?"

"It told His Majesty about the dreadful state of the textile industry in Lancashire and protested against doin' away with that law."

"Habeas corpus?" said Peter.

"That's the one, sir."

Others contributed with additional comments. A couple of the men had relatives in Manchester and knew how bad the rate of unemployment was there. They were quick to point out that Nottingham had similar problems. Peter was shocked at the degree of suffering endured. He began to appreciate the scale of their loss. To have their spokesman assassinated in London had been a hammer blow for them. Sir Roger Mellanby was irreplaceable. The only thing that would bring them succour was the arrest and execution of his killer.

The main door of the Black Horse had been locked by the landlord before the meeting. They wanted no strangers there. Expecting simply to sit and listen, Peter was surprised when, after opening the meeting, Hooper suddenly called on him to say a few words about the search he'd undertaken for the assassin. Peter responded by assuring everyone that neither he nor his brother would rest until they'd caught the person responsible. While trying to sound optimistic, he warned them that it might be a lengthy process. As he looked around the faces, he realised that he was talking to a cross-section of the local working and middle classes, family men with other mouths to feed who'd exercised their right of petition to the Prince Regent in a bid to achieve urgent political reform.

At the end of his speech, Peter was taken aback by a round of applause. He went off to sit at the very back of the room, allowing Hooper to step forward and take charge. Having been told that the brush-maker was a good speaker, he'd been looking forward to seeing him in action. Peter was disappointed. Hooper obviously had fire in his belly and the gestures of a born orator, but he was curiously halting. He stumbled over his words and had to repeat himself more than once. There was a general murmur of discontent. The men there were used to hearing Hooper in full flow. It didn't take Peter long to realise that *he* was the problem. In front of his friends and neighbours, Hooper was completely at ease. The presence of a stranger — a well-dressed, highly educated man from London — made him nervous. Peter decided that the kindest thing he could do was to slip out of the room so that the speaker could regain his confidence.

The Black Horse was an ancient inn with half-timbering, low ceilings and an abundance of spiders. It also had undulating floorboards with gaps between them. As he walked towards his room on the first floor, Peter could just make out the sound of Hooper's voice. When he reached the end of the passageway, there was far more clarity. The speaker was fluent, assured and in command of his audience. Since the door opposite his own room was slightly ajar, Peter looked in and saw that it was empty, so he went in. He was now directly above the bar in which Hooper was speaking and could hear every word clearly.

A distinctive aroma wafted into his nostrils. It was the lingering smell of tobacco. Only minutes before, someone had been smoking a pipe in the room. Tobacco ash had been left in the fireplace. Locking the door for the meeting had been a wise precaution but it was not enough. Whoever had been in the room had heard every word of what was said below. While he listened, the spy had enjoyed a pipe.

Hannah Granville was always nervous when she stepped upon the stage. It was a common feeling amongst actors. There was the constant fear of forgetting lines, mistiming cues, accidentally tearing a costume, knocking over part of the scenery or tumbling ingloriously to the boards. Ridicule was only one mistake away. Hannah was trembling. Once she came into view, however, there was such a buzz of delight in the theatre that she lost all her anxiety and blossomed. She brought more attack, more malice and more commitment to the role than she'd ever done before. Three witches had already appeared onstage, but it was her sorcery that beguiled the audience. Other members of the cast were caught napping at first and had to adjust accordingly, striving to match her power and intensity. Led by the indomitable Lady Macbeth, they were determined to make it the most memorable night of the entire run.

The whole cast came onstage for the curtain call but all eyes were on Hannah. She was the undisputed cynosure and luxuriated in the ovation. From that point on, she was in ecstasy. All her troubles had flown away and she floated on a sea of praise and wonderment. By the time she'd changed out of her costume, Paul had arrived to take her off to the party held to mark the end of a remarkable run. It was a joyous occasion. As the wine flowed and the compliments kept coming, she declared that Lady Macbeth was her favourite role. Paul was amused.

"You said that the Scottish play was cursed."

"That was a mistake," she said. "It's Shakespeare's masterpiece."

"You vowed that you'd never take part in it ever again."

"The manager has already approached me about reviving my performance some time next year. I told him that I'd be happy to discuss the possibility with him."

"What about all those nightmares it gave you?"

"They were never really serious, Paul. I exaggerated."

"Well," he said, "I won't tease you about the way you complained earlier. I'm just so pleased to see you happy again, Hannah. The stigma attached to the play has somehow miraculously disappeared." He raised his glass. "Let's drink to that."

"Again and again," she agreed, laughing. "I feel as if I'm in heaven."

"I hope that you're not feeling *too* angelic."

She laughed as she pushed him playfully away.

Celebrations continued until well into the night. It was only when the majority of people had drifted away that they realised just how tired and inebriated they were. After bidding farewell to the remaining few, they slipped out of the room and headed for the exit. A cab was waiting to take them home. Paul helped her up into the vehicle then took his place beside her. They set off at a steady pace.

"I was so fearful earlier on," she confessed.

"I told you before, Hannah. Forget all about the murder that took place outside the theatre. It was nothing to do with you."

"I've already dismissed it from my mind."

"Then what made you so anxious?"

"I was terrified that the Prince Regent would come again," she said. "I saw that look in his eyes. It was the glint of a hunter as he corners his prey. He *wanted* me."

"He'd have to get past me first," asserted Paul.

"When I saw there was neither a gift nor a message from him in my dressing room, I was thrilled beyond measure. I was safe. His Royal Highness was not going to be in the audience, gloating over me."

"He must have realised that you were beyond reach."

"I didn't *feel* beyond reach when he was standing only feet away from me. I tell you one thing. If Jenny hadn't been in the dressing room with me, I'd have been worried for my safety."

"Yet you must have known that I was coming for you, Hannah."

"You weren't there, Paul. The Prince Regent was."

He quickly changed the subject before her memories of a worrying experience cast a shadow over what had been an extraordinary performance. Paul told her about some of the compliments he'd heard about her, stressing how many people had compared her favourably to Sarah Siddons, the erstwhile darling of the theatre. Hannah glowed. Adored on all sides, she was in paradise once more.

"Miss Glenn described you as the finest actress ever," he said.

"That was very perceptive of her. Working with Dorothea has been a delight and I know that she's learnt a great deal from my example. I'm an inspiration to everyone."

"Does that include *me*?"

She tittered. "Your name is at the top of the list."

"I aim to keep it there," he said, squeezing her arm.

When they reached the house, Paul got out first so that he could help her down from the cab. After paying the driver, he took a firm grip on Hannah to stop her swaying to and fro. Though it was well past midnight, a maidservant was waiting to open the front door for them. They stepped into the hall. After a night of such delirious excitement, all that Hannah wanted to do was to go up to the bedroom and fall into Paul's arms. Then the servant pointed to the letter on the table and, at a stroke, everything changed for the worst.

"It arrived earlier, Miss Granville," she said.

"I can see that, girl. And I can recognise that royal seal."

"Read it in the morning," advised Paul, dismissing the servant with a gesture. "It's far too late to bother with it now. Besides, I'm not having you upset again."

"I can't just ignore it, Paul."

"Let's go to bed and forget all about it."

"How can I?" she cried, snatching up the letter. "The Prince Regent is the most important person in the whole country I can't just ignore it."

Opening the letter, she read its contents and blenched.

"What does it say?" asked Paul.

"It's an invitation to . . . Brighton Pavilion."

CHAPTER
ELEVEN

Peter Skillen spent a comfortable night at the Black
Horse, free from the guilt that had assailed him when
he stayed with Seth Hooper and his wife. Since it was a
Sunday he decided to attend a service at the village
church where David Mellanby was the vicar. Having
hired a horse, he rode into open countryside,
marvelling at the beauty of the landscape and relishing
the rural serenity that life in the heart of London could
never offer. The parish church of All Saints stood just
outside the village. Dating from the sixteenth century, it
had a strangely daunting appearance with battlemented
walls that looked like castle ramparts and a formidable
tower that might have been constructed as a keep. The
interior could not have been more different: welcoming, uncluttered and a positive haven of peace. The only
signs of architectural flamboyance were in the two side
chapels.

Given the circumstances, Peter feared the vicar
might have chosen to spend the day with his family, but
the Reverend David Mellanby was there to preach to a
full church. It was evident that he had the respect of the
congregation and — since word of his father's death
was now common knowledge — its profound sympathy.

123

Barrington Oxley was present but neither of David's siblings had turned up. Peter was pleased to see how grateful the vicar was that he had made the effort to get there. After collecting a smile from him, however, he had to settle for a scowl from Oxley, sitting near the front with his wife. Every pew was filled and Peter had to squeeze into one at the rear of the nave.

Understandably, it was a muted service with the air of a funeral. David's sermon was tailored to the occasion. It had a marked effect on those who'd known and admired his father and Peter noticed how many handkerchiefs were pressed into use. He took his turn kneeling at the altar rail during Holy Communion and felt the vicar's hand touch him lightly on the shoulder, an indication that they should speak at the end of the service. Before that, David had to stand outside in the porch and shake hands with each of the departing parishioners. It would be a long wait for Peter, but he was not left alone. Oxley strolled down the aisle to him.

"I didn't expect to see you here this morning," he said, reproachfully.

"Do you object, Mr Oxley?"

"How can I? The church is open to all. But I would have thought you'd be on your way back to London by now. That's where the murder will be solved — not in a sleepy village like this."

"I came to show my respects."

Oxley glared. "You hardly knew Sir Roger."

"I wish that I'd had that pleasure. He seems to have been an exceptional man in every way and championed a cause for which I have a lot of sympathy. That only

124

serves to stiffen my resolve to find those responsible for his death."

"How long are you staying in the area?"

"Why are you so anxious for me to leave, Mr Oxley?"

"It's because I think that your visit is pointless."

"That's for me to decide," said Peter. "Sir Roger's younger son is happy that I'm here and so are all the people at the meeting I attended yesterday evening. They were kind enough to show some gratitude. All that you've done is to obstruct me."

Oxley stiffened. "What are you implying?"

"You're an intelligent man. I'm sure that you can work it out for yourself."

"It's a base accusation. I talked to you at length only yesterday."

"I agree, but you carefully evaded most of my questions."

"You trespassed on areas that must remain private."

"Dead men don't have privacy, Mr Oxley."

Though Peter spoke softly, his words had a powerful effect. The lawyer's face was puce with anger and he looked as if he were about to strike. Unable to find a rejoinder, he turned on his heel and marched towards the door where his wife was waiting for him. They went out together. The church was almost empty now, so it was not long before Peter was joined by the vicar. Taking the service in such circumstances had clearly taxed him. He was almost sagging with fatigue. Peter walked towards him.

"Let's go into the vestry," said David. "We can talk alone in there."

A combination of drink, excitement and the lengthy celebrations had tired Hannah Granville. Once she'd recovered from the shock of the letter from the Prince Regent, she had to be helped upstairs by Paul and put to bed. She was almost instantly asleep and didn't wake up until mid morning. When she came downstairs, Hannah was just in time to stop Paul from leaving the house.

"Where are you going?" she asked.

"I have to pay a visit to someone," he explained. "Captain Golightly sent a message by hand."

"What about *my* message? Have you so soon forgotten that? Having hoped that I'd got free of the Prince Regent, I've now been summoned to Brighton Pavilion."

"It was only an invitation, Hannah. You can simply refuse it."

"Nobody can refuse a request from our next king."

"Then you must set a precedent."

"I'm worried, Paul," she said. "How did he know where I live?"

"I daresay he got someone to follow us back here."

She shivered. "That frightens me. What else has he been doing?"

"Finding out everything he possibly can about you," he told her. "That alone is reason enough to tear up the invitation. Pretend that it never came."

"But it's . . . in the nature of a command."

"You're not at his behest, Hannah. Ignore him completely and he'll soon go away." He saw the indecision in her eyes. "Oh dear, I think I can read your mind. You're actually tempted to go."

"Part of me is," she confessed. "I've heard so much about Brighton Pavilion. It's supposed to be absolutely sumptuous. Seeing it from the outside would be a delight but being allowed inside would be a magical experience."

"His Royal Highness has another magical experience in mind."

She laughed. "Don't be vulgar."

"Well, he's not asking you there so that you can discuss Shakespearean drama. We both know that Prinny has taken an unhealthy interest in you. He has a reputation, Hannah, and it's one that you should bear in mind."

"Common sense tells me that I shouldn't go."

"I endorse that decision."

"But I'll never get such an opportunity again, Paul."

"Is it that important to you, my love?"

She was honest. "The idea *is* growing on me . . ."

"Then accept the invitation," he said. "You can go in all your finery and I will be at your side to protect you."

"But you can't do that."

"Why not?"

"Don't you remember? Mr Yeomans came here to pass on that message. You must not interfere in the investigation of that murder outside the theatre. If he lays eyes on you at the Pavilion, His Royal Highness will have you instantly thrown out."

"He won't even think of doing that, Hannah."

127

"Yes, he will. You saved me from him once before. He won't forget that."

"I'll explain that it wasn't *me*. I didn't rescue you at the theatre. It was actually my brother, Peter."

"But it wasn't, Paul. It was you."

"*I* know that," he said, winking an eye, "but Prinny doesn't. Besides," he added, airily, "it's high time that Peter came in useful for once. The decision is made. *I'll* be taking you to the Brighton Pavilion in his name."

In the privacy of the vestry, David Mellanby let his emotions show. Flopping into the chair beside the desk, he buried his face in his hands in an attitude of sorrow. Loath to interrupt him, Peter stood there in silence and waited. David was in pain. Grief at the death of his father had been compounded by the cruel way in which his brother and sister had refused to attend the service. Because she was unwell, his mother could be excused, but his brother, sister and their respective spouses were in robust health. They knew how much their presence would have meant to the youngest member of the family, yet they shunned him. Their behaviour was a warning that he'd have to suffer similar disappointments in the future.

When he eventually came out of his reverie, David rose to his feet.

"I do apologise for drifting off like that, Mr Skillen."

"You're under intense pressure at the moment," said Peter, waving the apology away. "You coped with it extremely well."

"To be candid, I don't feel that I did. However, let's not talk about me. It's too unsettling. I want to hear how you got on yesterday after we parted. You told me you'd attend a meeting."

"It was more of a wake than anything else, I'm afraid. However, that didn't prevent some vigorous debate. They're more determined than ever to carry on the campaign."

Peter went on to tell him that he'd been mesmerised. When he learnt about the Blanketeers, he realised how ignorant he'd been about the problems with which Manchester had been struggling. Nottingham was in the same position. It was when Peter talked about his discovery at the Black Horse that David spoke once more.

"Someone was *spying* on them?" he asked.

"I believe so. When I entered the room, I could hear muffled voices directly below. If I stood next to the grate, however, the sound was crystal clear. Anyone standing there could hear the debate coming straight up the chimney."

"Did you warn them what you'd found?"

"Yes, of course," said Peter. "The landlord was aware of the way that sound was carried upstairs to that particular room, so he always kept it locked during a meeting. Someone had broken in and smoked a pipe while he was listening beside the grate. I only wish I'd got there soon enough to catch him."

"This is all very alarming, Mr Skillen."

"It might not have been the first time."

"That's very worrying."

"I've been wondering how his assassin knew that your father would arrive in London when he did. The answer is simple. He was acting on information that curled up that chimney like so much smoke."

Paul arrived at the house and was shown at once into the drawing room. Captain Golightly got to his feet and shook his visitor's hand.

"Thank you for coming so promptly," he said.

"There was a sense of urgency in your letter."

"I have news for you, Mr Skillen."

"Is it *good* news?"

"It may be — then again, it may not."

"I'm intrigued to hear it."

"Another murder has taken place," he said.

"That's hardly news, Captain. Unfortunately, it happens all the time. London is the most dangerous city in Europe. Corpses turn up much too often."

"This one is rather special."

"Why is that?"

"It was found in an alleyway in Covent Garden."

"Ah." Paul's curiosity was ignited. "Tell me more, I pray."

"When I first heard of the crime, I assumed that the victim was some scabby beggar or some bothersome trull who'd harassed a client once too much. The area is plagued by such wretches. In fact, it was a young gentleman in the best of health until someone plunged a dagger through his heart."

"How did you hear of this?"

"I felt it was unfair to leave all the work to you, Mr Skillen, so I took it upon myself to gather what I hope might be useful information."

"I need all the help I can get."

"Well," said the other, "the first thing I did was to visit the place where the body was found. It was less than twenty yards away from the Golden Crown, a tavern used primarily by actors from the nearby theatres."

"I know it well," said Paul, "and it is a haunt of thespians, especially those who are out of work. Theatre managers often drink there so it is a place where unemployed actors can court them with a view to securing an engagement." He looked at Golightly. "Are you telling me that the murder victim was an actor?"

"I've no means of knowing but it does seem possible. Since I'm acquainted with Mr Kirkwood, the chief magistrate, I went to Bow Street to learn what I could about the case."

"What were you told?"

"Simply this — a gentleman had been stabbed to death and had his purse stolen. There was nothing on him to indicate his name but the description of him as being flamboyantly attired was enough to interest me. He was killed very close to the place where Sir Roger met his death. Could he have been involved in it in some way?"

"That's sound thinking, Captain. You've done well."

"I'm not entirely without experience when it comes to snooping. I was trained to lead scouting expeditions in the army."

"Your skills have been put to good use."

"Be warned," said Golightly, "what I'm suggesting is based on an assumption. It could well be that the murder victim had nothing whatsoever to do with Sir Roger's murder. I just felt that I should bring to your attention what few details I've garnered."

"I'm very grateful to you."

"My first impulse was to go to the Golden Crown to see what I could learn but I'd be a fish out of water there. You, on the other hand, could easily pass for an actor and are familiar with their world. If there's anything of value that could be gleaned from the Golden Crown, you are much more likely to find it."

"I'll go there at once," said Paul. "There is a glimmer of hope, I believe, but I'm also braced for disappointment."

"What about the Runners?"

"I don't follow."

"Well, won't they make the same connection that I did? They, after all, will have seen the victim. Surely, they'll guess that he might have been an actor and reach the same conclusion that I did."

"There's no danger of that happening," said Paul, grinning. "Micah Yeomans and his men will be far too busy chasing shadows to make any sensible deductions. Besides, they'll have their hands full dealing with all the fraudulent claims from people with one eye on that reward money."

Eldon Kirkwood had been the chief magistrate for enough years to develop a keen insight into the criminal

132

mind. His proudest boast was that he could always tell when someone was lying to him. Even the most plausible confidence tricksters were soon exposed when they appeared in court before him, and they went off to serve their sentences with his acerbic comments ringing in their ears. Now he had finally met his match in the person of Harry Scattergood. Still hiding behind the alias of Giles Clearwater, he'd gone straight to the chief magistrate to tell his tale. As always, Kirkwood was highly suspicious at first, but his doubts were gradually dismantled one by one. Scattergood's account of what happened on the night in question was so convincing that Kirkwood believed that he had to have been a part of the throng outside the stage door. The clinching factor for the chief magistrate was that Scattergood didn't ask for money.

"I'm a man of means," said Scattergood with an expansive wave of the hand. "I'm happy to fund my search for the killer. When he is in custody, I'll take a share of the reward money but only so that I can dispose of it to a worthy charity."

"That's very noble of you, Mr Clearwater."

"I'll take up no more of your time, sir. I have a villain to find."

Getting to his feet, Scattergood took his leave and went briskly out of the office. Kirkwood was relieved that a sign of progress had finally appeared in a case that had so far completely perplexed the Bow Street Runners. He sent someone to track down Yeomans and Hale. Less than twenty minutes later, the two of them were standing before him. Sensing the chief magistrate's mood, they quailed.

"Tell me what your investigation into the murder of Sir Roger Mellanby has so far revealed," said Kirkwood. "What solid evidence have you gathered?"

"We've been working all hours, sir," said Yeomans.

"At this very moment," added Hale, "we have men combing London."

"It's only a matter of time before we catch him, sir."

"In other words," said Kirkwood, icily, "you have nothing of import to tell me."

"That's not true. Hale and I have made what we feel is a big stride forward."

"Yes," his partner chimed in. "We made contact with a gentleman by the name of Giles Clearwater who was actually there at the moment when Sir Roger was shot dead. Mr Clearwater saw the killer flee."

Kirkwood's eye kindled. "And will this gentleman lead you to him?"

"Yes, sir — we have a firm promise."

"It's only a matter of time, sir," said Yeomans. "At first sight, I judged the fellow to be another fraudster, but he soon convinced me that he was telling the truth."

"Then where is he now?" asked the chief magistrate.

"We are expecting him any moment, sir."

"Then you expect him in vain, Yeomans. He was so unimpressed by the way that you and Hale treated him yesterday that he came directly to me instead. I have heard the full story that you were too stupid to draw out of him."

"But we listened patiently to him," said Yeomans. "By questioning him closely, we heard all that he had to say."

"His account differs from yours and I'm bound to say that it's far more convincing. As a result, *I* have heard the salient details that you should have got from him. When a witness brings in such significant information, your duty is to gather it. Instead, you and Hale let Mr Clearwater slip through your fingers," said Kirkwood with withering scorn. "In other words, you were far too busy thinking about the ale and pies at the Peacock to do what you're paid to do."

Yeomans and Hale exchanged a despairing glance.

Harry Scattergood, meanwhile, was celebrating the apparent success of his plan between the thighs of a compliant woman with a lilting Welsh accent.

Peter Skillen was glad that he'd attended the church service. It had been a moving occasion and given him the opportunity for a lengthy private conversation with David Mellanby. The death of his father meant that there would be a shift in power within the family that wouldn't advantage the youngest member in any way. All that Peter could offer him was his sympathy. Notwithstanding his clash with Barrington Oxley, he couldn't believe for a moment that the lawyer was in any way linked to the murder. Apart from anything else, Oxley had nothing to gain. By clinging to Sir Roger's coat tails, he'd been given a fleeting eminence that he'd never have achieved elsewhere. He'd masterminded elections, been taken to London on a regular basis and become an auxiliary member of the family. He would now return to being no more than a humble lawyer in Nottingham. Even if Edmund Mellanby replaced his father in Parliament, Oxley's glory days were over. His grip on the family was effectively broken.

Since he'd found no evidence in the area of a plot to silence the Radical Dandy, Peter decided that he'd leave Nottingham that evening, travelling overnight so that the journey could be faster over largely unoccupied roads. What he'd learnt on his trip was valuable but the search for the full facts of the assassination had now to be moved back to London.

It was some time since Paul had been into the Golden Crown but he was nevertheless given a cheery greeting by the landlord. The place was quite full and his arrival caused some interest. Those who'd never seen him before were on their guard at once, fearing that he was an actor likely to be given parts in preference to them. All that Paul got from them were hard stares and cold sneers. Those aware of his identity as the companion of Hannah Granville were green with envy because he had a role that every man coveted. As he looked around, he saw a dignified old man with a white beard seated familiarly at a table in the corner as if he owned the tavern. Since he'd bought drinks for Simeon Howlett before, Paul knew exactly what his preference was.

"Dear boy!" said Howlett as the glass was placed in front of him. "This is a true act of kindness. Please do sit down."

136

"Thank you," said Paul, doing as he was bidden. "How are you?"

"I am still lying fallow, alas. Though I have more talent than anyone here, I am constantly undervalued and cruelly overlooked. I tell you, Mr Skillen, there is no justice in the theatre unless it comes from the mouth of Portia in *The Merchant of Venice*."

Howlett's eyes twinkled. Having seen him onstage, Paul knew what a brilliant actor he'd been in his day but age had played havoc with his memory and he was largely unemployable. The table in the corner was now a platform where he was able to recreate the performances of earlier years for anyone kind enough to listen. Patrons of the tavern all knew and respected Simeon Howlett but few of them ever took a seat beside him. It was the reason he was so grateful to Paul.

"Dare I ask about Miss Granville?" he ventured.

"She is in good spirits."

"Good spirits and deserved hands, I feel. Had I been younger, of course, *I'd* have had the delights that you enjoy. Time has robbed me of so many treasures."

"You still have your health and your sense of humour."

"I'd trade both in return for more teeth."

"And your reputation as an actor is still intact."

"What use is reputation if it doesn't bring in any work? However," he went on, "I won't burden you with my worries. What brings you here today?"

"I'm hoping that you can help me, Mr Howlett."

"Not if it's money you're after. My funds are precariously low. I can give you a speech from the

Bard," he said, brightening, "though I can only remember those with no more than eight or ten lines."

"I'm here to talk about a murder."

"Which play do you have in mind — *Othello, King Lear, Hamlet*? Each one has murders galore and the Roman plays are nothing but orgies of assassination."

"This murder occurred in the alleyway close by."

Howlett chortled. "Oh, many a lively time I had there in younger days with willing wenches who raised their skirts and bade me enter Elysium. That alleyway could tell some stories, I warrant you."

"A man was stabbed to death there yesterday," said Paul. "I'm told that he may well have been an actor."

"Then he must have committed suicide. It's an exit from this abominable profession that I've oft considered. I'd stab myself to death like a demented Julius Caesar. *Et tu, Simeon* would be the last line I ever uttered."

"I'm being serious."

"So am I, dear boy."

"I'm sorry to have disturbed you."

"Wait," said the old man as Paul rose to go, "do sit down again. I remember now. There was blood everywhere, I'm told. His wonderful costume must have been ruined." Paul lowered himself down again. "I was shocked, Mr Skillen. We all were, even though we are well acquainted with hideous sights here in Covent Garden. To lose one of our own in such a fashion was blood-curdling."

"He *was* an actor, then?"

"Who else would frequent this fleapit?"

138

"Do you know his name?"

"I can find it for you. Give me an hour or two, Mr Skillen."

"I need to know *everything* you can tell me about this man. It's very important, Simeon. You won't forget, will you?"

"Memory is a strange thing. It responds to alcohol. If you buy me a second glass of Canary wine, I can guarantee that I'll have found out what you want in the time specified. You have my word of honour."

Left alone for the rest of the day, Hannah Granville felt that the best way to forget the travails of playing Lady Macbeth was to concentrate on her next role. To that end, she studied the scenes from *Measure for Measure* in which she'd appear as the hapless Isabella, a role she'd always wished to play. She was so entranced by what she was reading that she was lost to the world. When the maid entered, therefore, Hannah was jolted.

"I did knock, Miss Granville," the woman said.

"What is it?"

"You have a visitor."

"Really? I wasn't expecting anyone."

"The young lady said that you told her to come for advice if ever she felt in need of it. Her name is Miss Glenn."

"Oh," said Hannah, getting to her feet. "It's Dorothea. Show her in at once."

After disappearing for a second, the maid ushered in the visitor. Dorothea Glenn was a short, slim, poised young woman with the kind of beauty that only came into its own when she was truly animated. Hannah spread her arms in welcome and the newcomer ran into them to receive a kiss on both cheeks. They sat beside each other on the sofa.

"I hope I'm not disturbing you, Miss Granville," said Dorothea.

"Not at all — I'm delighted to see you."

"I've been studying the play," said Dorothea, glancing at the copy of it on the low table. "And I see that you've been doing the same."

"I'm just easing my way into it and doing my best to shake off all trace of Lady Macbeth. I fancy that Isabella will suit my temper more appropriately. But you don't want to hear about me. You're here to discuss Mariana of the Moated Grange. It's only a small role but one in which you can make an impression."

"I do hope so."

"You have a wonderful chance to play on the audience's sympathies."

"Mariana is a victim. She's been shabbily treated."

Hannah sat back. "Tell me about your initial thoughts regarding the part."

"Well," said the other, "my feeling is this . . ."

For a couple of minutes, Dorothea talked quietly and intelligently about her role, then she began to falter slightly. Hannah was immediately alerted. As a rule, her visitor was always brimming with excitement at the fact that a distinguished actress was taking an interest in her. There was no trace of it now. Her voice was strained, her body tense and her eyes dull. Hannah raised a palm to stop her.

140

"You didn't come here to talk about the play, did you?"

"Yes, I did, Miss Granville."

"There's no need to lie to me, Dorothea. I'm your friend. I want to help."

"Thank you . . ."

"Is it Mr Sylvester? I've noticed the way he looks at you. Give him his due. He was a fine Banquo but he's well known for pestering female members of the cast."

"This is nothing to do with Mr Sylvester."

"Then what's troubling you?"

"Nothing," said Dorothea, jumping to her feet. "I must go. It's dreadful of me to burden you with my worries. I do apologise."

"I thought you trusted me."

"I do, Miss Granville. You've been so kind to me."

"Then please trespass on that kindness," said Hannah, rising to her feet. "Tell me what really brought you here today and don't insult my intelligence by trying to fob me off with lies."

"Oh, I'd never do that."

"Then tell me the truth." There was a long pause. "It's about a man, isn't it?"

Dorothea nodded. "Yes, it is . . ."

"Well, if it's not Mr Sylvester, it must be Mr Garland and that, I must confess, *is* a surprise to me. His preference in the past has always been for slender youths with fair hair and ready smiles. What has Mr Garland done to you?"

"Nothing at all," said Dorothea with an edge of desperation.

"Then what *is* going on?"

It was too much for the young actress. Lower lip trembling as she battled to control her emotions, she suddenly burst into tears and threw herself into Hannah's arms.

CHAPTER
TWELVE

It was time to collect his earnings. When the assassin had been hired, he was paid a quarter of his fee beforehand with the rest to follow after a couple of days. Since he wasn't permitted to know the identity of the person who provided the money, he had worked through an intermediary. The man had seemed trustworthy and promised that the balance of the money would be handed over at a specific time. All that the assassin had to do was to wait at the meeting place and the intermediary would walk past and slip a bag surreptitiously into his hand. It would contain enough money to fulfil an ambition of his to visit Paris for months on end. Now that the war was over, the French capital had a strange allure for him. Its main advantage was that it was a long way from the place where he'd shot Sir Roger Mellanby and was now being hunted for murder.

When his full fee was paid, he would be rich, happy and able to sail away from London until it was safe for him to return there. He could then go in search of a fresh commission to put someone to death.

Paul gave him ample time. It was almost two hours before he went back to the Golden Crown to speak to

Simeon Howlett. Meanwhile, he hoped, the old actor would have found out the name of the man who'd been killed in the alleyway nearby. There was, however, a problem. As he entered the tavern, he saw that Howlett was no longer there. The landlord had no idea if and when the old man would return. Paul began to feel that he might have been cheated. Having tricked a second drink out of him, Howlett had simply walked out and gone to ground somewhere. Instinctively, Paul went off in search of him, storming out into the bustle of Covent Garden. He got no further than the corner before he was hailed by a booming voice that rose above the tumult. Paul turned to see Howlett hobbling towards him.

"I'm sorry for the delay," said the actor. "It took longer than I estimated."

"I thought you'd let me down."

"Shame on you! I'd never let a friend down."

"Did you discover who the murder victim was?"

"Yes, I did, and it was a name unknown to me."

"What was it?"

"Orsino Price."

"I've never heard of him," said Paul, shaking his head. "Since I spend so much time around the theatres here, I'm familiar with most of the actors. Orsino Price is new to me. How old would he be?"

"He was still in his twenties, I was told."

"Did you get a description of him?"

Howlett chortled. "What a silly question!" he exclaimed. "The fellow was an actor. That immediately tells you that he dressed for effect and behaved at all

144

times as if he's in front of an audience. Add the fact that Price was young and you can safely assume that he was handsome into the bargain. Such a person would dedicate his life to searching for work in the theatre and pursuing the choicer members of the fair sex."

"What motive would someone have to kill him?"

"Jealousy is the first that comes to mind. Perhaps he was stalking a married woman or one who was already committed to another man. Then again," Howlett went on, "he might have defied someone trying to rob him and paid the ultimate price for his bravado."

"That alleyway is in more or less constant use," said Paul. "The killer went there deliberately to murder him. That means he bided his time until there was nobody else about, then struck quickly before taking to his heels. Within seconds, he'd have disappeared into the crowd."

Howlett cupped a hand to his ear. "Could you repeat that, please? I can't hear you properly in this pandemonium." He indicated the tavern. "Why don't we step into the Golden Crown and carry on this discussion over a drink?"

"I'm too busy, Simeon."

"Don't I deserve any kind of reward?"

"Yes, of course," said Paul, taking some money from his purse and pressing it into the old man's hand. "Enjoy a drink on me. And thank you for your help. What you've told me may turn out to be of great value. Goodbye."

Seth Hooper was disappointed to hear that Peter was planning to leave Nottingham late that evening. Having him there had been a source of comfort for Hooper and his fellow radicals. They felt that they had somebody on their side and, moreover, that he would be a link between them and the Mellanby family Peter was sorry to have to shatter their expectations.

"Things have changed dramatically, Mr Hooper," he said. "I'm afraid that you can no longer rely on the cooperation of the family. Sir Roger's elder son has no sympathy with your cause and neither does his daughter. Don't look to either of them for support."

"What about the younger son?"

"David Mellanby is a man of compassion who believes in the cause his father espoused. In essence, he approves of what you're doing in his wake but is unable to take an active part in your activities. He has his hands full with the duties of his calling and, if he were seen to be involved in politics, he's likely to get a stern reprimand from his archdeacon, if not from the Bishop of Nottingham."

"We don't want to get him into trouble," said Hooper.

"You'll have to settle for his tacit support."

"What does that mean, Mr Skillen?"

"He can't speak out in public but is on your side in private."

They were in the tiny living room of Hooper's house. The brush-maker's wife and mother-in-law had been banished while the visitor was there. Early that morning, Hooper had taken them both to church where they'd prayed for the soul of Sir Roger Mellanby For most of the city, Sunday had been a day of rest, but

Hooper had spent hours of it in discussion with other members of the local Hampden Club. He was sad to lose Peter.

"We'll miss you, Mr Skillen," he said.

"The feeling is mutual."

"I'm sorry we couldn't offer you better hospitality."

"You made me feel welcome," said Peter, "and that's the most important thing. I enjoyed my night at the Black Horse — until some of the rowdier customers started to sing. The landlord said that Saturday night is always noisy."

"It's got quieter of late. Lots of lads are out of work and have no money to spend on drink. Unless the government does something about places like this, it can only get worse." He forced a smile. "Thank you for speaking at our meeting. You did very well."

"I'm told that you did even better after I'd gone. You're a good orator."

"I just try to copy Sir Roger," said the other, modestly. "Now he were a *real* speaker and no mistake. All I can do is hold an audience. Sir Roger could inspire them. It were a treat to watch him."

"Did he realise that he'd been spied on from the room above?"

"He thought it were very likely. It's what happened in Manchester with them Blanketeers. Agents were sent from London to keep a close eye on them. That's where the order would have come for them to be attacked by dragoons."

"That would have been the local magistrates' doing, surely?"

147

"They were instructed by the government."

"Do you have any proof of that?" asked Peter.

"Sir Roger did."

"So who actually dispatched agents to keep people under surveillance?"

"The Home Secretary."

Peter was astounded. "Viscount Sidmouth?"

"That's what Sir Roger believed."

"Then I wish I'd met him because I'd have been able to tell him that it was highly unlikely. I happen to know the Home Secretary quite well because I was employed by him during the war to gather intelligence in France. I found him a decent and humane man," said Peter, "and he's been very helpful to me."

Hooper shrugged. "I can only say what I was told."

"Then you've been misled, I'm afraid. Any political meetings broken up and any marches prevented were victims of the local magistracy. They are the people to blame, Mr Hooper. I give you my word that the Home Secretary wouldn't dream of doing such a thing."

Though Peter spoke with passion, Hooper was unconvinced.

"Maybe it's time you *did* go back to London, sir," he said.

Harry Scattergood differed from the rest of the thieves who infested London. The majority of them stole in order to feed and clothe their families. Crime was a matter of survival. There were others whose exploits were more lucrative and who spent their ill-gotten gains on luxuries they couldn't otherwise have afforded. Very

148

few of them actually saved what they'd earned by the fruit of their brains and the quickness of their hands. The concept of insurance was foreign to them. Their lives were based on a philosophy of steal and spend.

What set Scattergood apart from the herd was that he kept much of what he'd stolen and took care to hide it in a variety of places. Whenever he needed money he could drop in on one of what he liked to call his private banks. Evading capture was his forte. He kept out of reach of the Runners by having a number of bolt-holes, each one equipped with several modes of exit in case he'd been tracked there. One of them had been a brothel where the talents of a beautiful young woman were reserved for his exclusive usage. It was with Welsh Mary that he was now lying naked on a bed. They were in the well-appointed lodging he'd bought when he decided to transform himself into a gentleman.

Welsh Mary had also undergone a complete transformation. Instead of the tawdry apparel of a prostitute, she now wore fine clothes and expensive jewellery. He had schooled her in speech, manners and deportment. Whenever she left the building on his arm, she looked the gracious wife that she was intended to be. If they needed to speak to anyone, Scattergood did all the talking, eager to hide the musical Welsh cadences of his lover. In private, however, he loved to hear them.

"How long are we going to stay here, Harry?" she wondered.

"We'll soon be moving to somewhere more suitable, my love."

"But I like it here."

"You deserve something better."

She giggled. "I've got everything I want."

"I've explained to you before," he said, stroking her cheek absent-mindedly. "We can't stay anywhere too long. It gets us noticed. People ask questions."

"I like to be talked about. It makes me feel important."

"You are important, Mary — to *me*."

She giggled again. He rolled over and kissed her full on the lips. Leaning on his elbows, he looked down at her with a fond smile.

"Something very big is in the offing," he confided.

"What are you going to steal this time?"

"It's not really a case of stealing, my love. I'm merely helping myself to some reward money for capturing a murderer."

She shivered involuntarily. "Don't put yourself in any danger."

"He's not a *real* murderer so there's no danger."

"Tell me more."

"No," he said, pushing her hair back gently from her forehead. "The less you know, the less you'll fret about my safety. All I will say is this. If everything goes as planned, I'll have the biggest haul of my career."

"I love you, Harry," she said, staring into his eyes. "Shall I tell you why?"

"Afterwards," he whispered.

Then he mounted her with his customary zeal.

The assassin had always liked St James's Park. It was the oldest of London's royal parks with a large acreage and a spectacular display of trees, flowers, shrubs, lawns and arbours. At that time on a Sunday afternoon, many people had flocked there to enjoy a stroll, trot on their horses or simply ride by in their open carriages to admire the view and be, in turn, admired. It was a place that held no danger for the assassin. Had there been a plan to betray him, he felt, he'd have been asked to meet after the city had been shrouded in darkness. As he watched the dandies and their ladies disporting themselves in the saddle or in their carriages, he promised that he would be doing the same when he reached Paris. Here he was just another pedestrian. When he got to France, he'd ride along the boulevards of the capital on a thoroughbred horse.

At that moment, another horse claimed his attention. He first caught sight of it out of the corner of his eye, cantering towards him from behind, then slowing to a leisurely trot. When it went past, it was only a matter of yards away, close enough for him to recognise the rider and to notice the black silk bag that hung from the pommel of his saddle by its tassels. By patting it, the rider confirmed what the man had hoped. The bag contained the final payment for services rendered. The assassin was thrilled. Paris suddenly seemed a great deal closer.

It was too public a place for the exchange, so the horseman cantered on to a stand of trees and disappeared from sight. He would be waiting near the fountain he'd designated. Heart pounding and stride lengthening, the assassin moved swiftly across the grass. He couldn't wait to get his hands on his money. But his

151

haste turned out to be a mistake because — when he'd almost reached the trees — his toe was caught in a clump of grass and he stumbled badly. The lurch forward saved his life. Out of nowhere a shot was fired so close to his head that he heard it whistle past his ear and end up in the trunk of an elm. He was on the defensive at once, seeking cover and pulling out a pistol from inside his coat. There was no silk bag stuffed with money. He'd been lured into a trap.

Having been hired to hunt someone, he was now the prey.

Captain Golightly was very impressed by what he'd been told. He congratulated Paul on the way in which he'd gathered a vital piece of information and thanked him for calling at the house to explain how he'd done it.

"Actors live in a world of gossip," said Paul, "and news travels like lightning. If anyone could find out the victim's name, I knew it would be Simeon Howlett. He's a veritable oasis of gossip."

"So this fellow earned a living in the theatre, did he?"

"That was his intention, Captain, but he failed abysmally. However good they are, most actors are out of work at various periods of their life. It's unavoidable. In the case of Orsino Price, it was not merely an occasional setback. He seems to have been permanently unemployed."

"What effect would that have had on his character?"

152

"It would have been very lowering. Imagine how a soldier would feel if he were never allowed to go into combat."

"I can think of some who'd have been delighted," said Golightly with a dry laugh, "but I take your point. When the profession he loved so much spurned him, iron must have entered this man's soul."

"That would have made him vulnerable to other offers."

"You think he'd stoop to murder?"

"No," said Paul, "I doubt that very much. The killer needed to be invisible. Price would never settle for that. Even in the middle of a crowd, he'd want to preen. There were dozens of others doing exactly the same thing outside the stage door."

"In that case, he must have been there simply to assist."

"We don't know that. It may be that Orsino Price was nowhere near Covent Garden on that fateful night. If I was an unemployed actor, I'd never go within a mile of a theatre at a time when crowds were pouring into it to watch people deemed to be better actors than me. It would remind me that I was an abject failure."

"You're quite right," said Golightly. "We're jumping to conclusions again."

"We're concentrating on the killer when the person or persons we really need to find are those who devised the plot in the first place. I think that I should take a second look at Oswald Ferriday."

"What about Hugh Denley?"

"Another word with him wouldn't come amiss," said Paul, "and I ought to speak to his estranged wife once more. During our first conversation, a great deal was left unsaid."

"Mrs Denley got closer to Sir Roger than anyone else."

"She was still dazed at the news of his murder when I met her."

"Then a second visit might be productive."

"We can but hope."

"You seem to have a way of extracting sensitive information out of people."

"I just listen, that's all."

"Ferriday, Denley and his wife . . . that leaves Sir Marcus Brough."

"The only thing I managed to extract out him was a lot of bluster."

"That could just be a smokescreen."

"Of all the people I talked to, Ferriday was the prickliest."

"Don't let that deter you," said Golightly.

"I won't."

"Thorns have to be grasped sometimes."

"I know," said Paul with a grin. "The trick is to wear thick gloves."

Peter Skillen got to the coaching inn hours ahead of the departure time. Having left Hooper with a promise that he'd work around the clock to find out who had instigated the murder of the Radical Dandy, he wanted time alone to consider the situation and to collate all

154

the intelligence he'd so far gathered about the Mellanby family and the activities of the local Hampden Club. Peter was worried that he and the brush-maker had parted on a sour note. The two men had enjoyed a friendly relationship until the name of Viscount Sidmouth was mentioned. They were suddenly on different sides of the argument. Hooper was adamant that the Home Secretary was directly responsible for the persecution of the Blanketeers and the decision to monitor political dissent in Nottingham. While not saying it in so many words, Hooper had come to believe that Sidmouth was somehow implicated in the murder of Sir Roger Mellanby.

The charge still hurt Peter like the sting of a wasp. He knew that Sidmouth had been party to the repressive legislation designed to clamp down on dissidents in a bid to stave off the danger of riots. Though Peter didn't agree with the severity of the laws that were drafted, he accepted that public order had to be preserved. Hooper had been embittered by the fact that, even though the Hampden Clubs were careful to work within the law, they were still considered to be enemies of society. That was why someone had been sent to eavesdrop on meetings at the Black Horse, a fact that Peter could hardly contradict.

Since he regarded the Home Secretary as a good friend, Peter had tried hard to absolve the man of being the monster he was portrayed in places like Manchester and Nottingham. His respect for Sidmouth was not only based on the work he did for him in France during the war. They had kept in touch ever since and Peter had been able to solve a puzzling crime at the Home Office itself, earning him the gratitude of Sidmouth. Could a politician whom he admired for his integrity really be the ogre Hooper had described? If that were the case, Peter realised, then he'd let friendship leave him blinkered. It was a salutary thought.

Further introspection was brought to a halt by the noise of the door creaking on its hinges. Two men entered. One was carrying a heavy valise but it was the other who caused Peter to sit up in surprise. It was Barrington Oxley, about to set off on a journey. When the lawyer caught sight of Peter, he walked across to him.

"Ah," he said with a smirk, "you've finally accepted what I told you. Coming here was a pointless exercise."

"I don't agree, Mr Oxley. It's been a journey of discovery."

"And what do you have to show for it?"

"To begin with," said Peter, "I have a far greater understanding of the work that Sir Roger was doing. I'm sorry that it wasn't endorsed by everyone in his family."

"That's none of your business."

"It must have been a source of regret for him."

"He was not a man to be troubled by regret. When you are driven by a passion, you don't let disappointment get in your way. Sir Roger always surged on regardless."

"I'd be interested to hear more about him, Mr Oxley. If you and I are to travel in the mail coach together, the time would pass more quickly if we had a civilised conversation for once."

"That won't be possible, I fear."

"Why not — you *are* travelling to London, I presume?"

"Indeed, I am, Mr Skillen."

"Are we simply going to glare at each other in silence?"

"I think you'll find that that would be quite impossible," said Oxley with a laugh. "By the time the mail coach departs, I will be well ahead of you on the road." He looked up as he heard the clatter of hooves and the noise of wheels on the cobbles outside. "It sounds as if my transport has just arrived." He clicked his fingers and the servant picked up the luggage again. "Goodbye, Mr Skillen. I doubt very much that we shall meet again. I'm going to London to arrange, amongst other things, for the return of Sir Roger's body. You, meanwhile, I predict, will be chasing your own tail and getting nowhere."

Oxley gave him a farewell wave and went breezily out through the door with his luggage following him. Peter was on his feet at once, crossing to the window to peer out. A coach was waiting to take a new passenger aboard. When its door opened, Peter saw that Oxley wouldn't be travelling alone. Beckoning him to climb into the vehicle was the new head of the family — Edmund Mellanby.

The assassin was pulsing with rage. He'd just had the narrowest of escapes from death. Instead of being paid for the murder he'd committed, he'd been destined to join his victim in the grave. Survival was now his priority. Since he couldn't actually see anyone about to launch a second attack, he ran quickly away from the trees and mingled with the crowd. He was safe there. He'd taken risks to earn his reward yet, the moment it was dangled in front of him, it was replaced by a murderous bullet. It meant that he was expendable.

His fury was tempered by caution. When he reached the gate, he hailed a cab and ordered the driver to whip the horse into a gallop. Instead of going straight back to his lodging, he took a circuitous route, asking the driver to stop at one point so that he could get out of the cab to make sure that nobody was following him. Clambering into the vehicle once more, he was driven off. Since the first attempt on his life had failed, he feared that a second might be made at his lodging. He therefore alighted from the cab a couple of streets away so that he could approach the address with care. One hand on his pistol, he walked past the building to see if anyone was keeping watch at the upstairs window, ready to open it. It remained shut. Only when he was convinced that nobody was lying in wait for him did he enter the house by the rear entrance and creep upstairs.

Unlocking his door, he opened it on a scene of complete destruction. The furniture had been overturned, the bed linen had been ripped to pieces and every item in his wardrobe had been shredded. Worst of all was the fact that the carpet had been pulled up to reveal a gaping void. The loose floorboard under which he'd hidden the money he'd already been paid had been yanked out. The space below was empty. Denied his second payment, he'd also been relieved of his first one. They'd taken everything and would be back to claim his life. Fondling his pistol, the assassin reached his decision. He had to kill or be killed.

When he'd left Captain Golightly's house, Paul made a detour so that he could call in at the shooting gallery to deliver an interim report. Charlotte and Ackford were struck by the amount of valuable work he'd already put in, but they differed on one point.

"I think that you should forget that actor," said Ackford. "I don't believe that he has any connection with the murder outside the stage door."

"I disagree," said Charlotte. "It's far too great a coincidence that a dead body turns up so close to the place where Sir Roger Mellanby was killed."

"It's a distraction."

"Why do you think that, Gully?" asked Paul.

"We're dealing with a political crime. You should be concentrating all your efforts on a search for the politicians behind it."

"That doesn't mean we ignore a vital piece of evidence when it falls into Paul's lap," argued Charlotte.

"I don't see it as evidence."

"Well, you should do."

"It's not convincing, Charlotte. All that we know is that someone was killed in that alleyway. A drunken old actor gave Paul a name. He could've invented it in order to get another free drink."

"Simeon wouldn't lie to me," said Paul. "I trust him."

"But there's no proof that the victim was linked to the earlier murder."

"Yes, there is, Gully," said Charlotte. "I feel it in my bones."

"Well, I don't, I'm afraid. What about you, Paul?"

"To be honest," said the other, "I'm in two minds. When I first heard his name, I felt elated. We finally had an important clue. Yes, it was a political crime but there was also a theatrical element to it. Orsino Price seemed to fit neatly into the picture, somehow. On reflection, however, I've scolded myself for getting too excited about what is — as Gully points out — rather flimsy evidence."

"But it isn't," urged Charlotte.

"It's beginning to look that way."

"You found out something of real value. Believe in it."

"If I do that, I'll allow myself to think that we've made real progress."

"You're only deceiving yourselves," said Ackford.

"We deserve a slice of luck."

"That's not what this is, Paul."

"Why not?"

"You're trying to connect two murders that may have nothing whatsoever to do with each other. Covent Garden is a bear pit. Everyone knows that. People get assaulted there all the time. Unfortunately, some of them die. Orsino Price happens to be the latest in a long line. That's his only significance."

160

"I wonder . . ." said Paul, mulling it over.

"Don't listen to Gully," advised Charlotte. "Be optimistic."

"That's what I'm trying to be, but my brain keeps issuing a warning."

"Ignore your brain and act from the heart."

"I did that once before," said Paul, chuckling.

"Yes, and look what happened. You finished up with the most beautiful actress in London. I've never heard you complain about that."

"You never will," said Ackford, grinning. "Paul had outrageous good fortune."

"It's happened again," she insisted. "Finding out about Orsino Price is a gift from God. We just need the courage to believe in it."

"Speak for yourself, Charlotte. In my view, it's sheer folly."

"Then we must agree to differ with you, Gully," said Paul, making his decision. "I agree with my lovely sister-in-law, I've stumbled on pure gold."

Peter Skillen was becoming impatient, fuming because Oxley and Edmund Mellanby had already set off for London. He accepted that there would be a post-mortem and an inquest before the body was released and that the two men had the perfect right to make their way to the capital. Peter's fear was that their presence there would only hinder the investigation that he and Paul were conducting. Oxley was bound to report to the Bow Street Runners that the Skillen brothers believed that only they could solve the heinous

161

crime. As a result, Yeomans and Hale would be issuing threats against them once more and hampering them in every way.

Peter also felt slightly embarrassed. His belief that Oxley would be cast aside by the Mellanby family was a misjudgement on his part. The lawyer was patently still in favour. To make matters worse, he'd been carried off in Edmund Mellanby's private coach. It was vexing.

As he sat there reviewing events, he eventually became aware that someone was standing directly in front of him. He looked up to see that it was Seth Hooper. The man's face was impassive. He was holding a small package and, after a moment, he gave it to Peter. After a brief handshake, Hooper walked out of the inn, leaving Peter to peel back the pieces of paper. Inside the package, he found a pie and some pickled onions, ammunition against the rigours of the long drive. It was a peace offering. Peter was relieved that they'd parted as friends, after all, and felt that his visit had been thoroughly worthwhile.

There was no point in staying because they'd certainly come back after him. The assassin had to flee. There were compensations. He still had a weapon to defend himself and enough money in his purse to pay for accommodation. London was full of hiding places. Once he'd chosen one, he could begin his search for the man who'd betrayed him and the accomplice who'd tried to kill him. He was already planning a slow and excruciating death for both of them.

CHAPTER
THIRTEEN

Since he was only a short ride away, Paul decided to go back home for a while to see Hannah. The days after a successful production had ended were usually difficult ones for her. With the excitement of performance taken away she was often morose, if not wholly depressed. The mental fatigue of a long run was complemented by physical exhaustion. In the past, she'd been known to sleep for half the day. As he dismounted from his horse, therefore, Paul was wary. He was more than likely to walk into a stream of complaints punctuated by extravagant yawns. While a servant took charge of the horse, Paul went into the house.

Hearing his footsteps, Hannah leapt to her feet and ran into the hall.

"Thank heaven you've come!" she exclaimed.

"It's nice to be welcomed," he said, embracing her.

"I need you, Paul. Come into the drawing room."

"What's going on?" he asked, as she pulled him by the hand. "And why are you leaping about? I expected to find you dozing."

"I'm far too anxious to sleep."

"Has something happened?"

"Yes, I had a visitor."

"Who was it?"

"Dorothea Glenn."

"What on earth did she want?"

"Ostensibly, she came here for advice about her role in our next play. That was simply an excuse to get to me. I soon saw through the deception."

"But she's always seemed to be a truthful girl to me," said Paul. "I can't believe that she tricked her way into the house."

"It was vital that she did so. Dorothea is in a terrible state."

"Why?"

"If you sit beside me," she said, patting the sofa, "I'll tell you."

"You don't need to, Hannah. I think I can guess." They sat down together. "The poor girl has been seduced by one of those powdered rakes in your company and there are the usual consequences."

"It's nothing like that. Well, it is, but not in the way you suggest."

"Stop talking in riddles."

"Dorothea is in love."

"That's perfectly natural for a young woman at that age."

"She really thought she'd found the man of her dreams. She's not a fanciful creature. Dorothea has both feet firmly on the ground. That's why she made sure that the friendship moved at a slow and steady pace."

"In other words, she wasn't swept off her feet by some adventurer like me."

164

She elbowed him. "Listen, will you? It's important."

"Let me have another guess. He's lost interest in her."

"No — or, possibly, yes. Dorothea is not sure and it's the uncertainty that's so maddening. After all the vows he made to her, he just disappeared. She said that it was completely out of character."

"He's a virile young man, Hannah. I'd say that it was absolutely *in* character."

"Don't keep interrupting. We're talking about a serious moment in that girl's life. I've never seen anyone in such distress. There was nobody else to whom she could turn. That's why she came here."

"What did you advise?"

"I told her to have more faith in him. She has to watch and pray."

"Suppose that her beau doesn't return?"

"He must do, Paul. He's professed his love a hundred times. She showed me some of the letters he'd written to her. A philanderer would never have done that. Well," she continued, "you've seen Dorothea. If *you'd* made promises to her, would you walk away from someone as beautiful as that?"

"No, I wouldn't. It would be an act of cruelty."

"So why did Orsino vanish into thin air?"

Paul gulped. "Is that his name?"

"Yes, he's an actor — Orsino Price."

"Oh dear!" he sighed.

"What's the trouble?"

"Dorothea is going to need a lot of help from you, Hannah."

"Why?"

"Orsino Price was stabbed to death in Covent Garden yesterday."

Embarrassed by their lack of progress, the Runners were also bruised by the censure heaped on them by the chief magistrate. As they walked side by side along the street, they were hurt and vengeful.

"I'd like to wring that scrawny neck of his," said Yeomans.

"Who do you mean, Micah?" asked Hale. "Are you talking about Mr Kirkwood or Mr Clearwater?"

"Both of them."

"I'd be afraid to touch the chief magistrate. There'd be repercussions. In any case, we can't really blame him. What made him so angry with us was what he learnt from Clearwater."

"Don't talk to me about that treacherous fop."

"Fancy going over our heads like that!"

"I'll never forgive him. If he has evidence, he should have handed it over to us and not tried to catch the killer on his own. We know how to track our prey. Clearwater will get nowhere. He's groping in the dark."

"Mr Kirkwood has faith in him."

"Our job is to restore his faith in us, Alfred. That means we have to find Clearwater and get the truth out of him even if we have to dip his head in the Thames."

Hale was shocked. "He might drown, Micah."

"I can't think of a better way for him to depart this world."

"What about our duty to uphold the law?"

166

"It gets in our way from time to time. This is one of them."

"I'm as mad at him as you are," said Hale, "but you have to take your hat off to him. He won Mr Kirkwood over. Not many people have ever done that to the chief magistrate. We never manage to charm him."

"We would do if we solved the murder of Sir Roger Mellanby."

"How can we do that if we don't have Clearwater to help us?"

"We concentrate all our efforts on catching up with him. We don't know where he lives, but he obviously hangs around the theatres and rubs shoulders with the rakes and dandies who flock there. Well," he continued, "you saw them flaunting themselves outside that stage door. And Clearwater was one of them."

"Yes, he was preening like a peacock, I daresay."

"We need someone to pick up Clearwater's trail, and, in my view, the best place to start is the Golden Crown."

"It's where all the actors go," said Hale. "If he likes the theatre that much, I'll wager that Clearwater frequents it as well. In fact, he might be downing a drink there at this very moment. Why don't we go there now, Micah?"

"I've got a better idea. You and I will enjoy the privileges of our seniority and send someone else instead."

"I agree wholeheartedly."

"A name is already being whispered in my ear, Alfred."

"I'm hearing it as well — Chevy Ruddock."

Harry Scattergood almost invariably worked alone because he knew that he had the ability to escape from any place or predicament. Others lacked his expertise in shinning up buildings and running along roofs. If he had someone else in tow, he reasoned, there'd be a weak link. It was better to take his chances alone than to engage a fellow thief who might be apprehended and betray Scattergood in order to secure a lighter sentence. He was not, however, without friends. Alan Kinnaird was the closest of them. Because he liked the man, Scattergood had given him useful advice over the years, even suggesting houses that were ripe for a clandestine visit after dark. As a result, Kinnaird had been able to reap the benefit of his friend's help time and again. He was eternally grateful and would do anything for Scattergood.

Kinnaird was a thickset man of middle years with the kind of constantly smiling face that won friends and deprived them of any suspicion. In spite of his bulk, he was extremely nimble and could squeeze through open windows with ease. As he got older, however, he preferred less strenuous ways of making an income and dressed in a way that allowed him to mix with crowds in theatres and at other public events. Like Scattergood, he'd learnt to look, sound and behave like a member of the class from whom his deft fingers took money on a regular basis.

When Scattergood called on him at his lodging, he was given a respectful welcome.

168

"It's good to see you looking so well," said Kinnaird.

"I could say the same of you, Alan. Business is clearly thriving."

"That's in no small part due to my mentor, Harry Scattergood."

"It's only because I trust you implicitly"

"What brings you here?"

"I have a proposition for you," said Scattergood. "It may frighten you at first, but the rewards on offer will ease your fears. All I ask is that you hear me out before you give me your answer."

"It will be in the affirmative," said Kinnaird, blithely. "Whatever you ask me, I'm more than willing to do. I owe you an enormous debt, Harry. It's time to repay it."

Scattergood smiled. "I was hoping you'd say that . . ."

Nobody was more aware than Paul Skillen of the fact that Hannah Granville was egotistical to the ultimate degree. Though he'd found it an unpleasant aspect of her character, he'd quickly adapted to it. He now witnessed a miracle. Hannah was actually putting someone else's needs first for once. Having talked obsessively about the invitation from the Prince Regent, she was so overwhelmed with sympathy for Dorothea Glenn that she forgot all about the possible visit to Brighton Pavilion. Hannah and Paul reached the same conclusion. Rejection by the man she loved would have been a dreadful blow for her but the news that he'd been murdered was far worse. Hannah feared that it

169

might destroy the poor woman and rob the theatre of a promising actress. On their way to Dorothea's lodging in a cab, Paul suggested a compromise.

"We first need to reassure her that Orsino Price would never have cast her aside. Evidently, he adored her. Only a serious obstacle would have prevented his coming to meet her."

"Murder is rather more than a serious obstacle, Paul," said Hannah, drily.

"We must acquaint her with the possibility of a mishap before we give her the bare facts. Prepare her gently for the truth."

"What if someone else blurts it out?"

"There's little danger of that, Hannah. From what I can gather, he had few friends. His ambition was to be an actor, but Simeon Howlett had never heard of him and his mind is an encyclopaedia of the profession. In view of the fact that she confided in you," he continued, "I'm surprised that you didn't suggest that she moved in with us so that you could look after her."

"I did make that offer but she refused. Dorothea was so afraid that he'd turn up at her lodging when she wasn't there that she insisted on returning."

"At a time like this, she shouldn't be alone."

"I know. She's in too delicate a state."

"The wonder of it is that she didn't mention this fellow, Price, to you earlier. Since they were that close, you'd have thought she'd have been burning to tell someone her good news."

"She did tell me," said Hannah, "but not in so many words. It was written all over her face. I was too absorbed in playing Lady Macbeth to notice but Jenny did. She misses nothing. Jenny observed that there'd been a big change in Dorothea. We now know exactly what it was."

"Poor creature!" he said. "We must find a way to soften the blow."

"The first thing to do is to get her out of that lodging. As long as she's there on her own, she'll only brood and mope. If I can persuade her to stay with us for a while, it will be a great help to her."

"What she needs most is a sympathetic woman friend. That's you, Hannah."

"I was touched that she turned to me."

"If she's under our roof, we can protect her from finding out the truth about Orsino, but she'll have to know the worst eventually. Is she strong enough to bear it?"

"I'm not sure, Paul."

"How long has Dorothea been in the profession?"

"It's almost three years."

"Then she's no shrinking violet. An actress has to have an inner core of belief to survive in what can be a testing world. You've often told me that."

"It's true. Sometimes you have to fight tooth and nail. Dorothea knows that."

"Good," said Paul. "It will help her through the ordeal to come."

Peter Skillen had arrived back in London the next morning much later than he'd hoped. Expecting a relatively swift nocturnal journey in a mail coach, he was dismayed when one of its wheels was badly damaged as it hit a rock invisible in the darkness. It had meant slowing to a snail's pace and — with the passengers trudging behind it — the coach limped into the next village like a wounded soldier returning from the war. Though extremely unhappy about being roused from his bed, the blacksmith was able to repair the wheel enough to make it serviceable until it could be replaced with a new one. Peter and the other passengers were grateful to climb aboard once more and resume their journey at last. It did, however, mean that he arrived in London hours later than intended.

After returning home to shave, change and consume a hasty breakfast, Peter went straight out again. Instead of going to the shooting gallery to make his wife and the others aware of his return, however, Peter rode straight to the Home Office. It was situated in Dorset House on Whitehall and was a place he'd visited many times in the past. While he was anxious to speak to the Home Secretary, he knew that he might have to wait some time — some days even — for an appointment. Since he was no longer employed by Sidmouth as an agent, he could no longer expect to be accorded special treatment.

Fortune smiled on him. The first person he met as he entered the building was the Parliamentary Under-Secretary. John Hiley Addington was the Home Secretary's brother and confidant. He recognised Peter immediately.

"How nice to see you again, Mr Skillen," he said with genuine cordiality. "My brother didn't tell me that you were coming to see him today."

"I haven't made an appointment yet," explained Peter, "but I'm hoping that I'll be able to do so. I'm fully aware of how busy the Home Secretary is. You and he are famous for your capacity for hard work."

"We are well matched by you and *your* brother, I fancy. The two of you have a reputation for being embarrassingly industrious."

"It's very kind of you to say so."

"Your triumphs have not gone unnoticed," said the other. "And yes, it's true that, like me, Henry is knee-deep in government business. But there's always room for manoeuvre where old friends are concerned. Let me have a quiet word with him. If I tell him that Peter Skillen is here, he'll be more than curious."

"I'm most grateful to you."

"Am I right in thinking that only a matter of some importance would have brought you here like this?" Peter gave a firm nod. "Leave it to me. Find yourself a seat and keep your fingers crossed."

After the trials of the journey back to London, it looked as if Peter's luck might have changed. It was a fillip he certainly needed. Until he'd confronted the Home Secretary, he'd never have peace of mind.

Because he was conscientious and proud of his position as a guardian of the law, Chevy Ruddock was often given difficult assignments. When it was explained to him at the Peacock Inn, the latest one sounded particularly demanding.

"Am I to work entirely alone?" he asked.

"Yes," said Yeomans. "This is a task ideally suited to you."

"That's why you were chosen, Chevy," added Hale. "We have faith in you. See it as a badge of honour."

"But I'm not sure where to start," admitted Ruddock.

"We've given you a detailed description of Giles Clearwater and told you that he's given to visiting theatres. Begin your search in Covent Garden."

"Clearwater is a dandy," said Yeomans, "and such men love to strut around the city to be noticed. You'll soon pick up his scent."

"I'll try my best," said Ruddock.

"It's important that we catch and shake the truth out of him. This fellow is actually daring to go in search of Sir Roger Mellanby's killer in order to claim the reward money and make us look foolish."

"That won't happen, Mr Yeomans."

"What do you mean?"

"Mr Clearwater will never catch the assassin before the Skillen brothers. They always seem to be better at solving murders than anyone else."

"Forget them," snarled Yeomans. "I've already warned Paul Skillen to keep out of this investigation. The killer belongs to *us*. Do you understand?"

"Yes, sir."

"Then get out there and find Clearwater. When I get my hands on that cunning devil, I'll put the fear of God into him. I'm not letting him steal the glory that rightly belongs to us."

"If I *do* find him," said Ruddock, hopefully, "and he does give us information that leads to an arrest, does that mean *I* get a share of the reward money?" The stony face of Micah Yeomans was an answer in itself. "I'd better be on my way, then . . ."

In the interests of his safety, he fled from the inn.

They found Dorothea Glenn at her lodging, a rather grim, cheerless room at the top of a crumbling house. In concealing the truth from her, Paul and Hannah felt that they were being cruel in order to be kind. They were also being practical. If they'd told her that her beloved had been stabbed to death in an alleyway, the young actress would have been inconsolable. She'd have been in such despair that they'd have been unable to get the crucial information they needed out of her. Since she refused to believe that Price would ever let her down, she'd come to accept that something serious must have happened to delay him. Hannah soon convinced her that it was wrong to put herself through the agony of waiting alone in the vain hope that he'd turn up, and that she should return to their house where she'd have someone to look after her. Paul, meanwhile, would go in search of the truth about what had actually happened to Orsino Price. The promise brought tears to Dorothea's eyes.

"Would you *really* do that, Mr Skillen?" she asked.

"Yes, I would," said Paul.

"But you hardly know me. Why should you care about somebody like me?"

"You're a friend of Hannah's. That's enough for me."

"I can't thank you enough," she cried, grasping his hands.

"Paul will need your help," said Hannah. "If he's to track down Orsino, he'll want details about him that only you have. We've no wish to intrude on your private life, Dorothea, but I'm afraid that it's unavoidable."

"I'll tell you *everything*."

"That's very sensible."

"First of all," said Paul, "let's get you back to the house. We can offer you comforts that this lodging of yours clearly lacks. More importantly, you'll have friends beside you to help you through whatever lies ahead."

Even with the intervention of the Home Secretary's brother, Peter had a wait of half an hour before he was conducted to the appropriate office. As he approached it, he passed the man who'd just left Sidmouth. Peter gave him no more than a cursory glance but, in return, he was the object of close scrutiny. The man stopped, stared and exuded an immediate hostility. When Peter turned to face the other visitor, the latter made a dismissive gesture with his hand, then walked off. Peter was bewildered.

The moment he entered the office, however, the incident was forgotten because Sidmouth came across to greet him with an outstretched hand.

"I'm sorry to have kept you waiting, Mr Skillen," he said.

"Affairs of state have to be dealt with, my lord."

"My brother and I seem to work all the hours that God sends us, yet we still make little impact on the problems that loom up before us on all sides. Political life is simply a well-dressed version of slavery. However," he went on, indicating a chair, "you didn't come here to listen to my woes. I suspect that you have some of your own you wish to ventilate."

"I do, indeed, my lord."

Sidmouth was a tall, square, rather bony individual of sixty with wispy grey hair. Not having seen him for some time, Peter was surprised at how much he'd aged. The lines on his face had increased in number and depth and his shoulders had become more rounded. What was unchanged was the air of decency and affability that Peter had always encountered in the past. Looking at him now, he couldn't believe him guilty of the charges Seth Hooper had hurled at him.

"Well," said Sidmouth, "what's brought you here?"

"I've taken an interest in the murder of Sir Roger Mellanby."

"He was a fine politician. I disagreed with most of what he had to say but I admired him for his commitment and fighting spirit. He came from Nottingham, I believe. They breed strong men in that part of the country."

"I know, my lord. I've just come from there."

Sidmouth's eyebrows lifted. "Really?"

177

"I was acting on behalf of a friend of his," said Peter. "The two of them had come to London to speak at the Hampden Club. Unfortunately, Sir Roger was killed on the eve of the meeting."

"He'll be a great loss to his family and friends."

"And to the cause that he championed, my lord. Nottingham worshipped him. The whole city is now in mourning." There was a long pause. Peter took a deep breath before continuing. "At a meeting of the local Hampden Club, your name came in for some . . . unkind treatment."

"What a pleasing euphemism that is," said Sidmouth with a laugh. "It's not one that Sir Roger would have chosen. Whenever we talked in private, he used much more colourful language."

"I felt obliged to defend you."

"There was no need. Insults run off my back like so much rain."

"They were more serious than mere insults, my lord," said Peter. "Accusations were made against you. I objected strongly to them."

"Then I'm very grateful to you for doing that." Sidmouth leant forward across his desk. "What exactly were these accusations?"

"It was said that you gave direct orders for the proposed march of the Blanketeers to be stopped in its tracks by dragoons. People were badly wounded in the process, my lord. They blame their injuries on you."

"That's both untrue and unfair."

"I used those very words in your defence, my lord."

178

"Reports of the clash did eventually reach me, of course, and I was pleased to see that the magistrates behaved correctly in breaking up that march. One can't have marauding bands of disaffected workers on the loose."

"We are talking about a peaceful demonstration, my lord," said Peter with a sudden passion in his voice. "The men from Manchester took great care to operate within the law and so did those whom I met in Nottingham. They are not unruly insurrectionists. They have legitimate concerns that they wish to have laid before Parliament."

"You're beginning to sound like one of them," warned Sidmouth.

"I take no sides in the matter. I just want the truth to be heard."

"And what do you conceive of as the truth?"

"Having the advantage of knowing you in person," said Peter, "I refused to accept that you had sent spies to places like Manchester and Nottingham so that you were aware of what people were planning."

"Thank you."

"I couldn't believe that the local magistracy was responding to direct orders from the Home Office."

"They know their job. I let them get on with it. As you can see from the way that my desk is covered," said Sidmouth, pointing to the piles of documents, "I have more than enough work to keep me busy. Where would I find the time to take a close interest in northern towns beset by dissidents?"

"Sir Roger Mellanby was no dissident, my lord."

"Indeed, he wasn't. He was a civilised man with a gift for debate that made him stand out from the general herd of parliamentarians."

"Some in that herd might have wanted him silenced."

There was an awkward pause before Sidmouth rose to his feet.

"Thank you for coming, Mr Skillen," he said. "It's always a delight to see you because it revives pleasant memories of times when we worked so well together. That is something we can't do on the matter you've brought before me today. Let me be clear. Agitators are at work throughout the country, trying to stir up trouble for us. As Home Secretary, I get reports on a regular basis from what are deemed to be places of incipient rebellion. I sent no spies to infiltrate those communities," he emphasised, "and resent being accused of doing so."

"Thank you, my lord," said Peter, getting to his feet. "You've told me all that I'd hoped to hear. I bid you good day." After heading for the door, he suddenly paused. "May I ask who was in here with you before me?"

"That was Mr Oswald Ferriday, the President of the Board of Trade."

"I see."

"Goodbye, Mr Skillen — and thank you for coming."

Peter was hurt. There was no hint of sincerity in the farewell.

180

* * *

Now that he'd dispatched Chevy Ruddock on his search, Yeomans felt that he could afford to relax. He and Hale had the greatest confidence in the younger man. When he'd first joined a foot patrol, Ruddock had been raw and inexperienced. They were defects he soon eradicated, going on to become one of the most efficient men under Yeomans' command. He was powerful, dedicated and tireless. In choosing him, they felt, it was only a matter of time before Clearwater was dragged to the Peacock to be interrogated by the senior Runners.

"Chevy is the best man we have," said Hale.

"I agree," said Yeomans. "It's because I trained him so well."

"He thrives on action, Micah. In some ways, he reminds me of how I was when I was that age. I loved it when villains resisted arrest because it gave me the right to use real violence."

"Ruddock has only one vice."

"I don't think he knows what vice is," said Hale with a snigger. "He's never even sniffed the vices that we've enjoyed. Chevy's too wedded to that wife of his."

"His vice is that he respects the Skillen brothers too much."

"He'll grow out of that in time."

"Well," said Yeomans, "you heard him earlier. He told us that Clearwater wouldn't claim that reward because Peter and Paul Skillen would grab it before him and — this is what upset me — before *us*."

181

"They won't do that this time, Micah. You warned Paul Skillen off this case and his brother hasn't been seen for days. For the first time in ages, we have no real competition — except what we're getting from Clearwater, that is."

"We'll soon crush *his* ambitions, Alfred."

"I'll enjoy doing that."

They replenished their tankards of ale and returned to their table. It was not long before they were interrupted. The door of the inn opened and in strode William Filbert, the oldest member of the foot patrols, a rather doddery, pipe-smoking man with an abundance of unwashed hair. Panting heavily, he'd obviously been running. His face was awash with sweat. He offered a letter to Yeomans.

"I was told to give you this," he said.

Yeomans snatched it from him. "Who sent it?"

"The chief magistrate — Mr Kirkwood said it was urgent."

Tearing open the missive, Yeomans read it then let out a howl of such fury that everyone in the inn took a precautionary step backwards. The Runner was shaking all over as if in the grip of a fever.

"What does he say, Micah?" asked Hale.

"He says that he's just had a visit from Sir Roger Mellanby's son who wants to know if we've caught his father's killer yet or if Peter Skillen is likely to do that before us. And do you know *why* he asked that?"

"I've no idea."

"It's because Peter Skillen went all the way up to Sir Roger's house in search of evidence. The son was outraged. He said it was *our* job to lead the investigation."

"He's quite right."

"Do you see what this means?" said Yeomans, grinding his teeth. "We'll not only have the son breathing down our necks from now on, we'll have the Skillen brothers to worry about as well." Tearing the letter to pieces, he threw it in the air so that it descended on Filbert like a minor blizzard. "This is *your* fault, Bill. Everything was going so well until you came through that door."

"I was only obeying orders," complained Filbert.

"Well, here's another order to obey." Grabbing him by the neck, Yeomans opened the door and flung him uncaringly into the street. "Get your disgusting old carcase out of here."

"Don't blame him," protested Hale. "He was only the messenger."

"That letter has put me right off my ale."

"Bill Filbert didn't write it."

"That makes no difference."

"What are we going to tell Sir Roger's son?"

"I'll think of something."

"The truth is that we've nothing at all to show for our efforts. That will make Sir Roger's son very angry."

"Forget him for the moment," said Yeomans, flapping a hand. "We have a far bigger problem in the Skillen brothers. They've been conducting their own inquiry behind our backs, and you know where that may end."

"Yes, Micah. They might show us up once again."

"We can't let that happen. It will take all the gloss off our reputation. Dealing with Peter and Paul Skillen must be our first priority. Whatever it takes, we have to stop them interfering once and for all."

CHAPTER
FOURTEEN

Once they'd taken her back to the house, Dorothea Glenn seemed to calm down slightly. Though still tense and anxious, she was no longer desperate and tearful. Grateful that they'd come to her rescue, she was ready to cooperate with Paul and Hannah in any way they suggested. Once the three of them had settled down in the drawing room, Paul let Hannah do most of the talking because Dorothea had complete trust in her.

"It's clear from what you told me earlier," said Hannah, "that Orsino was entranced by you."

"He was," confirmed Dorothea. "You saw the letters he wrote. They came from the heart. Unlike other gentlemen who'd taken an interest in me, Orsino was kind and considerate. He never tried to . . . lead me astray."

"I'm sure that he was the perfect gentleman you describe. But there were several things you didn't tell me about him. For instance, where did he live?"

"He didn't say, Miss Granville."

"Weren't you curious to know?"

"It wasn't something that we ever talked about."

"Did he mention his family?"

"He did make a passing reference to them," said Dorothea, "but I didn't press him. All I wanted to talk about was the time when we could be together for good."

"Was Orsino a man of means?"

"Oh, I think so. He always dressed so well."

"Yet, according to you, he hadn't established himself as an actor."

"It was not because he lacked talent," insisted Dorothea. "I've never met anyone with such presence and easy command of language. He was a born actor kept off the stage by envy and spite."

"Are you saying that he had enemies?" asked Paul.

"Yes, Mr Skillen. People conspired against him."

"Why was that?"

"He didn't go into detail. Orsino simply said that he would turn the tables on them all one day by blazing across the stage in the greatest parts ever written. Also," Dorothea went on, "he was kind enough to praise my own work."

"And so he should," said Hannah. "You've done well."

"He even went so far as to claim that I'd have been a memorable Lady Macbeth because my performance would have had subtleties of which most actresses were not capable."

Hannah was roused. "Did he not see *me* in the role?" she demanded.

"Oh, yes, and he was very impressed."

"Is that all?"

"Let me go back to an earlier question," said Paul, jumping in before Hannah's irritation got out of hand. "You don't know where Orsino lived, or if he had a source of income, yet you were ready to entrust your future to him."

"He promised to look after me," said Dorothea, simply, "and I had no reason to question that. As for money, he did mention it once."

"What did he say?"

"That he was about to earn a large amount for very little work."

"When was this?"

"It must have been three or four days ago."

"And where was this money coming from?"

"Orsino said it was from work as an actor, then he burst out laughing."

"Didn't you press him for detail?"

"No, Mr Skillen. I was simply delighted for him."

"Who was going to employ Orsino?" asked Hannah.

"I don't know."

"Did he say how much money he'd be receiving?"

"No, but he promised me that it would be a lot — enough for us to do all the things that we'd talked about."

She smiled for the first time since they'd picked her up from her lodging. Paul and Hannah were momentarily overcome with sympathy. They knew that the promises would never be delivered now. They also suspected that Orsino Price had deceived Dorothea completely, but they were careful not to mention their suspicions. In Dorothea's mind, Price had been her saviour and they didn't want to tarnish that image for her. Hannah put a consoling arm around her, but Paul was still thinking about what they'd just been told.

"Tell me about the boast he made to you," he said. "When exactly was it?"

Having sworn that he'd do anything that his friend asked, Alan Kinnaird was having second thoughts. He hadn't realised how much danger was involved. Seeing his hesitation, Harry Scattergood sought to dispel the doubts. His plan required an accomplice and Kinnaird was the only person he could trust. Instead of arguing with him, therefore, he took his friend on a short walk to a wall where reward notices were regularly pasted up. He pointed to the one relating to Sir Roger Mellanby's murder. When he saw the amount on offer, Kinnaird's jaw dropped.

"We'd get all that?" he asked.

"It would be shared between us, Alan."

"But *I'd* be the one taking the biggest risk."

"There's away that risk can be eliminated," said Scattergood. "Put your faith in me. Have I ever let you down before?"

"No, Harry."

"Does that mean you'll help me?"

Kinnaird looked at the reward notice. "Yes," he promised. "I may be putting my head in a noose but, after all you've done for me, I'll trust you to pull it out again."

Charlotte was alone when her husband returned to the shooting gallery and he gave her a welcoming embrace and a kiss. When he'd released her from his grasp, Peter gave her a concise account of what he'd learnt during his time in Nottingham. He also mentioned his disappointing visit to the Home Office.

"I'm not quite sure why," he confessed, "but I came away with a sense of failure."

"What happened?"

"It was just this feeling I had in the pit of my stomach."

"You've always got on so well with the Home Secretary before," she said.

"Perhaps I was expecting too much of him, Charlotte."

"Do you think he was dishonest?"

"Not exactly," replied Peter, "but I sensed that there was a distinct limit to his honesty. He was politely evasive, and I've never seen that side of Viscount Sidmouth before. He greeted me as a friend, yet he began to look at me as an interloper."

"You must speak to Paul."

"I can't wait to compare notes with him."

"He's been talking to a Captain Golightly, who was a good friend of Mellanby. Paul asked him a blunt question. If the government decided that Mellanby was a serious problem, who would give the order to have him killed?"

"What was Golightly's answer?"

"The Home Secretary."

"No," said Peter, "I can't believe he'd sanction an assassination like that."

"Captain Golightly said that he had to be the chief suspect."

"Did he offer any other names?"

"Yes, he did. One was a man who'd been injured in a duel with Sir Roger and had threatened to kill him. The other two were both politicians."

"Can you remember their names?"

"Let me see," said Charlotte. "One was Sir Marcus Brough, I believe. Yes, that's right. Paul had a long conversation with him. That didn't happen when he approached the other man. In fact, he was very rude to your brother."

"What was his name?"

"I've forgotten, I'm afraid but . . ." She racked her brains. "Wait a moment," she said, "I do remember his position in the Cabinet."

"Go on."

"He was the President of the Board of Trade."

"Oswald Ferriday."

"*That* was the name," she agreed. "However did you know it?"

"I met him at the Home Office," explained Peter, "and he stared at me as if he wanted to see me boiled in oil. I realise why now. Ferriday must have mistaken me for Paul. It's not the first time someone has done that," he added with a wry smile, "and I daresay it won't be the last."

Any reservations that Paul had had about keeping Dorothea Glenn ignorant of the truth about her beloved had been swept away. He and Hannah would

190

never have got the vital information that had emerged if the young actress had been stunned by news of his murder. From what he'd been told about Orsino Price, he was able to build up a picture of him. If he could win the confidence of someone like Dorothea, he must have been highly plausible, concealing far more about himself than he actually told her yet somehow persuading her that he was an acceptable suitor. Paul had met lots of failed actors like him: handsome, cunning, apparently agreeable young men who hung around on the fringes of the theatrical world in search of a way to advance their careers on the stage. Instinctively rejecting the advances she'd received in the past, Dorothea had somehow found Price irresistible.

Leaving her in Hannah's care, Paul paid a visit to Captain Golightly to make him aware of the latest development. The latter was delighted with the news.

"That's more than we could have hoped," said Golightly. "This wretched fellow was clearly the assassin's apprentice. One thing concerns me, however. If all that he had to do was to cause a distraction, he couldn't have been paid very much. Why was he boasting to Miss Glenn that he was about to enjoy a windfall?"

"I've been thinking about that," said Paul.

"And what did you conclude?"

"My feeling is that Price didn't realise exactly why he'd been hired. What he thought was a simple task turned out to have a sinister aspect. All of a sudden, he was an unwitting accomplice in a murder."

"That must have shaken him."

"I'm sure that it did at first. But it also gave him a weapon to use against the man who'd picked him out. He was in a position to name the killer. The first thing he'd do would be to demand more money from him."

"Blackmail can be a lucrative crime."

"That must have been where his sudden wealth was going to come from. To arrange the assassination of an important public figure would have cost a great deal of money. Price, I suspect, wanted a share of it."

"What amount would he have put on his silence?"

"A very high one, I fancy," said Paul.

"That would have irked the assassin."

"It's more than likely that he'd have decided the only way to escape Price's threat was to shut his mouth for ever. A knife through the heart was all that it took."

"Miss Glenn is going to be devastated when she learns the truth."

"We'll help her through it as best we can."

"And meanwhile . . . ?"

"I'll continue to hunt for the man behind the assassination."

"What about the killer himself?"

"I'll squeeze his name out of his paymaster," vowed Paul. "All I have to do is to find out who that paymaster is."

"You know my feeling. The Home Secretary is your man."

"I refuse to believe it. My brother, Peter, worked closely with him during the war and vouches for his

192

character. It wasn't Sidmouth but it may well have been another politician."

"Which one is it — Sir Marcus Brough or Oswald Ferriday?"

"I hope to find out very soon, Captain Golightly."

Though he could foresee scant hopes of success, Chevy Ruddock obeyed his orders and began his search in Covent Garden. It was as crowded and raucous as ever. Having memorised the description of Giles Clearwater, he was startled to find how many people it seemed to fit. He accosted almost a dozen men, demanding their names and getting everything from mild annoyance to snarling denial in return. In the end, he decided on a change of tactics that might save him from outright abuse. Aware of its appeal for actors and fops, Ruddock therefore adjourned to the Golden Crown, only to be met by another bevy of potential Clearwaters. Wisely, he didn't approach them, preferring instead to look around in order to assess his options.

The place was full of men, striking a pose or engaging in arguments that allowed them to raise loud, braying voices and to gesticulate wildly. Ruddock felt completely out of his depth. He then spotted the old man seated alone in a corner and nursing a half-glass of an amber liquid. In a room swirling with people and their deafening conversations, he seemed out of place. Ruddock went across and introduced himself. Simeon Howlett listened patiently then shook his head.

"I'm sorry, Mr Ruddock," he said, "I know of no Giles Clearwater."

"He'd be likely to come into a place like this."

"So are hundreds of others. I can't keep track of all their names."

"Where is the best place to look for such a man?"

"The Golden Crown is as good a place as any to start," said Howlett, "though there is a problem. If *I* haven't heard of this actor, nobody else will have done so."

"We don't know if he's an actor."

"Then what do you know about the fellow?"

Ruddock shrugged. "Very little, I fear."

"Then you've been sent on a fool's errand."

"No, Mr Howlett, that's not true at all. Clearwater really does exist. I've spoken with two people who've met him and were able to tell me about his manner and appearance. I simply must find him."

"Then I wish I could help. What was the name again?"

"Clearwater — Giles Clearwater."

"Let me concentrate for a moment." He downed the remains of his drink then handed the glass to Ruddock. "Tell the landlord it's for me. He'll know what to get."

"Oh, I see."

"Meanwhile, I'll put my thinking cap on."

Ruddock went off into the jostling crowd and eventually reached the bar counter. Since he was not a regular patron of the establishment, he found that he had to wait while those who were had the privilege of being served first. It was several minutes before he was able to fight his way back to the old actor.

194

"There you are," he said, placing the glass in front of him.

"Thank you, Mr Ruddock."

"Have you remembered anything?"

"Yes and no," replied Howlett. "I vaguely remember the name but I cannot, for the life of me, connect it to a human being. The mind plays tricks on you at my age. Things get horribly jumbled. Leave me to mull it over, Mr Ruddock. If I give it time, this tired old brain of mine might start to work again. It might even tell me who Giles Clearwater is or was." He smiled apologetically. "That's the best I can offer you, I fear." He raised the glass. "Good health to you, sir!"

While he was glad that he'd made the effort to go to Nottingham, Peter was relieved to be home again. Ackford and Huckvale were pleased to see him back at the shooting gallery and listened with interest to his account of his travels. Peter was not allowed to bask in their welcome for long. Two visitors arrived and the mood changed immediately. Yeomans and Hale were steaming with resentment when they came in.

"What's this about you going to Nottingham?" demanded Yeomans.

"It's a free country, isn't it?" said Peter. "I can go wherever I wish."

"We have it on good authority that you went there to get information about Sir Roger Mellanby."

"Don't bother to deny it," said Hale. "Sir Roger's son complained about you."

"He doesn't want you anywhere near his family," added Yeomans. "He wants this investigation to be in the hands of the people most likely to catch the villains involved. The Prince Regent said the same thing."

"I didn't hear him," said Peter.

"We have his ear."

"Then perhaps you can whisper something into it for me. Tell him that you're so incapable of handling a case as complex as this that you've called on us to help."

"We'd never employ our rivals," shouted Yeomans. "We're here to order you to stop interfering in our case."

"But we were expressly invited to do so."

"That's a lie."

"I'd suggest that you talk to Seth Hooper," said Peter, "except that it would involve a journey to and from Nottingham, and the pair of you never go far from the Peacock. Mr Hooper travelled to London with Sir Roger."

"We've never heard of the man."

"Yes, you have, but you didn't have the courtesy even to talk to him. When he was rebuffed by you, he came to us. In a sense, our invitation to take part in this case comes from the whole of Nottingham. We could hardly refuse it, could we?"

"Let me put it more clearly," said Yeomans, inflating his chest. "We don't want you meddling in this case, Sir Roger's son doesn't want you and His Royal Highness doesn't want you. Isn't that plain enough for you?"

"Show me the law that forbids a concerned citizen from trying to solve a murder. Explain to me the right by which Edmund Mellanby can prevent me from finding his father's killer. And," continued Peter, raising his voice, "let me have a copy of the royal decree that prevents my brother and me from plying our trade."

"It's *our* trade," bleated Hale.

"Then why don't you learn to do it properly?"

"We're experts. That's why we've gathered information about this case that you could never get. We know a man who was outside the theatre on the night of the murder."

"His name is Paul Skillen, my brother."

"This man actually *saw* the killer."

"Be quiet, Alfred," said Yeomans.

"But he needs to know that he can't compete with us. Giles Clearwater didn't come here, did he? He came straight to us."

"I told you to be quiet."

"Are you claiming that this man was a witness?" asked Peter.

"That's exactly what he was," Hale blurted out.

"Shut up!" roared Yeomans into his ear. "We're here to warn Skillen and his brother not to give away secrets." He turned to Peter. "Spare yourselves the time and energy," he went on. "This case is all but solved. Get out of our way or I'll be forced to use more direct measures."

"Take your pick," said Peter, indicating the weapons on display. "You can fight us with swords, boxing gloves or pistols. And the beauty of it is that we won't charge you a penny for whichever lesson we give you."

Unable to find a rejoinder, Yeomans grabbed Hale by the collar and dragged him out. Peter allowed himself a chuckle, then his brow furrowed.

"Who is Giles Clearwater?" he asked.

Because there was no entertainment on offer that evening, the theatre was deserted. When he took his friend to the stage door, therefore, Harry Scattergood could be confident that they wouldn't be interrupted. Having mastered the details of what had happened on the night of the murder, he had to pass them on to Kinnaird.

"You were standing there, Alan," he said, pointing.

"Was I?"

"Yes, that means you had a clear shot at Sir Roger Mellanby."

"But I've never even heard of the man."

"You'd been told exactly what he looked like."

"Had I?"

"No, of course you hadn't, but you must convince the Runners that you had. That's what I did. You'll be questioned closely time and again, Alan. You have to get everything absolutely right. Do you understand?"

"Yes, Harry." He moved into position. "I'm standing right here."

"Then this is what happened next . . ."

Since he'd been so pleasant and accommodating, Paul decided to take Sir Marcus Brough at his word. He therefore repaired to the House of Commons and waited patiently until the debate ended. The door of the chamber opened and Members of Parliament surged out like a herd of animals just released into the wild. Deep in conversation, they swept past Paul without giving him a glance. When he saw Sir Marcus coming towards him with a group of friends, he stepped boldly into his path. Taken aback at first, Sir Marcus quickly recovered and gave him a broad smile.

"It's good to see you again, Mr Skillen," he said, "but I didn't expect it to be just outside the Royal Chapel of St Stephen. It's in this chamber that the nation is governed, though some of the language used there is hardly suited to what had once been consecrated ground."

"You did say that I could call on you again, Sir Marcus."

"I did, indeed, and they were not idle words." He waved his friends away then took Paul aside. "Let's find somewhere less public, shall we?"

Sir Marcus was a big, red-faced man in his sixties with a sizeable paunch threatening to break clear of its moorings. His most significant feature was a mane of snow-white hair that cascaded down to his shoulders and gave him a leonine air. Surprisingly, his voice was quiet and confiding and seemed to belong to a much smaller man. He took Paul into the privacy of a recess.

"Now, then, what's brought you to the Palace of Westminster?"

"The same thing that made me seek you out in the first place, Sir Marcus, and that's the search for the truth. I won't rest until I've found out who ordered the assassination of Sir Roger Mellanby."

"Your tenacity is admirable, though I'm not sure why you've approached me. I've nothing to add to what I told you at our earlier meeting."

"You did promise to think things over."

"Did I?" asked the other. "Yes, I suppose I did, and, to some extent, I've been doing that. I've been looking around the benches to see which of Sir Roger's many enemies might be deemed capable of such an appalling crime."

"And did anyone stand out?"

"I'm not sure that they did, Mr Skillen. There are several Members who are secretly pleased that such a formidable speaker is no longer alive to fight for a cause they despise, but that doesn't mean they'd devise a plot to kill him."

"Who stands most to gain from Sir Roger's death?"

"It's difficult to pick out any individual," said the politician. "In a sense, the whole of the Tory government is the beneficiary because they will no longer have to face his thunderous criticism of the Corn Laws. As someone who believes strongly in that excellent piece of legislation, I must admit that — once I'd heaved a genuine sigh of regret at the news of his death — I felt a sense of relief."

"Were you involved in framing the Corn Laws?"

"Heavens, no!" he exclaimed with a laugh. "That was the work of sharper brains than mine. Expert lawyers like Oswald Ferriday were consulted. Since he owns a vast amount of land in Hampshire, he had a vested interest in protecting the income that is generated by it."

"Mr Ferriday's name was mentioned to me."

"In what context, may I ask?"

"He was felt to be particularly hostile towards Sir Roger."

"It's true," admitted the other. "But, then, he had good cause to be."

"Why was that?"

"Oswald made the mistake of challenging Sir Roger about his campaign for wider suffrage, daring to claim that it was only a pretence used to gain attention. In effect, he was impugning Sir Roger's integrity and that was akin to setting a light to a keg of gunpowder. The resulting explosion made the walls shake. I've never seen anyone as angry as Sir Roger became."

"What did he say?"

"It wasn't the content of the speech that was important. It was the way he delivered it. Oswald Ferriday was mercilessly excoriated," said Sir Marcus. "In the face of such a verbal hurricane, he was forced to apologise. He never dared to question Sir Roger's character after that."

"Are debates always that fiery?"

"This wasn't a debate. It was a duel between two men who loathed each other."

"It sounds as if Sir Roger was triumphant."

"Yes," conceded the other, "he certainly was. But his triumph was short-lived. Less than a fortnight later, Sir Roger was shot dead."

Paul detected the faintest note of approval in his voice.

* * *

Hannah Granville had adjusted quickly to the situation. Instead of being the centre of attention, she became a comforter, helping someone in distress to cope with her fear. It soon became clear that she didn't need to tell the truth to Dorothea Glenn because the latter already knew it in her heart. Orsino Price was dead. No other explanation could account for the way he'd failed to turn up for a crucial meeting with her. Just when she was on the cusp of committing herself wholeheartedly to the man she loved, she'd lost him for ever.

"You're so kind to me, Miss Granville," she said.

"I'm only doing what any friend would do."

"You and Mr Skillen are angels."

"I don't think that everyone would view us in quite that light," said Hannah with mild amusement, "but we've chosen the life that we want and ignore any narrow-minded criticism. But that's enough about us, Dorothea. Your plight is what concerns us most now."

"I'm so, so grateful."

"We couldn't just leave you to suffer alone."

"I was beside myself with anxiety," said Dorothea. "I've never felt so alone and helpless in my whole life."

"You're no longer alone and you're certainly not without help now. While I look after you, Paul will be trying to find out what exactly happened to Orsino."

"I hope he doesn't put himself in danger."

"He's rather accustomed to doing that," said Hannah.

"Doesn't that worry you?"

"It used to but I've come to accept it."

202

Dorothea fell silent and turned away. Fatigue was clearly creeping up on her. Hannah hoped that her friend could get some much-needed sleep but there was no chance of that happening. Dorothea sat up and turned to her.

"May I ask you a question, Miss Granville?"

"Of course you may."

"You won't keep the truth from me, will you?" asked Dorothea. "I'm not a child. I'd rather know the worst than sit here brooding on it."

"We're not keeping anything from you," said Hannah, soothingly.

"Thank you . . . I'm afraid that Orsino is dead."

"We don't know that."

"I do. I *feel* it. He's gone. Oh, I do wish you'd met him. You'd have seen what a wonderful person he was. It's unbearable," she cried, clinging to Hannah. "How could anyone want to hurt him?"

The assassin's anger continued to burn inside him. Since he was now being hunted, he first bought himself a complete change of clothing so that he became invisible. Those looking for the dandy he'd once been would never recognise him in the rough garb of a beggar. An exaggerated limp completed his disguise. While he didn't know who had actually ordered the murder of Sir Roger Mellanby, he knew the man who'd hired him and promised to hand over full payment. What he didn't have was his address because his paymaster had been careful to meet him well away from his house. Their deal was struck at the man's club, a place he visited on a daily basis. The assassin therefore went to the club and lurked outside in the shadows. Seated cross-legged against a wall with a begging bowl in front of him, he was able to watch everyone who went into or came out of the club.

His long, uncomfortable wait was eventually rewarded. Tall, lean and elegant, the man he sought came out of the building and walked along the pavement towards him. When he saw the beggar, he moved a couple of feet to his left so that he'd avoid him. Waiting for his moment, the assassin suddenly leapt to his feet and thrust his pistol in the man's ribs.

"Make a sound and I'll kill you," he warned.

Paul Skillen was glad that he'd spoken to Sir Marcus Brough the second time. On the first occasion, he'd found the man rather engaging and ready to talk freely about the assassination of a fellow Member of Parliament. There was a difference this time. While Paul had been given the same cheerful greeting, it was clear that Sir Marcus was unhappy about being accosted in front of his friends at the House of Commons. While he'd answered all the questions put to him, he hadn't done so with his earlier readiness. The bluff, hearty, adipose Sir Marcus revealed another side to his character. Paul began to see why he'd been named as one of the Radical Dandy's prime enemies.

When he left the building, he was too busy thinking about what he'd just learnt to notice the two figures standing a short distance away. They, however, were quick to see him and came across to intercept him.

Edmund Mellanby and Barrington Oxley stood in his way.

"What are you doing here, Skillen?" asked Oxley.

"I'm sorry," said Paul. "I don't believe I know either of you gentlemen."

"Then your memory is pathetically short."

"I find that remark offensive, sir."

"I am the one who should be offended," said Edmund, pompously. "I told you that I didn't want you prying into the affairs of my family, yet it seems you may still be doing so."

"Why else would you come to the House of Commons?" asked Oxley.

Paul stiffened. "I came because I chose to," he said, stoutly, "and I don't need your permission to do anything. Now please stand aside or I'll be forced to make you do so. I've never set eyes on either of you before and I sincerely hope that I never do so again." He looked from one to the other. "Well, are you going to move out of my way or aren't you?"

Before they could reply, he pushed them forcibly apart and walked between them, leaving both men spluttering with indignation.

CHAPTER
FIFTEEN

Having secured the unwilling cooperation of his victim, the assassin marched his prisoner through the backstreets until they came to St James's Park, the very place where he himself had been destined to die. Taking him into a wooded area, he pushed him hard against a tree.

"Don't kill me," pleaded the man. "I'll get you the money we owe you."

"It's too late."

"Then take my purse. Take anything I have about me."

The assassin was unmoved. "I'll take the most important thing you have."

"It wasn't *my* decision to betray you."

"Then whose decision was it?"

"I can't tell you that."

"In that case," said the assassin, pointing the pistol at him, "you're of no use whatsoever to me."

"No, don't, I implore you."

"You can't beg from a beggar. That's what I was reduced to being, thanks to you. Promises were made then forgotten. I was betrayed. To get close to you, I had to become the lowest of the low."

"I was only acting on someone else's orders."

"Give me his name."

"I can't do that," said the other, trembling with fear. "There's something I can tell you, however. When I met you here in the park, I had an accomplice in hiding. He was there to kill you."

"What was his name?"

"Will you let me go if I give it to you?"

"I might."

"I need a firm promise."

"Like the one you gave me?" asked the other, sourly.

"I spoke up for you, I swear it."

"You're lying."

"You did your job well. If it had been left to me, you'd have been paid and sent on your way."

"Yes — with a bullet inside me."

"On my word of honour, I argued against that."

"Who was the man who shot at me?"

"I'll need something in return."

"You'll get it," said the assassin. "I promise."

"His name is Robert Vane. He lodges at a house next to the White Lion in Gilbert Street."

"I'll find him."

"Does that mean I can go?"

"No," said the other, thrusting his pistol in the man's stomach. "If you want any mercy from me, you must give me the name of the person who set the plot in motion in the first place."

"I simply can't do that."

"Why not?"

"It's more than my life is worth."

"You don't *have* a life any more," said the assassin, using the butt of the pistol to club him to the ground. "Since you choose to keep your mouth shut, then I'll shut it for good. Say your prayers."

Putting the gun to the man's head, he pulled the trigger.

Chevy Ruddock was tireless. Reverting to his original plan, he stopped anyone who had the remotest similarity to the description he'd been given of Giles Clearwater and he questioned them. In every case, he drew a blank. Nobody had ever heard of the man. Several of those he approached were piqued at the way they were confronted and spoke sharply to him. He withstood all insults with unwavering bravery. Even though he was rebuked and sneered at by men from a much higher social class, Ruddock stuck to his task. When he'd made no progress in a couple of hours, he returned to the Golden Crown, only to find that Simeon Howlett was asleep in his usual chair. Unsure if he should wake the man or simply creep away, he stood there dithering for minutes. When he finally decided to leave the old man to his dreams, he was grabbed by a wrinkly hand.

"Don't go," said Howlett. "I've been waiting for you."

"Did you remember who he was?"

"What are you talking about?"

"I'm trying to find a man named Giles Clearwater."

"That name sounds familiar."

"You told me you'd try to remember why."

"Did I?"

"It's important that I find this man. He could help us to solve a murder."

"This is all very confusing, young man," said Howlett, scratching his head. "Give me a moment to collect my thoughts. A reviving drink would not come amiss."

"I bought you one earlier and got nothing in return."

"My brain always responds to alcohol."

"Give me the information I want," said Ruddock, asserting his authority, "and I might oblige you, but be warned — I won't be exploited. Stop playing tricks or I'll walk out of here."

"But I'm desperate to help you."

"Then let's have no more shilly-shallying."

"I've been cudgelling my brain for ages."

"And what's the result?"

"I *did* know the man you're after," claimed Howlett, "but I can't recall when and where I met him. But it will come back," he went on, clutching at Ruddock's sleeve. "It's shameful, isn't it? I was once lauded as one of the finest actors on the stage. I'd committed every great Shakespearean soliloquy to memory and could declaim them at the drop of a hat. Now, however, I can't even remember the name of a play itself, let alone any of its lines. It's embarrassing."

"In short," said Ruddock, "you've forgotten all about Clearwater."

"Not at all, not at all," said the other. "I have a vivid picture of him in my mind. He's just as you described. Give me more time to think. Meanwhile, leave me details of where I can reach you and, the moment my brain functions properly, I'll get in touch." He beamed, hopefully. "Will this content you?"

"Not really," said Ruddock, suspiciously.

"I give you my word."

"You'd better keep it."

"I won't let you down," said Howlett, hand on heart.

"No, you wouldn't dare!"

Peter Skillen was thrilled to be back in London again, but he had nagging memories of his time in Nottingham. He felt that he'd somehow let Seth Hooper and his friends down and resolved to make amends. Only the arrest and conviction of Sir Roger Mellanby's killer would vindicate him and he was determined to search for the man with renewed energy. He was alone with Charlotte in the storeroom at the shooting gallery when he had a second visit from the Runners. Strutting into the room, Yeomans and Hale were both smirking.

"You look as if you've just had good news," said Peter.

"We have," confirmed Yeomans.

"Does that mean you've finally made an arrest?"

"No, it means that we're just about to make one."

"What are you talking about?" asked Charlotte.

"We've come to apprehend your husband, Mrs Skillen," said Hale.

"You can't do that."

"Oh, yes we can."

"What possible charge can you bring against him?"

"It's one of assault," said Yeomans. "The incident took place recently outside the House of Commons."

"I've been nowhere near there," insisted Peter.

"It's true," said Charlotte. "He's been here for the last hour or more."

"We have it on good authority that he assaulted two gentlemen," said Yeomans, "and their evidence is clear. Sir Roger Mellanby's son and his lawyer have each given us a statement of what happened." He nodded to Hale who stepped in to take Peter's arm. "You've gone too far this time."

"This is ridiculous," protested Peter. "I did meet the two gentlemen you mention when I was in Nottingham, but I haven't set eyes on them since my return to London. Frankly, if I did so, I'd make every effort to avoid them."

"Ah," said Yeomans, eyes aglow. "So there's bad blood between you and them, is there? That might explain why you attacked them."

"I didn't attack *anybody*."

"Then why did Mr Oxley swear that you did? He's a lawyer. He'd only make such a claim if it had legal force. Lawyers are known for their honesty."

"This one isn't," said Peter. "He's shifty and treacherous."

"Mind your language," warned Hale, "or you could be adding slander to the charge against you."

"There *is* no charge. I simply wasn't there."

"Then why do the two of them claim that you were?"

"That's something I'd very much like to know."

"You'll have to come with us," said Yeomans.

211

"I refuse to do so."

"Are you resisting arrest?"

"I'm not being taken off to Bow Street for an offence I couldn't possibly have committed," said Peter, shaking Hale off. "Apart from my wife, there are two other witnesses — Gully Ackford and Jem Huckvale — who will swear that I've been in this building for the last hour or so."

"We'd rather trust the word of the two gentlemen," said Yeomans.

"I'll sue them for laying false information against me."

"They're waiting for you in Bow Street."

Peter folded his arms. "I'm not moving an inch."

Yeomans and Hale traded an uneasy glance. They were strong men but Peter was even stronger and much younger. It might take more than two of them to overpower him. In the event, no violence was necessary. The door suddenly opened and in walked Paul. Thrilled to see his brother, he threw his arms around Peter and they hugged each other warmly. Paul then noticed the Runners.

"What are these idiots doing here?" he asked.

"They're trying to arrest me," said Peter. "I'm supposed to have assaulted two men outside the House of Commons."

"The charge is that you pushed them apart with extreme force," said Yeomans, "and that's tantamount to assault." Paul started to laugh. "It's no cause for amusement. The two gentlemen are of good standing.

One is a lawyer and the other is the son of Sir Roger Mellanby."

"So *that's* who they are," said Paul. "They obviously confused me with Peter and you're doing the same. *I* was the person who brushed lightly past them outside the House of Commons."

"They described you as brutal and uncouth." Paul laughed even more. "It's no joke. You're in serious trouble."

"I doubt that," said Peter, easily. "It sounds to me as if this whole business can be sorted out in a couple of minutes. Come on, Paul. We'll both go to Bow Street to face the pair of them together and clear this matter up. Unless they're dripping with blood and covered in bruises, I don't think there's a case to answer."

The brothers went cheerfully out through the door.

It was only a suggestion but somehow it seemed to work. Rather than sit there with Dorothea Glenn and listen to her describing in detail her doomed relationship with Orsino Price, Hannah wondered if her friend would care to read some of the play in which they were next to appear together. Dorothea was uncertain at first. When she realised that she would be reading the part of Isabella, the leading female character, she changed her mind at once. It was an unexpected honour for her.

"But that's *your* role, Miss Granville," she argued.

"*You* are Isabella today," said Hannah, "and I'm sure you'll do justice to the part. Who knows? One day you may well play it yourself."

"That would truly be a miracle."

"They do occur sometimes."

"Orsino was my miracle. I'll never meet anyone like him."

"Let's forget him for a moment and concentrate on Shakespeare."

Seated beside each other, they had the play spread out before them. Hannah had turned the pages to the second scene between Isabella and Angelo, a man with absolute power during the absence of the Duke of Vienna. Isabella had come to him to plead for her brother's release from the death sentence imposed by Angelo on him for sleeping with his betrothed before they were married.

"Angelo is a puritan," said Hannah, "but he is strangely attracted to Isabella. As the scene develops, he has feelings for her that he is unable to control. As you know, he offers her a corrupt bargain. To save her brother's life, she must sacrifice her virginity."

"It's a terrible position to put her in."

"I agree, Dorothea, but it's a wonderful role for any actress, full of emotion and soaring verse. Are you ready to tackle it?"

"Yes, please."

"Then let's begin . . ."

Hannah deepened her voice and sharpened its edge so that she could sound like the peremptory Angelo. It took Dorothea a little longer to settle into the role. Nervous at first, she grew in confidence and improved steadily, handling the verse with great dexterity. In less than a minute, she was so committed to the play that

214

she forgot all about her troubles. Hannah, however, was aware of the faint connection between Isabella's plight and that of the young actress. If, as she believed, Orsino Price had been deceiving Dorothea, then the latter's virginity, as in the case of Shakespeare's heroine, was at the mercy of a lecherous man. There was a secondary parallel. Isabella was threatened by someone acting as a deputy to the absent Duke. Hannah was forced to remember that she, too, was being menaced by a man who'd assumed power in the absence of a ruler. No loss of virtue was involved in her case but that didn't detract from Hannah's discomfort when she recalled that she was, in effect, now playing the role of the Prince Regent.

For Dorothea, however, it was a totally different experience. The longer the scene went on, the more she grew into the part, and when she was confronted with the cruel ultimatum, she delivered her closing soliloquy with mingled pathos and passion. Hannah was so impressed that she clapped her hands in appreciation.

"That was brilliant, Dorothea!"

"Do you really think so?" asked the other, touched by the compliment.

"I could not have delivered that speech better myself."

"There's no higher praise than that."

"And, yes, I know that I was hardly a convincing Angelo, but the scene is really about Isabella and, like any good actress, you made the most of it."

"Thank you."

"How do you feel?"

"To be candid, I feel rather dizzy."

"That's only to be expected."

"But I'm so grateful that you suggested reading that scene, Miss Granville. It took me into another world. I actually forgot the demons assailing me."

"You've learnt a good lesson," said Hannah. "At times of crisis, you can always turn to Shakespeare. I've done so myself on many occasions. He may not be able to solve our problems, but he can always take us to a place where they aren't quite so oppressive. Remember that."

Harry Scattergood was a strict teacher. He rehearsed Alan Kinnaird for a long time until he was convinced that his friend would be able to hold his own under questioning from the chief magistrate. As a reward, Scattergood took him into the nearby Golden Crown for a celebratory drink. Secure in their disguises as men of fashion, their behaviour enabled them to blend easily into the crowd. The two of them drifted into a quiet corner. Kinnaird winked at his friend.

"We'd never have been able to do this in the old days, Harry."

"They wouldn't have let us in through the door."

"We've moved up in society."

"To make your living off fine gentlemen, you have to look like one of them."

"Look, smell and sound."

"That's right. All that practice we put in has paid off."

"Have you ever brought Welsh Mary here?"

"I wouldn't dare," said Scattergood with a grin. "I love her dearly but that accent of hers would give us away at once. Mary knows her place and that's beside, beneath or on top of me."

"Does she know about our plan?"

"It's best to keep her in the dark about such things, Alan."

"What if things go wrong?"

"They won't."

"Welsh Mary will be left high and dry."

"Don't even think such a thing. My plan is foolproof. Now that you've been properly rehearsed, we can choose our moment to strike."

"You're a genius, Harry."

"Giles, if you please," corrected the other. "Giles Clearwater."

"Where on earth did you get a name like that?"

"It was quite by chance, as it happens. I think it suits me."

"Well, I'm glad that I made your acquaintance," said Kinnaird, raising his glass. "I drink to you, Mr Clearwater."

"And I drink to our success."

The two of them enjoyed a first sip of their wine. Scattergood was brimming with confidence. He didn't notice the old man seated alone nearby and staring at him with great interest. Simeon Howlett's memory was starting to function again.

The visit to Bow Street was brief. Unable to decide which of the brothers had assaulted them, Edmund

Mellanby and Oxley settled on Peter. They claimed to recognise the sinister aspect in his character. Paul was highly amused, freely admitting that he had been at the House of Commons but denying that any assault had taken place. When he gave his version of what had happened, the chief magistrate concluded that no crime had occurred and chided the visitors from Nottingham for wasting his time on such meaningless trivia.

"What were you doing there in the first place?" demanded Oxley.

"I was in pursuit of the man who ordered the death of Sir Roger Mellanby," said Paul. "Instead of having me hauled here, you should be thankful that someone is on the trail of the assassin."

"The Bow Street Runners have mounted their own investigation."

"It remains to be seen who achieves a satisfactory result."

"We don't need you involved at all," said Edmund.

"In that case," interjected Peter, "you will wait for ever before you discover who shot your father and at whose command."

Taking their leave, the brothers walked out and left the two men fuming. On their stroll back to the shooting gallery, they caught up on each other's news. Paul was fascinated to hear about Peter's trip to Nottingham, and how the Mellanby family was not uniformly in favour of his commitment to solve the murder on their behalf. For his part, Peter was astonished at the amount of evidence that Paul had already assembled. Now that he was back in the capital,

218

he wanted to throw himself into the search. He told Paul what his first move had been.

"You went to the Home Secretary?" asked Paul in surprise.

"He's responsible for law and order in this country."

"That must make him a very busy man. However did you get access to him?"

"His brother contrived an appointment for me."

Paul grinned. "Brothers do come in useful from time to time," he said. "But tell me about Sidmouth. Was he pleased to see you, or did he object when he realised the purpose of your visit?"

Peter gave him a concise account of the interview and confessed that he'd left the Home Office in a state of confusion, refusing to believe that Sidmouth had direct involvement in the suppression of radical movements further north, yet sensing that the man was somehow guilty of actions Peter detested. At all events, he didn't expect to be allowed anywhere near the Home Secretary again.

"You've lost an important ally," said Paul.

"In times as stressful as this, all friendships come under strain."

"You're being very philosophical, Peter."

"I'd say that I was being pragmatic."

"You always did like to quibble."

"What do you propose to do next?"

"Ideally," said Paul, "I'd like some time alone with our renowned President of the Board of Trade but I doubt if Oswald Ferriday will let me within a mile of him."

"He obviously has something to hide."

"You could say that of all politicians — even Sir Roger Mellanby."

"Who was this mistress of his that you met?"

"Kitty Denley. There's much more to come from her yet. Seeing her again is one of my priorities."

"What about me?"

"I'd like your opinion of her husband, Hugh Denley. I certainly haven't crossed his name off the list of suspects yet. Losing a duel rankles, especially if it means you lose your wife into the bargain."

Peter came to a sudden halt.

"What's wrong?" asked Paul.

"I've just thought of something," said Peter. "Sir Roger's son and his lawyer came to London to attend the inquest before taking the body home. What were the two of them doing at the House of Commons?"

Reading a play with an actress she held in the highest regard had not only taken Dorothea's mind off her anxieties, it had tired her. The performance as Isabella — albeit only a first reading of the role — had required effort and concentration. It had taxed her emotions. Worried about Price earlier on, she'd been unable to sleep but she was now close to exhaustion. Her eyelids now began to flutter and she drifted gently off.

Hannah was glad to see her getting some of the rest she so obviously needed. As she looked down at her friend, she was reminded of herself at that age. She, too, had been a young actress, struggling to make her mark in an unforgiving profession. Her beauty had

220

attracted unwanted attention from men in the company and aroused jealousy in the women. Like Dorothea, she had once fallen in love with a man who had deceived her but, in her case, she had realised her mistake in time.

Without disturbing her friend's slumber, she got up and went to the bureau to take out the letter she'd received from the Prince Regent. It still left her in a state of indecision. The invitation was carefully worded and there was a real flourish to the signature. It had been sent by someone who was used to being obeyed. Hannah was still poring over the invitation when Dorothea came instantly awake.

"Oh," she said, sitting up with embarrassment, "I do apologise."

"You've nothing to apologise for, Dorothea. You're fatigued and overwrought. How you stayed awake this long I don't know. Your body was telling you that you needed a rest. That's why you fell asleep."

"It was dreadful of me, Miss Granville."

"I'm not complaining. To be honest, I was glad that you were able to let yourself go like that." She held up the letter. "While you were getting some long-overdue sleep, I've been wrestling with a problem of my own. This is an invitation from the Prince Regent to go to Brighton Pavilion."

"What a wonderful honour!" cried Dorothea.

"In one sense, it is. In another, I feel that it would make me beholden to him."

"But you want to go, surely?"

"I'm tempted. I'll admit that."

"I'd accept the invitation at once. Everyone says that the Pavilion is like nothing else in this country. How can you even think of turning down His Royal Highness?" said Dorothea, excitedly. "It would be an insult."

Gilbert Street was a thoroughfare in the more affluent part of Marylebone. He could see that the White Lion was a public house of some distinction. The adjacent house, a detached property of fairly recent construction, had a pleasing symmetry to it. What interested him was that it also had a side gate. He was no longer disguised as a beggar. Having disposed of one of the men ordered to kill him, he felt confident enough to wear his usual apparel. He walked on past the house, then, having reached the end of the road, he waited ten minutes before strolling past it again on the opposite pavement. His reconnaissance was complete.

Thanks to his brother, Peter had some idea what to expect when he called on Hugh Denley. He was a tall, spare, agitated man in his fifties with a bulbous forehead and a wispy beard. Though a servant allowed Peter to step into the hall, he got no further. Denley came out to see who his visitor was.

"What are you doing here, Mr Skillen?" he asked, inhospitably. "I've told you all that I'm prepared to say. You may as well leave at once."

"Before I do that," said Peter, "there's something you should know. The person you talked to earlier was my twin brother, Paul. He was grateful that you felt able to

222

be so frank with him. When reviewing his notes of the conversation, however, he felt that there were one or two gaps. I'm here in the hope of filling them."

"Then you're going to be disappointed."

"Don't be too rash, sir."

Denley opened the front door again. "Goodbye, Mr Skillen."

"If you turn me away, I'll feel duty-bound to pass on your name to the Bow Street Runners. Their questioning won't be half as respectful as ours. For a start, they'll insist that you're hauled before the chief magistrate and then," Peter went on with a cautionary smile, "there's the small matter of your illegal duel."

"There's no need for them to know anything about that."

"If we tell them that you fought — and lost — against a man who was later murdered, they'd be bound to take a keen interest."

Denley shut the door. "Come into my study," he growled.

Peter followed him down a corridor and into a large room with a desk under one window. Ledgers were stacked on top of each other. Paul had told his brother that Denley was a successful wine merchant and that he owned a warehouse on the Thames that stocked the wine imported from abroad. Since the end of the war, the vineyards of France had resumed their supplies.

Denley was brusque. "What do you wish to know?"

"Tell me about your relationship with Sir Roger Mellanby."

"Your brother asked me that."

"Yes, but he's not here, unfortunately. So I'd be grateful if you could humour me. Where and when did you first meet him, for example? And why did you suspect him of taking liberties with your wife?"

Denley grimaced.

Paul was given a much more cordial welcome when he called on Kitty Denley. Now that the initial shock of her lover's murder had worn off, she was able to take a measured view of her position. Being the mistress of a Member of Parliament had brought some excitement into her life for the first time.

"The last time I was here," said Paul as they settled down in the drawing room, "you weren't ready to talk freely. Is there anything else that you wish to tell me now?"

"Yes," she said.

"What is it?"

Kitty wet her lips before speaking. "My husband has a thriving business but I wasn't allowed to know anything about it. 'Women don't understand such things,' he used to say. So it remained a closed book to me."

"Didn't you meet any of his suppliers or clients?"

"No, I never did."

"You must have felt left out."

"It was a cross I learnt to bear, Mr Skillen, and in some ways I was grateful. The wine trade would have bored me. Hugh loves that world. The happiest time of all for him is when his latest imports are unloaded at

224

the docks. He stands on the wharf and checks them carefully."

"Does his work mean that he has a large social circle?"

"Yes — but I was kept on the fringe of that as well. For most of my marriage, I was a wife in name only. That's why my . . . attention waned. I can see what you're thinking. Why did I marry him in the first place? The answer is simple. Hugh was kind and attentive to me in those days. He offered me stability and companionship."

"Yet you had no children."

"That was the thing that disappointed me most. With a family to bring up, I'd have been happy and fulfilled. As it was, my life was empty."

"You said that you had something to tell me."

"I do, Mr Skillen. Do you remember asking me if my husband has any political affiliations?"

"You told me that he doesn't."

"I was wrong. I learnt yesterday that he has a friend in Parliament."

"What is his name?"

"It's one that you mentioned during your first visit."

"Oswald Ferriday?"

"No," she said. "Sir Marcus Brough."

CHAPTER
SIXTEEN

Robert Vane was a short, slight, soberly dressed individual in his thirties with a nondescript appearance that never attracted a second glance. He might have been a banker, a merchant or a minor functionary in the government. Nobody would have suspected what his profession was in reality. When the cab dropped him outside his lodging, there was a muted hilarity coming from the White Lion. Vane decided that he would join the other patrons in due course. In the anonymity of a public house, he was easily accepted. No questions were ever asked about his work.

He rented two rooms on the first floor of the adjoining house. Letting himself in through the front door, he went soundlessly up the stairs. A separate key was needed to admit him to his lodging. Once inside, he pushed the bolt in place. Vane was about to remove his hat when he became aware that something was not quite right. Certain objects had been moved from the usual place. The clock on the mantelpiece had disappeared altogether. He resolved to confront his landlord. Before doing so, he wondered if anything had been shifted in the bedroom.

Opening the door, he came to an abrupt halt. Propped up on pillows, a man lay indolently on his bed. The assassin gave him a broad smile.

"We meet again," he said, patting the pistol beside him. "Only this time, *I'm* the one with the weapon."

"I've never set eyes on you before," claimed Vane.

"You tried to kill me in St James's Park."

"I'm sorry but you must be mistaken. And what are you doing, moving my things around and lolling on my bed? Get out of here at once."

"I can't do that, I'm afraid."

"Then I'll have to make you."

With a sudden burst of energy, Vane leapt towards a bedside table, yanked it open and pulled out a pistol. He pointed it at his unwanted visitor.

"Get up!" he ordered.

"I'm perfectly comfortable here, Mr Vane."

"If you don't do as you're told, I'll shoot."

"I very much doubt that. I took the precaution of removing the bullet. All that you will get is a disappointing click." He snatched up his own weapon. "My pistol, however, is loaded, so you might as well put yours down." Vane hesitated. "Do as you're told or I'll kill you. It's the least you deserve." Vane put his pistol aside. "That's better. Now we can talk."

"Look, there must be some mistake."

"I agree and you're the one who made it."

"You're confusing me with someone else."

"The man who hired you to kill me gave me your name and address. I shot him dead by way of a thank you." Vane backed away. "Stay where you are or I'll

227

drop you as well." He got off the bed and stood upright. "This place of yours is very comfortable. You're obviously well paid for your work. I was promised a large reward as well, then I was betrayed."

"That wasn't my doing. I didn't make the decision."

"Then who did?"

"The man you claim to have killed."

"He was only a link in the chain," said the other. "I want the name of the person who hatched this plot in the first place. Give me that and I might show you some mercy by simply shooting at one your kneecaps." He aimed the pistol at Vane's leg. "Who is he?"

"I don't know," said Vane, shrinking away.

"Your friend must have told you."

"But he didn't. I was only hired to kill you."

"What about my lodging? Who broke in there and stole my money? Who wrecked the place out of spite?" Vane was writhing. "What malevolent little toad destroyed almost everything I owned?"

"I hated having to do that."

"Ah, so you admit it now."

"I was told to recover the money."

"You did a lot more than that, Mr Vane. That's why I vowed that I'd kill the pair of you. This may be a pleasant lodging but it's remarkably easy to break into. I've been here for over an hour, waiting for you. I passed the time by rearranging some of your things. Oh, yes," he added, "and I found most of the money you stole from me. You should have found a better hiding place than that trunk of yours."

228

"I'll get much more," said Vane, gabbling. "Take me to my bank and I'll withdraw all I have. It's yours for the taking."

"So is your life."

"No, *please* — we can come to some arrangement."

"Get down on your knees and beg."

"If I knew the name you want, I'd tell you at once."

"Get down!" snapped the other.

Vane fell to his knees and started jabbering. Standing behind him, the assassin put a bullet in his skull. Exulting in his rage, he left the house swiftly through the upstairs rear window he'd used to get into it.

Peter's estimate of the man was very much the same as that of his brother, Hugh Denley was spiky, secretive and rancorous. Answering some questions with obvious annoyance, he refused even to consider the rest. Time and again, he insisted that he had a right to privacy.

"Privacy doesn't exist in a murder investigation," said Peter.

"I had nothing whatsoever to do with what happened."

"You had a definite link with Sir Roger Mellanby."

"I only met the man once and that was on Hampstead Heath at dawn."

"You went there to kill him, Mr Denley."

"It was a matter of honour."

"It should have been a matter of common sense. From what I've heard, Sir Roger was an expert swordsman."

"I was not aware of it at the time."

"You should have taken the precaution of finding out. Very well," said Peter, "let's look elsewhere. I believe you have a flourishing wine business."

"It's the fruit of hard work over many years."

"I'm told that people in high society are numbered amongst your clients."

"They want the best wine available so they come to me."

"Do any members of the government buy their stock from you?"

"I don't see that that's any concern of yours."

"It's a natural assumption, Mr Denley. It may be, for instance, that the Home Secretary drinks wine purchased from you. Then there's the President of the Board of Trade, Mr Ferriday. Might he also be one of your customers?"

"I don't keep track of individual accounts. All I know is that my stock is popular and that business is brisk."

"Let's go back to Sir Roger," suggested Peter.

Denley sighed. "Must we?"

"What was your opinion of his stance on suffrage?"

"I've no time for politics."

"He wanted to widen the franchise considerably. Sir Roger felt that those at the mercy of government decisions regarding their livelihood ought to have a say on who was elected to Parliament. Don't you think that cause is laudable?"

"It's irrelevant as far as I'm concerned."

"Why do you believe that?"

"The lower orders must be kept in their place," snapped Denley, "or we'll have anarchy. Power must

230

remain in the hands of the people best qualified to exercise it. We can't let a rabble run the country."

"I thought you had no time for politics."

"I'm only saying what every decent Englishman would say."

"Then let me tell you something," said Peter, sharply. "I've met some of the people you call a 'rabble' and, to a man, they were decent and hard-working. Denied education, they've made every effort to educate themselves. They don't have the money to sit around drinking your wine and decrying the major section of the population. They fight for the few rights allowed them and I find that admitable."

Denley sniggered. "You're a second Sir Roger Mellanby."

"How would you know?"

"I heard him speak on one occasion at a public gathering."

"What were *you* doing in the audience?"

"That's my business."

"You told me that the only time you met Sir Roger was at the duel."

"I was just one face in the crowd. We never spoke."

"Why were you there in the first place?"

"I wanted to know a little more about him."

"Was this before or after the duel?" asked Peter.

"It doesn't matter."

"It does to me. It was afterwards, wasn't it?"

Denley lowered his head. It was an acknowledgement.

Paul's second interview with Kitty Denley had been instructive. She had talked more openly about her marriage and how she'd felt bored and disregarded. What interested him most was the link she established between her husband and Sir Marcus Brough. Moving in different spheres of society, they were hardly natural friends. Paul wondered what had brought the two of them together. She was unable to tell him. He thanked Kitty for being so honest with him, then rode home to see how Hannah was coping with Dorothea. To his relief, the latter was no longer distraught and fearful. Something had happened to calm Dorothea down. Paul decided that it might be time to tell her the truth. Holding it back any longer could be seen as an act of wilful cruelty.

"Well," asked Dorothea, getting up. "Have you found anything out?"

"Yes," he said. "I have."

"I can see from your face that it's bad news."

"I'm afraid that it is. Why don't you sit down again?"

"I'd rather stand, if you don't mind. Please tell me the worst, Mr Skillen. I will be able to cope with it, I promise you."

"Dorothea is much stronger now," said Hannah, rising from the sofa to stand beside her. "We've been reading together."

"What have you discovered, Mr Skillen?"

"The body of a man was found in an alleyway in Covent Garden," he said, softly. "He'd been stabbed to death." Dorothea tensed and Hannah put an arm

232

around her shoulders. "He's not been identified yet, but there's every possibility that he might be Orsino Price."

"Thank you for telling me," said Dorothea, holding back tears.

"There's still a chance that it might not be him, of course, but I don't think it's wise to nurture that hope."

"You've only confirmed something I already knew, Mr Skillen."

"Have I?"

"Orsino was a saint. He'd never break a promise to me unless . . ."

"You have our deepest sympathy."

"I think I'd like to go to my room now," said Dorothea.

"Let me come with you," said Hannah, putting an arm around her and helping her upstairs. A few minutes later, she returned.

"How is she?" asked Paul.

"She's surprisingly calm."

"I thought that the news would destroy her."

"Dorothea is more resilient than she looks."

"At least, we're not deceiving her any more."

"His family will need to be informed."

"We don't know that he has one, Hannah. He said nothing to Dorothea about parents. She wasn't even told where he lived. Then there's another problem."

"Is there?"

"Orsino Price may not even be his real name. You know how vain actors are. They prefer a name that has a ring to it."

"Does Hannah Granville have that ring?"

He spread his arms wide. "It's a peal of bells in itself."

They shared a laugh. Sitting down together, they caught up with each other's news. Hannah was fascinated to hear about his visit to Sir Marcus Brough and his subsequent encounter with Edmund Mellanby and Oxley. She was amused when she heard how Peter had come close to arrest.

"I can see how it happened," she said. "After all this time, *I* still can't always tell you apart."

"I'm the devilishly handsome one."

"And so is Peter."

"Charlotte can tell the difference between us immediately."

"Then I'll have to ask her the secret."

"I want to hear *your* secret first," he said. "How did you teach that poor girl to master her emotions like that? When she first came here, she was a wreck."

"I tried to take her mind off her worries."

"Well, whatever you did, it seems to have worked."

"It was a two-way process, Paul. She was able to help *me* in return. You know that I've been fretting about that invitation to go to Brighton Pavilion."

"You keep changing your mind about it."

"Well, I didn't know if it was a threat or a mark of distinction."

"And what do you think now?"

"I think we should go," she said. "With you by my side, I'll feel completely safe. In any case, how often will I get an invitation from the next king? This may be my one and only chance. I should seize it with both hands."

234

Alone in her room, Dorothea knelt beside the bed and prayed for the salvation of Orsino Price's soul. Eyes still closed, she thought about the times they'd spent together, the plans they'd made and the promises he'd given her. She couldn't believe that her dreams had been snatched away so quickly. All that she had left were some precious memories of a love that had steadily deepened over the weeks they'd been together. A memory of a different kind then surfaced.

Back in the shooting gallery, Peter was telling Gully Ackford about his meeting with the wine merchant because he valued his friend's opinion. Ackford gave it bluntly.

"Mr Denley has something to hide," he said.

"I agree. And I'll warrant that he knows the name of every single person who buys his wine. It's the sort of thing he'd commit to memory."

"Then conceal from you."

"Yes, Gully. He struck me as the kind of man who never confides in anyone, even his wife. Wine has made him wealthy and that's all he cares about."

"Is he quiet, reclusive, self-centred?"

"He's all of those things."

"Then how did he have the spirit to challenge Sir Roger to a duel? It shows that he has a reckless streak in him."

"It was very nearly a suicidal decision."

"How did he learn that his wife had gone astray?"

"He refused to tell me."

"And why did he go to a meeting addressed by a man he hated?"

"It may be that he wanted to turn that hatred into something more positive," said Peter, "such as an assassination."

"Would he have the courage to arrange such a thing?"

"He'd need someone else's support. That's why I questioned him about politicians with a grudge against Sir Roger. He denied even knowing who they were."

"Did you include the Home Secretary's name?"

"Yes, I did."

"I thought he was your friend. Has your opinion of him changed?"

Peter sighed. "I'm not sure."

"But he'd never stoop to anything like this, surely?"

"Until today, I'd have said the same thing, Gully. When I met him, however, he was evasive. He's always been so honest with me before. The trust between us has gone. I'm almost sure that he had Sir Roger watched in his constituency."

"Why? Was he such a danger to the government?"

"Sir Roger had a powerful voice. It could drive people to take action."

"Is there a chance that Denley and the Home Secretary worked together?"

"I wish I knew," said Peter. "But I also questioned Denley about Sir Marcus Brough and Ferriday. After what happened today, I might have added the name of Edmund Mellanby."

"Surely you don't suspect Sir Roger's own son?"

"According to his younger brother, he's long coveted a seat in Parliament. That might be why Paul met him outside the House of Commons. It's conceivable that he'd gone there to gloat."

"He might equally well have wished to meet members of his father's party. From what you've told me, the Whigs have lost their crusader. Perhaps the elder son wanted to offer himself as a replacement."

"Edmund Mellanby never offers, Gully — he simply *takes*."

"People of that class often have the same attitude."

"What sticks in my mind about him is that he and the family lawyer have gone out of their way to hamper my investigation. Why? Are they afraid that I might find out family secrets that could embarrass them? Is that the reason they've dismissed me as an irrelevance?"

Ackford cackled. "Then they certainly don't know Peter Skillen," he said. "The more they try to brush you aside, the more determined you become."

"It's true. Anyway, thanks for letting me air my thoughts. It's enabled me to get them into perspective."

"Will you be seeing Mr Denley again?"

"It's possible."

"Then pass on a message to him. The next time he decides to fight a duel, advise him to take some lessons from me beforehand. I can at least teach him the rudiments of swordplay."

When he called at the house, Paul fully expected to be sent on his way. To his amazement, he was invited in. It was almost as if his arrival had been foreseen. He was ushered into the drawing room where Oswald Ferriday was ensconced in a leather armchair.

"I had a feeling that you'd show up again, Mr Skillen," he said. "How did you get hold of my private address?"

"I'm used to finding things I regard as important, sir."

"Evidently," said Ferriday. "I saw you briefly at the Home Office. You looked as if you had no idea who I was."

"I'll think you'll find that it was my twin brother, Peter, who went to see the Home Secretary. He worked as one of his agents in France."

Ferriday was surprised. "There are *two* of you?"

"Yes, and we're both engaged in this enterprise."

"So your brother was one of those brave men who worked behind enemy lines, was he? I'm impressed. Espionage is an important tool of government."

"Is that why innocent members of Hampden Clubs are under surveillance?"

"I'll ignore that jibe and suggest that you sit down." Paul settled into a chair opposite him. "Now, please don't abuse my hospitality."

Ferriday was a middle-aged man who looked much older than his years. Time had twisted his body out of shape and given him a pronounced hump. His face was colourless and criss-crossed with deep lines. His voice, however, was crisp and his gaze searching.

"I'm sorry that I shrugged you off earlier," he said. "Sir Marcus Brough scolded me for doing so. We may have fought against everything Sir Roger stood for but, in spite of that, we had a sneaking fondness for him. And we certainly want his killer brought to justice very quickly."

"It will take more than a few pious words to achieve that end."

Ferriday was stung. "Do you doubt my sincerity?"

"I've seen no sign of it so far, sir."

"Then what would you have me do?"

"Cooperation with me and my brother would be a good place to start," said Paul, "and you've so far treated me like a leper."

"That was a mistake for which I've already apologised."

"It was only because Sir Marcus chided you. Without his intervention, you'd have kept me at arm's length indefinitely."

"Listen, Mr Skillen," said the other, controlling his irritation, "I've agreed to speak to you even though I'm under no obligation to do so. If you have any questions for me, please ask them but don't you dare badger me."

"I'll do my best not to do so."

"Thank you."

"May I ask if you know a man named Hugh Denley?"

"He's not a close friend of mine, if that's what you mean."

"But you are aware of who he is."

"Anyone who enjoys a glass of wine as much as I do is aware of Denley. I get my supplies from his company on a regular basis."

"Have you ever met him?"

"I'm not sure," said Ferriday. "I think it unlikely somehow. Mr Denley is in trade and — despite my position in the Cabinet — I never invite people like him into my social circle. What on earth would he and I *talk* about?"

"So you know nothing of his family?"

"Why should I? A wine merchant exists to sell wine. That's enough for me. I don't require an insight into his private life."

"Let's turn to Sir Roger," said Paul, watching him carefully. "I understand that you and he had some battles in the House of Commons."

"I'm a Tory and he was a Whig. Disagreements between us were inevitable."

"I accept that. However, I've been told that there was rather more than a disagreement between the two of you, sir. It's my understanding that you and he clashed over the imposition of the Corn Laws. Sir Roger launched a personal attack on you."

"He did that to anyone who didn't agree with him, including members of his own party. I was one of many who felt the lash of his tongue."

"Why were you picked out?"

"It was for no particular reason," said Ferriday, airily. "I was a member of Lord Liverpool's government. That made me fair game."

"Oh, I fancy that it went deeper than that. He pilloried you time and again. Because you own extensive farmland, you represented everything he despised about the Corn Laws. You stood to gain from legislation that caused misery in the general population. Sir Roger hounded you."

Ferriday's face darkened. "You've been talking to Sir Marcus, haven't you?"

"He was more approachable than you."

"Sir Marcus is a good friend of mine but he does have a love of hyperbole. If you take his words too literally, you'll be led completely astray. Besides, what possible connection can there be between my support of the Corn Laws and Sir Roger's murder? Unless, of course," he added with a cautionary glint, "you're alleging that a few harsh words from him provided me with a motive to have him killed."

"I didn't say or imply that."

"Then what *is* your position regarding me?"

"It's not *my* position that brought me here," replied Paul, "but that of Sir Roger himself. The three politicians he regarded as his arch enemies were the Home Secretary, Sir Marcus Brough and you. It's only natural that I would take an interest in all three people."

"I could name you dozens of other politicians who loathed Sir Roger."

"I'm only interested in the trio he specified."

"And what's your conclusion?" asked Ferriday. "Your brother has spoken to the Home Secretary and you have interviewed Sir Marcus and me. Have you obtained any evidence that the three of us were engaged in an assassination plot?"

"It's too early to say."

"Then the answer is that you haven't and, I can assure you, that you never will because such evidence doesn't exist. Not to put too fine a point on it, we regarded Sir Roger Mellanby as no more than a parliamentary nuisance. His oratory enlivened debates but we'll manage quite well without it, thank you very much. Can you hear what I'm telling you?" he continued. "We had no conceivable motive to silence his voice. It was simply a disagreeable noise in our ears."

"The people of Nottingham viewed him as a hero."

"That's their prerogative."

"They'll mourn him for a long time."

"Then perhaps they should take a closer look at the circumstances of his death," said Ferriday, nastily. "What was a married man doing outside the Covent Garden Theatre that night? Why was their hero hoping for a glimpse of one of the most beautiful women in London? That's how the so-called Radical Dandy should be remembered — as a pathetic figure in the grip of his sexual fantasies."

Paul got to his feet and left abruptly.

While their arrest of Peter Skillen had been a mistake, Yeomans and Hale did have some reason to be pleased. They'd managed to convince Edmund Mellanby that they were getting ever closer to his father's killer and that it was only a matter of time before he was caught. Back at the Peacock Inn, they had to face facts.

"We haven't really made much progress," admitted Hale.

"Yes, we have. Fresh information comes in every day."

"It's also coming in to the Skillen brothers. Perhaps it was a mistake to turn that man, Seth Hooper, away. We could have learnt a lot from him, Micah."

"He's irrelevant," said Yeomans. "We have someone who can be of practical use because he was actually there when Sir Roger was shot."

"But Giles Clearwater has refused to help us."

"Yes, Alfred, and we know why. He has his greedy eyes on that reward. Well, we won't let him get away with it. That's why I set Ruddock on to him."

"That was several hours ago. He should have been back by now."

"Don't panic, man. Buy me a pint of ale while we wait."

They were soon settling down with their drinks. Hale was becoming increasingly pessimistic but he rallied when he saw Ruddock coming in through the door. He rushed over to him.

"Thank goodness you've come, Chevy. We need you."

"It's kind of you to say so, Mr Hale."

"Where is he?"

"Who?"

"Giles Clearwater, of course."

"We were hoping you'd bring him here," said Yeomans, joining them. "We need to have a serious talk with the man."

"That won't be possible, Mr Yeomans," said Ruddock. "I could find neither hide nor hair of him.

Nobody had ever heard of Clearwater, let alone befriended him."

"Are you daring to tell us that you *failed*?"

"It was not for want of trying, sir. I spoke to hundreds of people."

"Clearwater is the only one who interests me."

"He's vanished into thin air, Mr Yeomans."

Hale was aghast. "Didn't you find out where he lived?"

"No, sir, I didn't."

"We expected more from you than this, Chevy."

"I'm sorry, sir. I kept at it for hours." He brightened. "There is one small ray of sunshine, however. In the Golden Crown, I met an old man who said that he vaguely remembered the name."

"What use is that?" demanded Yeomans. "We need more than some old fool with a bad memory."

"He felt sure that it would come back to him. He asked me to leave my name and address so that he could send word when his mind cleared. I told him to contact me here."

"Who exactly is this man?"

"His name is Simeon Howlett. He's a retired actor."

"I'll wager that he tried to cadge money off you."

"No, he didn't," said Ruddock. "It was a drink."

"And you were stupid enough to buy it for him, I daresay."

"You're far too soft-hearted, Chevy," said Hale. "People take advantage of you. This old man you talk about used you. He's never heard of Clearwater and he's not going to send you a message to confirm that

244

he's remembered something about the man. You were well and truly hoodwinked."

"I'm sorry, Mr Hale," said Ruddock, head bowed in apology. "I did my best, sir. The truth is . . . he made me believe in him."

Yeomans laughed cruelly and Hale rolled his eyes. They were about to admonish him together when the door opened and, right on cue, a boy entered.

"I'm looking for a Mr Ruddock," he said.

"That's him," said Hale, pointing.

"I'm to deliver this letter from Mr Howlett."

"There you are," said Ruddock. "What did I tell you?"

"You're to read the message and I'm to take your reply back to him."

He handed the letter over and waited. Ruddock opened it and read what had been written in a spidery and barely decipherable hand.

"Well," said Yeomans, "what does the fellow say?"

"He says that he's finally remembered who Giles Clearwater is."

"And who is he?"

"He'll only tell me if I go to the Golden Crown."

"It's a trick," sneered Yeomans. "He just wants to get another free drink out of you. Tear up the letter and give this lad a clip around the ear for being party to this deception."

"It's no deception, sir," said the messenger. "My parents own the Golden Crown. We know Mr Howlett very well. I've taken messages for him before. He's always ready to help people. He said that Mr Ruddock was kind to him."

"I was," agreed Ruddock. "He deserved respect."

"So what are you doing to do, Chevy?" asked Hale.

"I'm going to walk back to the Golden Crown with this lad and see what Mr Howlett has to say. In sending this message, he's kept his word. He obviously wants to pass on the information to me in private. So — if you'll excuse me — I'll be on my way."

"Report back as soon as you can," ordered Yeomans.

"I will, sir."

"And don't you dare buy the old devil a drink."

"If he tells me what I want to know," said Ruddock, defiantly, "I'll buy him two glasses of whatever he chooses. I'm as anxious as you are to find this man and Mr Howlett knows exactly who Giles Clearwater is."

Alan Kinnaird was beginning to lose heart. A light shower had driven him into the shelter of a doorway. For over an hour, he'd been keeping vigil on Newgate Prison, the most feared gaol in the entire city. Having adopted a more suitable disguise, Harry Scattergood had deliberately started an argument with two of the turnkeys and got himself locked up for his pains. It was supposed to be a demonstration of how easy it was to escape from the prison but, Kinnaird believed, his friend had for once failed. Instead of walking out of the place, Scattergood would be taken before a magistrate and given a sentence to make him show more respect to those employed to keep villains behind bars.

When the shower turned into rain, it was as if the weather was confirming Scattergood's failure. The demonstration was over so there was no need to lurk outside the prison. Keeping to the shadows, Kinnaird made his way home, arriving there soaking wet. Having unlocked the door of his lodging, he went gratefully in.

"What kept you?" asked Scattergood, reclining in a chair.

Kinnaird gaped. His friend had done exactly what he'd promised. No prison could hold Scattergood for long. The demonstration had been a success, after all.

CHAPTER
SEVENTEEN

When he took a cab to his club that evening, the first person Captain Golightly met was a man he'd once put forward for membership. Stephen Quine had been the doctor in Golightly's old regiment and the two had become firm friends. After leaving the army, the doctor had been given a series of promotions and was now in charge of the most urgent post-mortems carried out in the city. His cheerful disposition was unusual in a surgeon but he always claimed that the dissection of the human body was an uplifting and educative experience and that he felt privileged to be involved in medical science.

Ordinarily, he rarely talked about his work when at the club because most of its members found a discussion of death to be far too morbid a subject over a companionable brandy. Golightly was the single exception. Having witnessed carnage on the battlefield, he had developed a thick skin. Quine was delighted to know someone to whom he could pass on what he felt was a significant discovery.

Once they'd ordered drinks, they sat side by side in armchairs.

"How is life treating you?" asked Golightly.

"Very well," replied the other, "but death — that's been giving me the real excitement of late. However, you may not be in the mood for tales from the morgue. Please stop me if you find the subject inappropriate."

"That depends what the subject is."

"Guns."

"In that case," said Golightly "talk as long as you like. Guns and rifles have saved my life on more than one occasion. I regard them as friends."

"You wouldn't find this particular gun friendly."

"Why not?"

"It's in the wrong hands."

"Could you be more precise?"

"I stumbled on an extraordinary coincidence."

"Then please let me hear about it . . ."

His visit to Robert Vane's lodging had been profitable. In addition to giving in to the opportunity to wreak his revenge on a man who'd tried to kill him, the assassin had recovered much of the money taken from his own lodging and was able to confiscate Vane's small collection of weapons. There was an even greater bonus. Sifting through a pile of correspondence, he found a letter from the man who'd actually hired him to murder Mellanby. It gave details of how and when he himself was to be disposed of in St James's Park. Unlike the missives he'd received from the same man, this one had an address. It put him one step closer to the person who had originally devised the plot to have Mellanby shot dead.

Once he'd made his escape from Vane's house, he went to the address he'd found to weigh up the possibilities of breaking into it. It was a large, detached property with a garden at the rear. The rain was his accomplice, keeping many people off the streets. Under the cover of the darkness now falling, he climbed into the garden and inched forward towards the house so that he could try to work out the disposition of rooms. His paymaster had been in his thirties. He'd have a wife and, most probably, some children. There'd also be servants to bear in mind. The assassin had to move with care. He reasoned that the only safe place to enter the building was by means of the study. It would probably be on the ground floor and, since the man to whom it belonged had been so secretive by nature, it would certainly be locked. If he could gain access to it, the assassin might well be undisturbed. That, at least, was his hope. He was intending to make only a hasty visit. Once he'd found the name he was after, he would search for the money that should have been paid to him for his services.

He could then declare the contract over and done with.

Chevy Ruddock arrived at the Golden Crown with the messenger. Both had been caught in the rain. When he took off his hat to shake it, he set a small shower into the air. While the messenger went off to his parents, Ruddock looked around and was upset to see that Howlett's usual chair was empty and that there was no sign of the old actor anywhere else in the room. His alarm was temporary. A door opened on the far side of the room and Howlett came shuffling in with a bag slung over one shoulder. Seeing his visitor, he gave him a wave.

"Call of nature, my dear fellow," he explained. "Comfort restored."

Howlett went to his table and Ruddock sat opposite him. The actor stared at him as if he'd never seen him before. He raised a quizzical eyebrow. Ruddock took out the letter he'd received and waved it in front of him.

"You sent for me, Mr Howlett."

"Ah, yes, I believe I did."

"You said that you'd remembered that name at last."

"Indeed, I did."

"Did you know the man?"

Howlett chortled. "That was beyond even *my* fabled capacities."

"Then how did you recall his name?"

"Are you a theatregoer, Mr Ruddock?"

"I don't have the time or the money for entertainment of any kind."

"That's a pity. It would enrich your mind."

"Feeding my family comes first," said Ruddock, "and it always will. Now, who *is* this man? I'm desperate to find out."

"Then the waiting is over," said Howlett, taking the bag off his shoulder and plunging a hand into it. "I am not simply a supreme actor. I am an unacknowledged historian of the profession. For long decades, I have religiously collected material about it and here is one

251

example." He took out a playbill and handed it over. "What do you see?"

Ruddock needed a moment to work out what he was looking at, then his eyes glowed with pleasure. His search was over.

Peter Skillen called on his brother so that they could discuss what each other had found out. Paul was interested to hear his opinion of Sir Marcus Brough and told him what Ferriday had said about his glib colleague. For his part, Peter was amazed that a member of the Cabinet had given so much time to someone he'd earlier treated with disdain. It was telling.

"He's worried, Paul," he said. "He's afraid of what you might find and so he's pretending to cooperate with you in order to divert attention from himself."

"He ended up doing the opposite. The only reason he agreed to speak to me again was that Sir Marcus persuaded him to do so. Although," added Paul after a moment's consideration, "it may be that Sir Marcus was not acting of his own volition."

"Somebody else instructed him?"

"Yes, Peter, and we can both guess who it might have been."

"The Home Secretary?" His face clouded with doubt. "Can this conspiracy really go all the way up to that level?"

"You've already found out that he had spies watching Sir Roger."

"It's a strong possibility, alas."

252

"Their reports may have been directly responsible for his death."

"Don't jump to conclusions, Paul."

Before he could offer his own opinion, Peter was stopped by the sound of the doorbell being rung with some urgency. The brothers listened while one of the servants answered the door. They heard a man's voice. The servant came immediately to the drawing room and knocked before entering.

"There's a Captain Golightly who is very anxious to speak to you, sir," said the maidservant.

"Then show him in at once," said Paul, getting up and turning to Peter. "Only something important could have brought Golightly here."

"After what you've told me about him, I'll be interested to meet him."

Peter also rose to his feet so that the two brothers were side by side when Golightly entered. The newcomer recoiled slightly. The resemblance was so striking that he had no idea to whom he should speak. Paul introduced his brother, then suggested that they all take a seat. Once they'd settled, Golightly took over.

"I've not long come from my club," he told them.

"I wish that we had time for such a luxury, Captain, but our work seems to keep us far too busy."

"Being involved in it has been a revelation to me, Mr Skillen. However, let me pass on my news. I met an old friend of a mine at the club. Stephen Quine was our regimental doctor and an excellent one at that. Don't worry," he went on, "I'm not going to bore you with military memoirs. Dr Quine now makes a living dissecting the bodies of murder victims."

"Was he involved in Sir Roger's post-mortem?" asked Peter.

"Indeed, he was. More recently, he dealt with the case of a man who was shot dead in St James's Park and, almost as soon as that had been done, he was summoned to look at a murder victim being examined by a colleague."

"I don't quite see what relevance this has," said Peter.

"Bear with me and you will. The second case I mentioned refers to a man shot dead later today in a house in Marylebone."

"So?"

"Including Sir Roger, we have three men shot through the skull."

"Go on."

"Dr Quine believes that, in each case, the same pistol was involved."

"That's a very big assumption to make," said Peter, sceptically.

"Surgeons never make assumptions, Mr Skillen," said Golightly. "They deal in hard facts. I find the evidence compelling. The bullet that was taken from Sir Roger's brain was of an unusual shape and so was the one taken from the victim in St James's Park. Since they were identical, the bullets must almost certainly have come from the same mould. But there's another clinching detail."

"What is it?" asked Paul.

254

"Each bullet had a letter 'D' scratched into it."

"Was that the initial letter of the killer's name?"

"I've no idea," said. Golightly, "but let's move on to the third victim. Dr Quine had mentioned what he'd found to a colleague so you can understand why the man called him in. What he'd extracted from the brain of the third victim was a bullet of the same unusual shape and bearing the same signature. That's irrefutable evidence in my mind that the assassin who took Sir Roger's life went on to murder two more victims. I thought you'd find that interesting."

"It's fascinating," said Peter.

"And it raises the question of who those victims are," said Paul. "My guess is that they might be people involved in the plot. The assassin was ruthless. He works on the principle that the best way to ensure his own safety is to eliminate the only people aware of his guilt."

"Wait a moment, Paul. You're forgetting Orsino Price. He was also an accomplice, yet he wasn't shot through the skull. Someone stabbed him to death in an alleyway."

"In that instance, a dagger was as quick as a bullet and far less likely to attract attention. Hired killers are usually adept with a range of weapons."

"What's your view, Captain Golightly?" asked Peter.

"I suspect that the same man is responsible for all four deaths."

"And they've come in fairly close succession."

"It's almost as if the killer is out of control."

255

"Oh, I think he's very much in control, Captain," said Paul. "He's systematic and deadly. There's only one thing we need to ask."

"And what's that?"

"Who is his next target?"

Getting inside the house was more difficult than he'd hoped. His first problem came with four legs attached. A servant brought a dog into the garden to relieve itself and the intruder had to dive into the bushes to hide. The animal then scampered around the lawn, barking aloud. When it came towards him sniffing the grass, the assassin reached for his dagger so that he could parry it away but it was a false alarm. It got within yards of him. The servant whistled and the dog trotted obediently back to him. Wet and cramped, the man in the bushes had had a narrow escape.

He could now tackle the second problem. After he'd established that the study was not at the rear of the house, he realised that he'd have to enter it at the front. Even though the weather kept most people away, a passer-by might notice someone trying to climb in through a window. It was a chance that had to be taken. He consoled himself with the fact that — safely back inside the house — the dog wouldn't be able to attack him. He simply needed to work fast. Creeping to the front, he was able to pick out the study at once because it was the only room in which there was no light. He first looked up and down to make sure that nobody was about, then he took out his dagger again and attacked the window. A minute later, he was inside the house.

As he'd suspected, the door of the study was already locked. Groping his way in the darkness, he reinforced his security by jamming a chair under the knob. It made him feel confident enough to light an oil lamp so that he could take stock of his surroundings. Though it was relatively small, it was exquisitely designed. Oak bookshelves lined two walls and were packed with volumes in identical binding. Over the mantelpiece there was a portrait of a dignified old man in the uniform of a major. He bore a clear resemblance to the person the assassin had murdered in St James's Park. The desk was close enough to the window to profit from any daylight. Predictably it was locked.

Since he was sometimes required to enter a property illegally, he always carried a selection of skeleton keys with him. Taking them out, he got to work. It took almost ten painstaking minutes before he finally succeeded. He rifled quickly through the drawers but found nothing that really interested him. There was no money, no correspondence and no address book. The assassin was patient, knowing that desks of that kind often had hidden cavities in them. Searching for a spring, he explored each of the drawers in turn. At his third attempt, he heard a ping and a secret drawer suddenly appeared.

He had no time to count the wad of banknotes but estimated that he'd found several hundreds of pounds. It was the pile of correspondence that really interested him. Leafing through it, he came across a letter from Robert Vane, agreeing to be in St James's Park as requested. But there was another name that he'd come

257

for and he eventually found it. Written in a looping hand, it offered congratulations on the way that Sir Roger Mellanby had been killed, then ordered that the man responsible for his death should himself be murdered.

When he saw the signature on the letter, the assassin was baffled.

It was worthy of a celebration. Having demonstrated his skill at escape, Harry Scattergood took his friend to the nearest tavern and let Alan Kinnaird buy the drinks.

"How did you do it, Harry?" asked Kinnaird, raising his tankard.

"It takes a lot of practice."

"And are you sure that I can learn everything necessary?"

"Yes, I am. Then you'll feel confident that you can walk out of anywhere they lock you up. Newgate is the most likely place."

"You went in one door and out through another."

"When I've wet my whistle, I'll tell you exactly how I did it."

"And do you really think that we'll get all that reward money?"

"We won't, Alan. It will belong to Giles Clearwater. He's the one who's going to get his hands on it."

"You promised to tell me why you chose that name."

"Yes," said Scattergood, "I did. Well, it was quite by accident, really. I was in a shop that sold maps, cartoons and old theatre posters . . ."

Yeomans glowered across the table at the Peacock.

"Could you say that again?" he asked.

"He's in *The Provok'd Husband*," said Ruddock, beaming.

"And what, in the bowels of Christ, is that?"

"It's a famous play, Mr Yeomans. At least, the author thought it would be famous but it more or less died after its first performance. Mr Howlett explained that there's a much better play, written well over a century ago. It was called *The Provok'd Wife* by Sir John Somebody and another playwright thought he could copy him. It's in *The Provok'd Husband* that Giles Clearwater appears."

Yeomans bristled. "You're dealing with a provoked Bow Street Runner at the moment," he warned, "so don't you dare try my patience any further. We send you out to find a flesh and blood human being and you bring back a character from a play that's never performed."

"Are you teasing us, Chevy?" asked Hale.

"I'm telling you what Mr Howlett told me."

"Then *he* must be teasing us."

"And you bought him another drink, I'll warrant," said Yeomans, angrily.

"He deserved thanks for helping us," argued Ruddock. "If it hadn't been for his collection of theatrical memorabilia, we'd never have known who Clearwater was."

"We still don't. We're after a real man."

"Shame on you, Chevy," said Hale. "You've let us down badly this time."

"But I haven't," said Ruddock. "Don't you see what this means?"

"Yes, you've taken leave of your senses."

"I thought you'd both be pleased."

"*Pleased?*" echoed Yeomans. "You tell us that a man we've actually met and spoken to at length is a character in a play and expect us to be pleased? What kind of half-witted thinking is that?"

He paused to guzzle down a drink. Ruddock was hurt because he wasn't getting the congratulations he'd expected. Instead, they were furious with him.

"Get back out there and continue the search," said Yeomans.

"But it's pouring with rain."

"I don't care if there's six feet of snow on the ground. Disappear."

"At least, let me explain," pleaded Ruddock. "You owe me that chance."

"All we owe you is a punch on the nose."

"Don't be too harsh, Micah," said Hale, showing sympathy for the younger man. "Chevy did his best. He just got confused, that's all. Let him explain."

Yeomans gave a low animal growl. Hale gestured to Ruddock. The latter cleared his throat and took a nervous step towards them.

"My mind works different to yours," he began.

"Oh, so you actually *have* a mind, do you?" sneered Yeomans.

"When I saw that name, I knew I'd made a discovery."

"Yes, you found a dull play that died after one performance."

"I found out something more important than that, Mr Yeomans. With the help of Mr Howlett, I learnt that the man you sent me to find is an impostor." The two Runners were taken aback. "Don't you see? He must have stolen the name of Giles Clearwater from the play."

Hale's jaw had dropped. "How do you know?"

"Well, it's such an unusual name. How many Clearwaters do you know?"

"None, Chevy."

"None at all," admitted Yeomans, eventually.

"There you are, then," said Ruddock. "I could be right, after all. Mr Howlett was reminded of *The Provok'd Husband* by a man who walked into the Golden Crown. He'd actually seen the first performance — Mr Howlett, that is, not this stranger. It was the cut and colour of his clothing — this stranger's, not Mr Howlett's — that jogged his memory."

"You're not making much sense, Chevy," said Hale.

"Didn't you tell me that the Giles Clearwater you met had the air of an actor?"

"Yes, we did."

"And he was outside a theatre when Sir Roger was shot dead?"

"That's right."

"If he needed to use a false name, the chances are that he might filch one from a play. And where better to go to than to a play known by very few people?"

"This is beginning to sound interesting," said Hale.

"No, it isn't," said Yeomans with a wave of his arm. "There are two Giles Clearwaters — the real one and the one from the play. Indeed, there may well be more than two. There could be three, four or five."

"Then why has nobody ever heard of any of them?" asked Ruddock.

"That's a fair point, Micah," said Hale.

"No, it isn't," retorted Yeomans. "We met Clearwater in person and — though I took against him on sight — he seemed to me to be exactly who he said he was. Even if he pulled the wool over *our* eyes, he'd never have got past the chief magistrate. That's three of us with endless experience of dealing with confidence tricksters and Giles Clearwater is definitely not one of them."

"I second that," said Hale.

Ruddock was unrepentant. "I still think I'm right," he said under his breath.

After their visitor had left, Peter and Paul continued to talk about the coincidence that had come to light. There was an identical pattern to the way that three different people were murdered. The killer was ruthlessly methodical.

"I'm so glad that Captain Golightly came to us," said Peter.

"It's not the first time he's given me vital information," said Paul. "It was from Golightly that I got the names of Sir Roger's worst enemies, and he also told me about the murder victim who turned out to be Orsino Price."

"Yes, he was the odd man out — killed by a dagger."

"Given the choice, I think I'd prefer a bullet in the head."

"You're quite safe, Paul," said his brother. "With me guarding your back, nobody will get close enough to stab or shoot you."

"And you can always count on *me*, Peter. However, there's one thing we mustn't forget. The very fact that we're searching for this man puts us in jeopardy. Whoever hired him won't welcome our interest. If we get too close, he'll want us killed."

"Yeomans and Hale would be delighted if we were shot dead," said Peter. "They'd have a clear field for once. And there's also Sir Roger's son. He'd shed no tears over our demise."

"I think he'd applaud."

"And yet we're trying to help him and his family."

"Edmund Mellanby sees us as obstacles. We're in the way."

Peter was adamant. "And we mean to stay there."

"Well, we're not moving for his benefit," said Paul, stoutly.

"I keep thinking of the way that his father treated Seth Hooper. Sir Roger accepted him as a friend — though the social chasm between them remained, of course. The elder son, by contrast, dismisses Hooper and his fellow members of the Hampden Club as if they're something he picked up on his boot by inadvertently treading in it."

"Why is he so different from his father?"

"He won't let us close enough to ask him," said Peter. "However, I must be on my way," he went on, rising. "Charlotte will wonder where I am."

"Thank you for coming."

"I'm glad that I did. If I hadn't, I'd have missed what Captain Golightly had to say. I found it intriguing." He moved towards the door. "Give my love to Hannah."

"And pass on mine to Charlotte," said Paul, following him into the hall. "Let's meet at the shooting gallery early tomorrow and decide what our next steps are."

"I'll be there," said Peter before turning round. "You know, I keep thinking about the letter 'D' on those bullets."

"What do you think it stands for?"

"The obvious thing is that it's the initial letter of the killer's name."

"I fancy that it's a case of 'D' for Destiny."

"There might be a far simpler explanation, Paul."

"What does it stand for, then?"

"Death."

While the two brothers had been downstairs, Hannah had been in the guest bedroom with Dorothea. The latter was delighted to have her company but, curiously, she didn't want to talk about her romance. In fact, there was no mention at all of Orsino Price. All that Dorothea was interested in was some advice about her career in the theatre. Hannah was more than ready to wax lyrical about her experience in the profession and to offer suggestions.

264

"I think that you should invest in some singing lessons," she said.

"But you said that I had a sweet voice."

"You do, Dorothea, but it lacks variation. A good teacher would help you to acquire that and to improve your projection into the bargain. It's a problem I had at your age and I had the sense to seek instruction."

"Singing teachers tend to be expensive, Miss Granville."

"I'll be happy to pay for the first half-dozen lessons."

Dorothea was elated. "You'd really do that for me?"

"Well, I don't see anyone else in this bedroom," said Hannah, laughing.

"That's so generous of you."

"There's very little you need to be taught about acting but you must have another string to your bow. When work onstage becomes scarce, you can offer yourself as a singer. First, of course, you must build up a repertoire. It's what I did. When managers realised how well I could sing," said Hannah, "I began to be given roles in plays that had songs and music in them."

She was about to go on when she realised that Dorothea was no longer listening. Eyes fixed on some imaginary object, the young actress was staring up at the ceiling as if in a trance. Hannah watched her for a couple of minutes before she touched her on the shoulder. Dorothea was jerked out of her reverie. Guilty and flustered, she began to apologise profusely. A gesture from Hannah silenced her.

"I'd much rather have an explanation than an apology," she said. "What's going on, Dorothea? Earlier

265

on today, you couldn't say a sentence without Orsino's name in it, yet you haven't said a word about him since I've been here."

"I know."

"Has it begun to hurt when you mention him?"

"Yes, it has."

"That will pass in time."

"I'm not sure that it will," said Dorothea. "What hurts me is that I'll never know the truth. Did he really love me or didn't he?"

"Of course, he did. You showed me his letters."

"When I first read them, I was transported. But now I have doubts."

"I don't see why."

"It was when I said my prayers earlier, Miss Granville. I prayed for Orsino's soul and hoped that he'd find solace in heaven. I remembered all the wonderful things he said to me then I recalled something that was very different."

"What was it?"

"We were talking about why we wished to have a career in the theatre," said Dorothea. "I told him that I'd been inspired by the example of people like you. I had this uncontrollable urge to be up onstage in front of an audience."

"All actresses have felt that urge."

"Orsino told me that he didn't idolise other actors because he knew that he was better than them. He couldn't understand why others were employed when he was always turned away. Then, all of a sudden, his mood changed. He shook with anger. The theatre was his birthright, he shouted, and he'd beg, borrow or steal to become a leading figure in the profession. *Nothing* would stop him," she recalled. "He was adamant, Miss Granville. It frightened me."

"I can see why. Dedication is one thing but what you've just described is an obsession, and that can be destructive."

"It was the only time I saw Orsino behave like that."

"Did he apologise for his outburst?"

"No, he didn't."

"Then he meant what he said."

"Thinking about it earlier made me wonder," said Dorothea, wistfully. "I loved him dearly but . . . was Orsino *really* the man I took him to be?"

Sir Marcus Brough had always been popular. Arriving at his club, he was met with a polite fusillade of greetings from staff and members. He shared an individual word with each one of them before going into the dining room. He was pleased to see that his guest was already seated at the table he'd reserved for them. After a ritual handshake, they sat opposite each other. As they perused the menu, they resorted to idle chatter. Once the meal had been ordered and they had a glass of wine in their hands, real conversation could begin. Sir Marcus sat back complacently.

"Everything seems to be falling into place," he said.

"We do still have one fly in the ointment."

"Strictly speaking, there are two of them — the Skillen brothers."

"They've no right to trespass on private property," said Edmund Mellanby. "One of them had the audacity to come to Nottingham on the expectation that we'd welcome him with open arms. I soon relieved Peter Skillen of that delusion."

"His brother, as you saw, had the gall to pop up in front of me in the House of Commons. One has to give him credit for tenacity. It was the second time he'd accosted me and I made it quite clear that there would not be a third."

Mellanby tasted his drink and indicated his approval with a nod.

"What about *my* situation?" he asked.

"Well, it is a little tricky, to be honest."

"Politicians have crossed the floor before."

"Indeed, they have. On many issues there's very little to divide the Tories from the Whigs. But your father was *above* party. He frequently upset his colleagues as much as he upset us. The universal love felt for him in Nottingham was not replicated on any of the benches. Sir Roger rampaged around like a mad elephant."

"You don't need to tell me that. I grew up in his shadow. I saw him practising his speeches and rehearsing his gestures. I watched the effect he could have on a spellbound audience. I could never do that," confessed Mellanby, "and I've no wish to learn how to do it. What I covet is an opportunity to serve my country at what is a very dangerous time."

"That's putting it mildly. The Home Secretary is getting daily reports of unsettling behaviour. There's a disgusting whiff of revolution in the air."

"Then let me stand beside you to suppress it."

"With respect, you're not even a Member of Parliament yet."

"It's only a matter of time, Sir Marcus."

"Are you that confident?"

"Nobody would dare to oppose me for selection and there's a more than adequate majority. Getting into the House of Commons is not the problem. It's being in a party of government."

"So you'd stand as a Whig and defect to the Tories, is that it?"

"There would naturally be an interval while I learnt the ropes. When that's done, I could begin talks with your party — if you think it feasible."

"It's not up to me, Edmund."

"Your voice is listened to."

"My wife doesn't think so," said the other with a throaty laugh. "As for your request, you *are* aware of the likely consequences, aren't you? The voters will feel betrayed."

"I'm man enough to withstand their anger, I can assure you."

"Won't there be complaints from within your own family?"

"My brother, David, will bleat at me, but I can handle him. This is not a sudden decision on my part," he went on. "I've thought about it for years."

Sir Marcus sat back and appraised him. He sipped some more wine.

"This meeting never took place," he insisted. "You never approached me and I never invited you here."

Mellanby nodded in agreement. "I must admit that luring a Mellanby into our party is in the nature of a *coup*, but these are early days yet. I don't foresee our needing to speak again for . . . twelve months."

"I accept that, Sir Marcus."

"Then let's put the matter aside and enjoy our meal. Unless, that is, you wish to ask a question."

"I do but it's a very simple one."

"What is it?"

"How do I stop the Skillen brothers from getting in the way?"

CHAPTER
EIGHTEEN

Peter and Charlotte arrived at the shooting gallery next morning soon after Gully Ackford had opened it. It was not long before the first customer turned up, a sinewy young man seeking instruction in pugilism. Ackford took him off to another room. Then Jem Huckvale came in, looking tired and worried. He seemed to have lost all of his usual vitality. They gave him a cheery welcome but his response was subdued.

"What's the problem, Jem?" asked Peter. "As a rule, you come bounding in every morning like a dog that's just been let off the leash."

"I feel like a dog who wants to go to sleep in front of a warm fire," said Huckvale. "I've never been so exhausted."

"It's only to be expected," explained Charlotte. "Jem has had to take on a lot of the work that would normally be done by you and Paul. Yesterday, he spent six hours teaching pupils how to fire a pistol, then a further three supervising archery practice. Then there were two evening sessions."

"I'm not complaining," said Huckvale, bravely.

"The investigation is really testing us," admitted Peter.

"Have you any idea when it will be over?"

"I'm afraid not. It may drag on for weeks." Huckvale groaned. "Don't worry. When this case is over and done with, we'll make amends to you."

"Thank you. I could do with a rest."

"Well, you won't get it now, Jem," said Paul, walking into the room. "Mr Aveley has just arrived for some fencing lessons. I sent him upstairs."

Huckvale yawned. "Then I'd better go."

Peter and Paul were sorry for the extra pressures put on him. But they felt that solving a murder was more important than improving someone's skill with a weapon. It also brought in a lot more money and kudos.

"How is Hannah?" asked Charlotte.

"She's fine," replied Paul. "It's Dorothea who is the problem. The poor girl is very fragile. Hannah is handling her with great care. She's like a surrogate mother."

"What about Dorothea's real mother?"

"Oh, she and her husband live in the wilds of Lincolnshire. While they did relent in the end, they didn't approve of their daughter's wish to enter such a volatile profession. They felt that she'd be exposing herself to danger. If they knew about her friendship with this fellow, Orsino Price, they'd be horrified."

"But that friendship has been abruptly terminated."

"I hope that her parents never find out how," said Paul. "However, let's put Dorothea aside. We have work calling us. Where should we start, Peter?"

"I'd like to confront Sir Roger's son again."

"Do you know where he's staying in London?"

"No, I don't."

"Then let me suggest you try the Clarendon Hotel first. His father always stayed there. It's more than probable that Edmund Mellanby will also choose it as his base in the capital."

"Thank you, Paul. Where will you start?"

"I'd like to meet this friend of Captain Golightly's."

"Dr Quine?"

"Yes, what he discovered has proved just how mercenary the assassin is. The doctor has given us evidence that we'd never obtain elsewhere."

"When shall I see you again, Peter?" asked Charlotte.

"We'll meet here around midday," replied her husband.

"I agree," said Paul. "We need to share what we've found out."

"Let's just hope that we have something worth sharing."

Over a late breakfast at the house, Dorothea was unusually silent. When she'd first confessed to Hannah that she'd formed an attachment with a man, the words had gushed out of her like a waterfall. She then entered a more reflective phase, only mentioning Orsino Price's name when she recalled a memory she hadn't mentioned. The previous evening, she'd told Hannah something about her supposedly devoted admirer that made the latter adjust her opinion of him. Price had clearly been in the grip of a mania. He'd use any means and exploit anyone in order to achieve his goal.

Dorothea might believe that she was the goddess he portrayed her as in his letters, but Hannah was convinced that she was simply his latest victim.

"What would you like to do today?" she asked.

"I don't know, Miss Granville."

"Do you feel well enough to go for a walk, or would you rather stay here and rest? It's entirely up to you, Dorothea. I won't feel at all upset if you'd rather be on your own. On the other hand, you might prefer to have company."

"I do," said the other, decisively.

"Then I have a suggestion to make."

"What is it?"

"You may have noticed the pianoforte in the salon. It's always kept tuned. I've used it myself to practise when I'm performing in a play that requires me to sing. Don't forget that I did encourage you to take singing lessons."

"You did and it was good advice."

"Then you can begin right here. If you'll trust me, I'll act as your teacher."

"I trust you implicitly. You sing so beautifully."

"When you've finished your breakfast," said Hannah, "we'll make a start. Are you happy with that idea?"

"Yes, I am," said Dorothea, producing her first smile of the day.

In leaving her husband, Kitty Denley had come to see that there were losses as well as gains. She had flounced out of the family house after a fierce row and moved into a much smaller dwelling as a temporary measure.

Money was no object. A wealthy woman in her own right, she could well afford to buy a new property when she found one that suited her. For the moment, she was happy enough in her new abode with the servants she'd taken with her. The sense of freedom was breathtaking.

Set against the benefits, however, there were disadvantages. Kitty had walked out on the multiple luxuries provided by a husband who was a highly successful businessman. In doing so, she'd fractured the small social circle in which she moved. Her few women friends secretly admired what she'd done, but their husbands ordered them to have nothing whatsoever to do with her. When she'd lived under his roof, Hugh Denley had giving her the countenance of respectability. It had vanished instantly. She'd become an outcast.

As she reflected on the losses, she decided that, on balance, they were outweighed by the gains. She could start a new life elsewhere, one in which she wouldn't be required to be on her husband's arm in church every Sunday. Kitty was her own woman at last. Nothing could dull the pleasure she drew from that thought. Unimpeded by someone else's demands, she could plan her day exactly the way she wanted. And then, to her chagrin, her husband called at the house.

Kitty wrestled against her initial instinct to send him on his way. Whatever the hostility between them, however, civility had to be preserved. She therefore agreed to see him. Denley was in a testy mood.

275

"What do you mean by setting those terriers on to me?" he demanded.

"I've no idea what you're talking about."

"First, it was Paul Skillen, treating me as if I was a suspect in a murder enquiry. No sooner had he gone than his brother, Peter, came snapping at my heels. You had no right to give them our address, Kitty."

"I didn't send either of them."

"Don't lie. They were dispatched by you."

"That's not true. I admit that I answered a few questions from Paul Skillen, then I sent him on his way. As for his brother, I didn't even know that he existed. I certainly didn't meet this Peter Skillen myself."

"They're two of a kind — *twin* brothers and twin nuisances."

"Well," said Kitty, "I won't pretend that I'm pleased to see you but, while you're here, you might as well sit down."

Denley gave her a long stare before lowering himself into a chair.

"How is business?" she asked, sitting down herself.

"It continues to thrive."

"So it should. Half the nobility get their wine from you."

"Don't exaggerate."

"Buying and selling were the only two things you could do well."

He winced. "Let's not descend to insults," he said. "How are you?"

"Do you really care?"

"You're still my wife, Kitty."

"Oh, no, I'm not. I left you a long time ago, Hugh. Because you had your head in your account books, you never even noticed."

"People still ask after you."

"What do you tell them?"

"I tell them the truth," he said, awkwardly. "I miss you."

Her eyelids narrowed. "I can't say that the feeling is mutual."

"There's no need for us to fall out, Kitty."

"We already *have*," she said, acidly, "and it was all because of the foul accusation you hurled at me about Sir Roger Mellanby. I hardly knew the man."

"I saw the way he looked at you."

"Lots of men look at me that way, Hugh. It's in their nature. I ignore them in the same way that I ignored Sir Roger. You said earlier that people still ask after me. Well, it may interest you to know that some of the men amongst them do more than simply enquire about me."

"What do you mean?"

"How they found out my new address, I don't know, but two of your friends took the trouble to call on me to see if I was — in the words of one — managing without the company of a man."

"Give me their names," he yelled, angrily.

"I'm not having you fight any more duels, Hugh."

"I have the right to *know*."

"With regard to me," she said, "you don't have any rights at all." She waited until his wrath slowly subsided, then she pointed a finger at him. "You came in here to hurl an unjust accusation against me. Let me ask you one question."

"What is it?"

"Were you in any way involved in the murder of Sir Roger Mellanby?"

His mouth began to twitch.

Chevy Ruddock was not a contemplative man. He had neither time nor inclination for such things. His strength was that he knew his limitations. He accepted the world as he found it and took his allotted place without complaint. In his early days on foot patrol, he'd been ridiculed by Yeomans and Hale, slowly gaining their respect by learning his trade. The fact that he was trusted with individual assignments showed that they now had faith in him. As a rule, he was able to justify that faith.

Once again, he believed, he'd done so. He'd toiled in the rain for hours to get the information they'd demanded, yet it was thrown back in his face. Ruddock had spent money he couldn't afford on drinks for Simeon Howlett without the slightest regret because he trusted the old actor to help him. He'd been duly rewarded with the discovery that Giles Clearwater was a character in a play and that led him to believe that someone had stolen the name to hide behind it. So convinced was he that Ruddock wondered if he should go above the heads of Yeomans and Hale and speak to their superior. Then he realised the possible consequences.

If Yeomans and Hale knew what he'd done, they would make his life an utter misery. In any case, Eldon

Kirkwood, the chief magistrate, had actually met Giles Clearwater and judged him to be genuine. Ruddock's conviction that the man was an impostor would be dismissed out of hand. All that he could do was to bide his time and hope that the truth would finally come out. Until then, Ruddock would keep his head down and his mouth shut.

Peter didn't stand on ceremony. When he saw the two men leaving the dining room of the Clarendon Hotel, he stepped boldly in front of them and held both arms out so that there was no way past him. Barrington Oxley was fuming but Edmund Mellanby remained calm.

"If I were so minded," he said, superciliously, "I could ask the manager to have you thrown out into the street."

"Your request would certainly be denied," Peter told him. "As it happens, the manager is a close friend of my brother's. He'd never dare do anything so rash as to upset Paul."

"What do you want, Mr Skillen?"

"I wish to speak with you, please."

"We don't have time for an idle chat," said Oxley.

"*You* are not included in the conversation."

The lawyer blanched. "I beg your pardon!"

"Leave us alone, Oxley," said Mellanby.

"But you need me there."

"Have you gone deaf, man? Disappear."

Hurt and offended, Oxley walked away. Mellanby indicated the lobby and went into it with Peter. They settled down in high-backed leather chairs. Mellanby was having difficulty trying to conceal his annoyance.

"I'm a busy man," he said. "If you have anything to say, please say it quickly then leave me alone."

"First of all," said Peter, "thank you for getting rid of Mr Oxley. I find his manner unpleasant."

"Forget him, Mr Skillen. He's disposable."

"Does *he* realise that?"

"He will do in due course. Now, what do you want?"

"I'd like to know what you were doing at the House of Commons when my brother saw you there."

"Mind your own damned business!"

"Oxley told me that you'd come to London specifically to attend the inquest, then take the body of your father back home for the funeral."

"I also came in the hope of seeing my father's killer caught."

"Then why did you refuse to help me catch him?"

"Because you want to root around in my family's affairs when there is no need to do so. It's an unwarranted interference. The Bow Street Runners agree with me. They don't want to intrude on our privacy."

"That's why they'll never find the evidence necessary."

"Have *you* found it, Mr Skillen?"

"We've unearthed quite a bit of it, as it happens."

"Then it's your duty to hand it over to the Runners."

"My brother and I were engaged by a friend of your father to conduct our own investigation because we have an unrivalled record of success. Had you cooperated with us, we'd be much closer to making an arrest."

280

"I have no faith in untrained amateurs like you and your brother."

"Talking of brothers," said Peter, "I had the good fortune to meet yours. He was much more amenable. He told me that you had ambitions to replace your father in Parliament. Is *that* why you went to the House of Commons? Did you wish to look at the place that might well become your alternative home?"

"Replacing my father is a natural desire," said Mellanby. "It's what happens in political families. The baton is passed on to the next person in line. That's what should occur in my case."

"But the baton was not passed on, was it? It was viciously snatched from Sir Roger's hand because his campaign caused too much disquiet in certain quarters. It was a reasonable assumption that you'd eventually replace your father," said Peter, "but Parliament would not be changing like for like. You had severe reservations about Sir Roger's radical principles. Your brother told me so."

"David knows nothing about politics."

"He recognises punitive legislation when he sees it. If anyone should pick up the baton in the Mellanby family, it should surely be him. At least his views are aligned with those of your father."

Mellanby got to his feet. "I don't have to listen to this nonsense."

"Then let me ask you one last question," said Peter. "Sir Roger was murdered some days ago. When are you going to start mourning him?"

Refusing to answer, Mellanby swept out of the room.

281

★ ★ ★

Challenged by his wife, Hugh Denley got into such a state of indignation that she felt she had to calm him down. She ordered tea and one of the servants soon came in with a tray. Denley's ire slowly began to recede. He watched his wife pouring the tea and felt a surge of regret.

"You don't have to live like this, Kitty."

"It's only until I buy a more suitable property in Dorset."

"Dorset?" he repeated. "I assumed that you'd be staying in London."

"I've always wanted to live on the south coast."

"You'd be bored to death in a matter of weeks. Dorset is a backwater. *This* is where things happen."

"Yes," she said, "things like an unnecessary duel that could have cost you your life. I want to be in a place far away from here where I don't have to put up with your insane jealousy I'm the innocent party in all this, Hugh, and I'm fed up with being made to feel guilty."

"I did apologise."

"Your apologies always come far too late."

"Will I be allowed to visit you?"

"What's the point? We have nothing to say to each other."

"We're still married, Kitty."

"Not in any real sense of the word."

"Do you hate me so much?" he asked.

"I've just accepted that a phase of my life has ended. It wasn't something that I sought but I have to adjust to it. My parents used to take me to Dorset on

282

holiday. I love the seaside. I'm sure that I can find a new life there. Apart from anything else," she added, "it will put me out of reach of those friends of yours who seem to feel that I'm available to satisfy their desires."

"I'm ashamed to have put you in that position."

"At least you recognise that it was your fault. That's progress."

He sipped his tea. "Thank you for this. I needed it."

"When you've finished it, I'd like you to leave."

"But I came here to talk."

"We've talked more than enough."

"I have something else to say."

"Then please say it and be on your way."

Denley was hurt. "Why are you being so hostile towards me?"

"I believe that I've been quite polite."

"Listen," he said, taking a deep breath before going on, "the real reason I came here was to make a confession. I miss you." She pulled a face. "Don't be like that, Kitty. I've done my best to give you a good life. I've admitted that I accused you unjustly of being involved with . . . someone else, and I had a rush of blood to the brain when I demanded a duel with him. However . . . that's all in the past."

"Oh, no, it isn't," she said, firmly

"I'm not asking you to come back . . . well, not immediately, anyway."

"Then what are you asking for, Hugh?"

"I want us to reach an amicable agreement."

"That can't happen yet. The wound is still smarting."

"I was injured as well, you know," he said, irritably. "My wounds were physical as well as emotional. They still haven't healed."

"Don't ask me for sympathy."

"Do you have to be so harsh?"

"No," she conceded, tone softening. "I don't, and I must school myself to be more understanding. When a marriage breaks up, husband and wife both suffer. My feeling is that the pain will get worse."

"There are ways to reduce it, Kitty."

"That will only happen if I move away."

"Do you really have to go that far?"

"I need a feeling of safety," she said, "and I can never have that here. In a strange way, I'm touched that you want me back but it's something I couldn't even begin to consider. Goodbye, Hugh. Please don't call again."

She rang for a servant to show him out.

Hector Golightly was pleased when Paul Skillen called on him. It gave him the opportunity to apologise for arriving at Paul's house the previous evening without notice.

"You couldn't have been more welcome," said Paul. "The news you brought has given us food for thought."

"One pistol — three victims."

"I don't think that they were the only ones. A man who takes the trouble to embellish his bullets has doubtless killed before. I made that point to Dr Quine."

Golightly was startled. "You've met him?"

"I spoke to him earlier. It's obvious that he's a brilliant surgeon but how can he work in such foul conditions? The stink was almost overpowering."

"Human bodies decay, I'm afraid."

"Dr Quine showed me one of those bullets."

"What was it like?"

"It was exactly as you described. It was an unusual shape and had the letter 'D' scratched carefully into it. Since it had penetrated a skull, its nose was slightly bent out of shape. It had lodged in the brain."

"Why did the killer autograph his bullets?"

"Perhaps it's an example of his vanity."

"Can someone really be so proud of shooting people dead?"

"A soldier like you shouldn't need to ask that question," said Paul. "You must have had people in the army who joined for the sheer pleasure of killing."

"We did. Whenever battle was joined, they became almost frenzied. But tell me what else you and your brother have been doing."

"We're going over old ground in case we've missed anything. Peter had a crack at Hugh Denley and I paid a second visit to Sir Marcus Brough. Behind his bluff exterior is a very shrewd politician."

"We've thought from the start that this was a political assassination," said Golightly. "The person who initiated it might be higher up in government than Sir Marcus. The name that keeps coming back to me is that of Viscount Sidmouth. I remember Sir Roger saying that he could be merciless."

"He's still our prime suspect."

"Proving that the Home Secretary was involved is well-nigh impossible."

"It won't stop us trying," said Paul. "When you were in public with Sir Roger, did you ever get the feeling that you were being watched?"

"*I* didn't but he certainly did."

"Wasn't he worried by that?"

"On the contrary, he gloried in it. Sir Roger loved the idea of being viewed as a threat. But what of the Runners?" asked Golightly. "While you've been gathering evidence, they've been doing the same thing. How far have they got?"

"They claim to have found someone who witnessed the murder."

"So did you."

"This man, apparently, saw who the assassin was and had the wit to follow him. When the reward notice appeared, he went to the Runners."

"How did they react?"

"Knowing Yeomans and Hale as well as I do, I expect they tried to steal his evidence and use it for their own ends."

"What was the name of this witness?"

"Giles Clearwater."

Harry Scattergood. refused to let him off the hook. Even though he'd interrogated Kinnaird five times in a row, he insisted on doing it again.

"But you said that I was word perfect," moaned Kinnaird.

"Let's try it once more."

"Why?"

"Six is my favourite number."

"I'm tired, Harry."

"One last time," decreed Scattergood. "Are you ready?"

"I suppose so."

"What's your name?"

"Alan Kinnaird?"

"No, you buffoon!" shouted the other. "That's your *real* name. At a stroke, you've given the game away."

"I'm sorry. I wasn't thinking."

"Let's start again. What's your name?"

"Charles Mifflin."

"And what's your occupation?"

"I'm a gentleman of independent means."

"What were you doing at the Covent Garden Theatre on the night in question?"

"I went to watch a performance of *Macbeth*."

"Why did you do that?"

"I wanted to see Hannah Granville in the role of Lady Macbeth."

"Was that the only reason?"

"No, I was following Sir Roger Mellanby."

"Why?"

Kinnaird gave the answer he'd rehearsed many times. There were no mistakes. He was clear, well spoken and convincing. Scattergood gave him a slap on the back.

"Well done, Charles Mifflin. You'd fool anybody."

"There's only one thing that worries me, Harry."

"What is it?"

"The reward is for the arrest and *conviction* of the killer. We don't get a sniff of it until I've been tried and found guilty."

"I've told you before. Once I have the money, I can use some of it to buy you out of Newgate. I know exactly who to bribe." Scattergood laughed. "Clever, isn't it? Having escaped from Newgate more than once, I'll be breaking into the place to help you get out."

"When?"

"When the time is ripe, of course."

"And when is that, Harry? I don't want to be stuck in there for weeks on end. You know the black-hearted villains who'll be locked up in there. One of them might try to do the hangman's job for me."

"The way it works is this," said Scattergood, speaking slowly. "Sir Roger was a well-known figure. They'll want his killer punished as soon as possible. That means a speedy trial during which I'll give evidence against you. Then you'll be dragged from the court and taken out past a mob howling for your blood."

"That's the bit I'm not happy about."

"Before you know it, you'll be inside the safety of Newgate."

"And what will you be doing?"

"I'll be counting the reward money," said Scattergood. "As soon as I've done that, I'll get into the prison to rescue you. I'll have to wait for the right moment, of course. That goes without saying." Kinnaird's face fell. "Trust me, old friend. Nothing can possibly go wrong."

"It had better not."

"Giles Clearwater will come to your rescue."

The previous day, they'd found a means of escape into one of Shakespeare's plays. That morning it was music that offered them a source of relief. With Hannah seated at the piano and Dorothea standing beside her, they sang a series of duets. Each one was carefully discussed afterwards. The second time they sang it, Dorothea put the advice that Hannah had given her into practice. Before the first hour was over, there was a marked improvement in the younger woman's voice. Hannah was discovering a talent for teaching that took her by surprise.

"How are you feeling now, Dorothea?" she asked, breaking off.

"I feel exhilarated."

"That's as it should be. Music uplifts the soul."

"It didn't work completely, though," confessed Dorothea. "When we read from *Measure for Measure*, I was in a different world where nothing else mattered. This time it was different. An image of Orsino kept floating past my eyes."

"Was it a pleasing image?"

"It was both pleasing and disturbing. I was momentarily glad to see him again, yet relieved when he went away."

"Did you dream about him last night?"

"No, and that was odd. Ever since I met Orsino, I've dreamt about him and the life we'd have together. I always awoke refreshed and happy."

"And now?"

"Something has changed in me, Miss Granville. Since the moment when I remembered what he said about dedicating his life to the theatre, I felt used. Was he really as sincere as he seemed to be?"

"Only you can answer that question, Dorothea."

"I know." She walked away, then swung round to face Hannah. "When are you going to Brighton Pavilion?"

"The date has yet to be set."

"Oh, I thought you were invited to a ball."

"No, it was simply an open invitation to meet the Prince Regent in Brighton. I'm to name the day that's most convenient."

"Just think," said Dorothea, excitedly, "a letter that you write will actually be read by His Royal Highness."

"It will be very formal."

"Yes, but it's *yours*. I'm sure that he'll treasure it."

"The Prince Regent must get dozens of letters every day."

"They don't all come from a famous actress. Oh, it will be a magical experience for you, Miss Granville. I'm so jealous. You will tell me what the Pavilion is like, won't you?"

Hannah smiled. "I'll bore you to death with excessive detail."

"Orsino promised to take me to Brighton one day. He said that it's the ideal place for actors to promenade. I used to dream of walking along on his arm and turning heads. Sadly, that will never happen now."

290

"There'll be other opportunities, Dorothea . . . with someone else."

"I'm not ready to believe that yet."

Hannah got up from the piano and crossed to her. She could see the doubt whirling in the other's eyes. Dorothea was still torn between believing the fantasies that she and Price had created and accepting fully that she'd been a victim of his wiles. There seemed to be no chance of her ever finding out the truth.

Dorothea suddenly became animated. "Do it now," she urged. "Reply to that royal invitation and say that you'd love to accept it. What's holding you back?"

Hannah shrugged. "I wish I knew."

When the Prince Regent walked slowly into his study, the first thing he did was to look at the pile of correspondence on his desk. He turned to his secretary.

"Has Miss Granville replied to my invitation yet?"

"No, Your Majesty."

"Then send someone to make sure that she does."

CHAPTER
NINETEEN

The assassin was becoming restive. Instead of being in France and enjoying the large amount of money he'd earned, he was stuck in England still being sought by the Bow Street Runners and by those excited by the size of the reward offered for his capture. Sooner or later, somebody would catch up with him. He realised that he simply couldn't go on killing people indefinitely. Three had already been shot dead and a fourth had been dispatched with his dagger. The last of his autographed bullets had been intended for the person who had concocted the plot to assassinate Sir Roger Mellanby. The problem was that he couldn't decipher the signature on the letter he'd stolen. Also, the letter bore no address. He'd come up against a blank wall.

In the safety of the room he'd rented, he counted out all the money he'd so far acquired. The haul from Robert Vane was supplemented by the takings from the man who'd hired the assassin then — when Mellanby was dead — engaged Vane to shoot him in St James's Park. Though there was a substantial amount of money, the assassin felt that he deserved more. The only way he could get it was by confronting the person whose name he'd found after breaking into that study. So far, his luck had held but he couldn't count on it doing so for ever. After his next strike, he'd have to flee the country. London was becoming too uncomfortable a city in which to stay. Paris would be far safer and allow him the freedom for which he yearned.

Taking out his pistol, he used a cloth to clean it. Then he selected a bullet.

On his own initiative, Peter Skillen decided to call on one of their suspects. His brother had given him the home address of Oswald Ferriday and Peter was pleased to learn that the President of the Board of Trade was there that morning. Getting to speak to him was another matter. When the servant answered the door, he said that his master was not receiving any visitors.

"He might receive *me*," said Peter. "At least, give him my card."

"I'm sorry, Mr Skillen," said the servant, refusing the card offered to him. "I have my orders. You are to be turned away."

"There must be some mistake."

"The decision was made after your first visit here."

"Ah," said Peter, "I see what's happened. You're confusing me with my brother, Paul, who did ruffle Mr Ferriday's feathers somewhat. That's the last thing I intend to do." He flashed a smile. "I'm a much more agreeable individual."

"The answer remains the same, sir."

"Your master might change his name if he realises I am a friend of the Home Secretary." The servant dithered. "Go and tell him, man. Turn me away and you might come in for reproach."

"I'm only obeying orders."

He tried to close the door, but Peter got a firm hand to it, deliberately raising his voice so that it might be heard by Ferriday himself. His strategy yielded the desired result. The Cabinet minister came out of his study to see what the noise was.

"Our conversation is ended, Mr Skillen," he snapped.

"That's what you might say to my brother, Paul, but I'm *Peter* Skillen and I have some rather different questions to ask you."

"I'm too busy."

"Viscount Sidmouth told me that you'd be more accessible."

"Did he send you?"

"No, but he realised how eager I was to speak to you."

"It will be on the same subject that your brother raised."

"Not quite," said Peter.

"I had nothing whatsoever to do with Sir Roger's death," said Ferriday.

"I accept that, sir. I wish to talk to you on a related matter."

The older man eyed him up and down. Inclined to shun him, he remembered that Peter had worked as an agent in France during the war. That was worthy of respect. It swayed Ferriday's judgement.

294

"Oh, very well," he said, reluctantly, "but I can only give you fifteen minutes."

"That will be more than enough."

Peter stepped into the house and followed him down the passageway to the study. He sat in the chair that Paul had occupied the previous day. Ferriday was behind his desk. He squinted at his visitor.

"You look remarkably like your brother," he decided, "but you lack his air of ostentation. I should have remembered that when I saw you at the Home Office. I wouldn't have confused you with your brother then."

"Paul and I have taken different paths in life."

"Yet I understand that you work together."

"We do indeed, sir."

"Someone, I believe, asked you to investigate the murder. Sir Roger was unique in many ways, though I can't say that I'll miss that booming voice."

"He had important things to say and made sure that he was heard."

"I was deaf to his entreaties," said Ferriday, coldly. "So please don't spend any more of your fifteen minutes by extolling his virtues."

"You, I hear, were critical of his vices."

"I'm a family man who lives by Christian principles. I disapprove of those who pretend to do the same until they are away from home."

"Would you say that the government's policy of denying people basic rights was in line with Christian principles?"

"I'm not interested in a theological discussion, Mr Skillen."

"You've seen what the Home Secretary has done."

"I've seen what he's been *forced* to do," said Ferriday, pointedly, "and I support him to the hilt. Since the war ended, floods of discharged soldiers have returned here to find that they have no jobs. Bands of them roam around this city and cause endless problems."

"I'm more concerned with factory workers and people on low pay."

"Don't tell me you're a Luddite."

"I have sympathy for anyone unemployed."

"The march of progress must go on, even if it entails the loss of jobs. New machines can do the work of human beings so they had to give way. And what was their response?"

"They wrecked the machines."

"And they were duly punished for their crime."

"Was that when it started, Mr Ferriday?"

"What are you talking about?"

"This vast network of spies that's been set up," said Peter. "The Luddite riots were at their height five years ago. Since then, manufacturing towns have been infiltrated by government agents who report directly back to the Home Office."

"I shouldn't have thought you'd object to that," said Ferriday. "You were a government agent yourself at one time and sent your reports to the same source."

"In my own small way, I was helping to win the war."

"That's exactly what these alleged spies are doing — fighting to save this country from another kind of war.

If such revolutionaries are not suppressed effectively, the whole country will suffer."

"Would you call Sir Roger Mellanby a revolutionary?"

"He had the same hot blood in his veins."

"That comes from having passion and commitment."

"How would you know? You never met the man."

"I've met those who were closest to him," said Peter, "and I've spoken to both of his sons. Neither of them, incidentally, wishes to follow in his footsteps."

"That's a relief."

"Edmund has political ambitions but they are of a very different hue from those of Sir Roger."

"Who do you think might have killed him, Mr Ferriday?"

Peter's question caught him unawares and there was a stony silence. When he spoke, Ferriday's voice was much more measured. He rose to his feet so that it would have more force.

"I don't know, Mr Skillen," he said, "but I resent the fact that you and your brother have selected me as a potential suspect. What was my motive — hatred, fear, envy of the Radical Dandy's compulsion to show off his new waistcoats in the House? I daresay you can dream up half a dozen other reasons why I would contrive his death. Your efforts, however, would be futile. The truth is that I never took Sir Roger seriously enough to consider him anything more than a confounded pest. Please tell that to your brother." He glanced at the clock on the mantelpiece. "Your fifteen minutes has expired," he said, icily. "A man with your proven expertise will surely be able to find his way to the front door."

297

Having gone to the coroner's office to discuss the terms of the inquest, Edmund Mellanby and Barrington Oxley came out to a windswept morning. There was a fundamental disagreement between them.

"I don't want him involved in the inquest," said Mellanby.

"But he was there at the time," Oxley pointed out.

"So were the Runners and so is that man who wishes to claim the reward."

"Giles Clearwater?"

"That makes three witnesses. If we dared to ask the Prince Regent to attend that would push the number up to four," said Mellanby. "We simply don't need Paul Skillen to be there as well."

"But he's put his name forward."

"Contrive a way to have it removed."

"It may be difficult."

"That's what my father paid you for, wasn't it?" said the other, sharply. "You were retained to smooth out any difficulties. Start earning your fee."

Oxley was offended. "Sir Roger wouldn't have spoken to me like that."

"I'm in charge now, Oxley."

"He always called me by my first name," protested the other.

"That's changed."

Hailing a cab, they asked to be taken back to the Clarendon Hotel. As the vehicle set off, Mellanby was decisive.

"And I want to avoid any more meetings with Peter Skillen," said Mellanby. "The fellow is beneath contempt."

"Why did he wish to speak to you?"

"Why do you think?"

"Since you refused to let me stay," said Oxley, "I haven't a clue."

"He taunted me about the fact that I don't believe in my father's radical agenda. I never did and I never will. What this country needs most is peace and stability. If it means stamping on a few toes to achieve those objectives," continued Mellanby, "then I'm all in favour of it happening. My father was an extraordinary man but he had a fatal softness of heart. He cared for people I regard as good-for-nothings. Peter Skillen is the same. He takes nonentities like Seth Hooper seriously."

"Hooper thought your father was a kind of god."

Mellanby was harsh. "That's not a mistake I'd ever make."

"You . . . didn't really get on with him, did you?"

"I saw the defects that he so cleverly hid from everyone else. You spent all that time trotting at his heels. What's your opinion, Oxley? Did you really think that Sir Roger Mellanby was the Messiah he strove to be?"

"Well," said the lawyer, weighing his words before uttering them, "your father was a gifted politician, but he was not without his foibles."

Mellanby laughed. "Foibles?"

"We have to make allowances for them."

"You can do that, if you wish, but I won't. My mother is far too ill to be told the truth but it's one I'll never forget. Obituaries will praise my father to the skies," he said, "and omit the embarrassing fact that he was shot dead while hoping to ogle a beautiful actress as she left the theatre. The Radical Dandy was a disgrace," he went on with vehemence. "When he was away from home, he rarely slept alone and took advantage of an unknown number of women. I know this because I had suspected it for some time and hired someone to follow him to London. The report I received shook me rigid. My father, whom I'd loved and respected, turned out to be nothing more than an incorrigible lecher."

"He loved female company, that's all," said Oxley.

Mellanby was fuming. "Don't you dare try to excuse him," he snarled. "He was a monster. That's why I was so determined to stop Peter Skillen from prying into his life. I know the hideous truth about my father and wanted to keep it to myself. Let the world remember him as a resolute politician that he became. I know, to my cost, what his true measure was."

Chevy Ruddock arrived at the Peacock to find a pleasant surprise awaiting him. Alfred Hale was there alone for once. The younger man seized his opportunity to win him over.

"*You* believe what I told you yesterday, don't you?" he asked.

"I'm afraid not, Chevy."

"At least you had the kindness to hear me out. As soon as I told Mr Yeomans what I'd found out, he jumped on me as if I'd committed a crime."

300

"In a sense, that's what you did. You raised our hopes before dashing them."

"I did exactly what you asked me to do, Mr Hale."

"We trusted you and you let us down."

"But I didn't — don't you see that? I discovered that you and Mr Yeomans had been duped by this man."

Hale gave him a push. "Say that again and I'll hit you."

"I meant no disrespect," said Ruddock. "We all make mistakes — even the chief magistrate. When I first joined a foot patrol, what did you keep telling me?"

"I said that there were times when you had to act on instinct."

"That's what I did. In talking to Mr Howlett, I was relying on my instinct for telling the truth from arrant lies, and I found out something that's very important. Giles Clearwater is an impostor."

"And which Giles Clearwater are you talking about?" asked Hale, sarcastically. "The one in a long-forgotten play or the man Mr Yeomans and I have both met?"

"There *is* only one. He stole his name from *The Provok'd Husband*."

"That's only wild guesswork, Chevy."

"My instinct tells me that I'm right."

"Then I admire you for sticking to your guns. But let me give you a word of advice. Don't try to convince Mr Yeomans. He's not as tolerant as I am. And if you dare to suggest again that he was tricked — along with me and the chief magistrate — he'll seal you in a barrel of herrings and throw it into the Thames. Besides," he went on, sharpening his voice, "what are you doing here

301

when you should be continuing your search for Clearwater?"

"I've already found him for you," insisted Ruddock.

"We'd like the *real* one this time."

"Don't you understand? There *is* no real one. The name is an alias that someone is hiding behind."

He was about to develop his argument when the door was flung open to admit Yeomans. The Runner was even more intimidating than usual, and he made Ruddock quiver inwardly. Yeomans gave him a prod.

"What are *you* doing here?" he demanded.

"He's on his way to resume the search," said Hale, gesturing for Ruddock to get out. "He called in to apologise for the mistake he made yesterday. He regrets it now, Micah. Don't you, Chevy?"

Ruddock's resolve weakened. "Yes," he said, meekly. "I do."

But he was saying something very different to himself.

It was a complete change of tack for Harry Scattergood. Having spent his entire life dodging magistrates, he was now sitting in the office of the most senior one of them all. Eldon Kirkwood would accept nothing until he'd interrogated his visitor with his customary thoroughness. Scattergood answered every thorny question to the chief magistrate's satisfaction. Kirkwood gave an approving nod.

"Is there anything you wish to ask me, Mr Clearwater?" he said.

"As a matter of fact, there is."

"Go on."

"If I divulge the information I've taken such trouble to gather, can you confirm that I will get the credit for the arrest of the man?"

"You have my word."

"May I also have your guarantee that I will be able to claim the reward and that you won't allow any of your Runners to try to take it from me?"

"I give you my guarantee readily."

"Then it's time to proceed," said Scattergood. "The man who shot dead Sir Roger Mellanby is named Charles Mifflin. He doesn't live in London but comes here regularly and always stays at the same hotel."

"Do you know which one it is?"

"I do, sir. Naturally, I'll make the arrest myself with your men in support. It will need a group of us — perhaps ten or more — to surround the hotel once we know that he's inside. Can you recommend Runners who are well versed in such operations?"

"The best men at my disposal are Yeomans and Hale."

Scattergood pulled a face. "I'd sooner anyone than them," he protested. "When I first approached the pair with my evidence, they refused to believe that it had any significance. That's why I came to you instead. I knew that your judgement would be less affected by the desire for personal gain. Yeomans and Hale want the glory of capturing this man without taking the trouble of hunting and unmasking him."

"You've done that in exemplary fashion, Mr Clearwater."

"I want Sir Roger's death avenged."

"So do we all," said Kirkwood, "but I can't have you dictating how I should deploy my men. If I choose Yeomans and Hale, you must respect my decision."

"Yes, sir," said Scattergood, ruefully.

"They are experienced officers and — if violence is involved — you couldn't have two better men at your side."

"Then I withdraw my objection, sir."

"Good — when will the operation begin?"

"I'll have to wait until Mr Mifflin returns to his hotel," said Scattergood. "Once he's safely inside, I'll send word and we can surround the building. Led by *me*," he emphasised, "we'll enter the hotel to make the arrest."

Kirkwood rose to his feet. "I'll be the first to congratulate you."

Peter and Paul arrived at the shooting gallery at more or less the same time. Charlotte was delighted to see them back and listened to what they had to say. She was astonished to hear that Peter had called on Edmund Mellanby at his hotel.

"You surely don't consider him as a suspect, do you?" she said.

"As the son of a murder victim," replied Peter, "he's behaving in a strange way. I wondered why."

"What sort of reception did you get?"

"It was frosty. Anyway, after I'd left him, I decided to have a look at Mr Ferriday for myself."

"I'll warrant that he slammed the door in your face," said Paul.

Peter laughed. "By the time I left, he wished that he had."

He gave them an account of the conversation he'd had with the politician and said that Ferriday's name should certainly remain amongst their suspects. It was Paul's turn to talk about his visits to Dr Quine and Captain Golightly, respectively.

"I met the doctor as a total stranger," he explained, "but left as a friend. He was as interested in *our* work as I was in his. Quine will be a useful man in any future murder investigations, Peter. He's a genuine find."

"What did you do after you'd seen Captain Golightly?" asked Charlotte.

"I went back to Covent Garden," said Paul. "I walked down that alleyway where Orsino Price was stabbed to death. After that, I went around to the stage door where Sir Roger met his death. It was rather eerie being back there. In less than a minute, a man was shot dead, the Prince Regent was rushed to safety inside the theatre and everyone else ran for their life. After that experience, escorting Hannah out of the stage door will feel rather dull."

"What was eerie about going back there?" said Peter.

"I saw two men there, shuffling about for some reason. One was giving the other one some orders. They stopped when they saw me and rushed away. The weird thing was that I *knew* one of them but couldn't remember who he was. It was maddening. I've been trying to place him ever since."

"Do you think he recognised you, Paul?"

"Oh, I'm certain of it."

"Then it might have been someone you arrested."

"I have a good memory for faces, Peter, but I failed this time."

"The theatre is dark at the moment," observed Charlotte, "so what were they doing there? Hannah wasn't going to come out of the stage door and neither was anybody else."

"You should have challenged them, Paul," said his brother.

"I didn't get the chance. The moment he saw me, the man who'd been giving the orders dragged his friend away. I was left wondering," said Paul, brow corrugated, "who the devil was he?"

The distance between Brighton and London was less than fifty miles, as the crow flies, but the messenger dispatched by the Prince Regent was riding a horse that didn't have the benefit of wings. Nevertheless, he pressed on hard and, by changing his mount at intervals, he made good time. He reached his destination and tethered his horse at the gate. He then took out his letter and walked up to the front door. Hearing the doorbell, a maidservant opened the door to see the man standing there.

"I have a message for Miss Granville," he said.

"I'll be happy to give it to her," she said, extending her hand.

"My orders are to deliver it in person. I've travelled here from Brighton."

"Oh, I see," she said, flustered. "In that case, I'll fetch her." She hurried off to the drawing room and knocked before entering. Hannah looked up from the book she was reading.

"Yes?"

"There's someone here with an important message for you."

"How do you know it's important?"

"He's ridden all the way from Brighton."

Hannah was shaken but recovered her composure very quickly and went to the front door to find the man standing there. He handed her the letter.

"This is from His Royal Highness, the Prince Regent."

"Thank you very much," she said. "I'll read it in due course."

He was insistent. "I'm to wait for an answer, Miss Granville."

It was Hannah's turn to be flustered.

Despite boasting about the way that he'd won the confidence of the chief magistrate, Harry Scattergood was also ready to chide himself.

"It was a mistake to go back to the theatre in daylight," he admitted.

"We needed to go through it all one more time, Harry."

"Yes, but we should have done it after dark. Nobody would have seen us then, especially Paul Skillen."

"How do you know it was him?" asked Kinnaird. "You told me that he has a twin brother who looks identical."

"Paul is the one with a good reason to visit the Covent Garden Theatre," said Scattergood. "In fact, it's the best reason possible. He is Hannah Granville's beau. That makes him the envy of every red-blooded man in London."

"But he didn't recognise you, did he?"

"We didn't stay long enough for him to take a good look at me."

"He still wouldn't realise that it's you. Didn't you say that he looked you full in the face the night you mingled with the others outside the stage door?"

"The light was poor on that occasion. That would have helped."

The two friends were in the hotel they'd chosen as the place where Charles Mifflin was going to be apprehended. Situated near Piccadilly, it was the kind of establishment where a wealthy visitor might be expected to stay during his time in the capital.

"You've no need to worry," said Kinnaird, eyeing him up and down. "Even *I* didn't recognise you when you chose to go up in the world. Besides, when you were caught by the Skillen brothers, you looked completely different. Paul Skillen could peer at you a hundred times and still not know who you were."

"You underestimate him, Alan."

"Do I?"

"He only caught a glimpse of me this time but it was enough to make him stare. If we hadn't bolted, he'd soon have worked out who I was. I'll take no more chances," said Scattergood. "I've fooled him twice. Paul Skillen is not going to let me do it a third time."

Charlotte Skillen was not merely employed to handle the bookings at the shooting gallery. Ever since they'd offered their services as detectives, she had become their archivist, keeping details of every case in which they were involved. She was also a talented artist. Whenever she attended trials of those arrested by Peter and Paul, she drew sketches of the miscreants in the dock. Her record books therefore had the advantage of being illustrated. As a result, her brother-in-law was eager to leaf through her archives in a bid to identify the person he'd seen outside the theatre in Covent Garden.

"Was it Ned Greet?" asked Peter.

"He's still in prison," replied his brother.

"What about Humphrey Iliffe?"

"He was too short. This man was tall, lean and almost debonair."

"You've just described yourself, Paul."

Peter and Charlotte laughed. Seated beside Paul, she watched as he turned the pages over, marvelling at how many villains they'd caught and seen convicted. When she kept apologising for the defects in her sketches, Paul assured her that her portraits had caught the essence of each individual. As a new face appeared before him, he suddenly shouted in triumph.

"That's him!"

"Are you sure?" asked Charlotte.

"No wonder I couldn't remember him at first. Harry Scattergood has changed so much. But he was definitely one of the men I saw in Covent Garden today."

"But you told us that they were both well dressed," said Peter, "and that was hardly typical of Harry. The last time we arrested him, it was in a brothel. He used to rub shoulders with low company."

"It was him, Peter. I swear it."

"Then why was he skulking around the theatre? The only reason Harry would go to see a play would be to pick the pockets of anyone foolish enough to get close to him. As a rule, your eyesight is remarkable, but not this time, Paul."

"I'd stake anything on it. Because I'm used to seeing him in seedy pubs and squalid leaping houses, that face of his never really registered with me. But it has now. Harry Scattergood has decided to rise in society."

"From what I recall," said Charlotte, "he was an exceptionally good thief."

"He was," agreed Peter. "Those light fingers of his made him rich. The only time we managed to get him in court, he escaped custody."

"How did he do that?"

"We still haven't worked it out. He's very clever."

Paul's mind was whirring. He knew that Scattergood wouldn't do anything unless there was a prospect of gain in it. When he'd seen the two men outside the stage door of the theatre, they had been moving around to alter their positions. Had Paul stumbled upon some kind of rehearsal? If so, why did it take place in a deserted spot like that? More to the point, who was his companion? Since he was a friend of Scattergood's, he had to be a criminal associate. Unfortunately, Paul didn't have such a good look at the other man so there was no point in hunting for him in their archive. He was still puzzling over what had been going outside the theatre when there was a knock on the outer door.

"I'll go," said Peter, leaving the room.

Unlocking the door, he opened it wide then stepped back in amazement. Standing outside with a valise in his hand was a man he never expected to see again. It was the Reverend David Mellanby.

Alfred Hale was having second thoughts about what Ruddock had told him. As they waited in Bow Street Magistrates' Court for the summons from Giles Clearwater, he dared to think that they might be making a mistake. Alone with Micah Yeomans, he took time to pluck up enough courage to raise a possibility.

"I've been thinking, Micah," he said.

"That's a nasty habit — warps the mind."

"Chevy is an intelligent man. To be honest, I sometimes think that he may be more intelligent than us. I believe we should take him seriously."

"Ruddock is still a raw beginner in my book."

"That's unfair. Look at the things he's done for us. He got a letter of commendation from Kirkwood for the way he acted when there was an attempt to rescue a prisoner from a cell here." He sucked his teeth noisily. "That's more than we ever got from him."

"I know," said Yeomans with vehemence, "and it's just not right."

"Mr Kirkwood sees something in Chevy that we don't."

"There's nothing there to see. Ruddock is strong, willing and follows his orders. That's all that can be said in his favour. On the debit side, he's slow, clumsy, easily gulled by villains and prone to have wild ideas."

"His ideas are not *all* wild, Micah."

"What are you trying to say?"

"Supposing that he's right about Giles Clearwater?"

"He's not."

"But supposing that —"

"Stop right there," ordered Yeomans, getting up to threaten him. "Don't let that poisonous idea enter your brain. If you think that Ruddock is right, you're saying that you, me and the chief magistrate are hopelessly wrong. Between us we've racked up over ninety years of dedication to law enforcement. Compare that to Ruddock's experience. What is it — one, two, three years at most? As an officer, he's still wet behind the ears."

"It's just that he's so . . . well, convinced."

"I'm even more convinced, Alfred. What we're dealing with here is a simple coincidence. There's more than one Giles Clearwater. If you went through the last census, you'd probably find that there are lots of them. There are certainly more people called Micah Yeomans in a city as big as this and you could probably form a cricket team out of all the Alfred Hales at large." He put his face close to that of his friend. "Does that answer your question?"

"Yes, it does."

"And do you promise not to mention Chevy Ruddock again?"

312

"I do, Micah — on my word of honour."

When Peter invited their visitor in, David was astonished to meet Paul. He looked from one brother to the other, wondering how they could be told apart. He was introduced to Charlotte and, from the look he gave her, clearly wondered what someone like her was doing in a shooting gallery. She read his mind.

"I know what you're thinking," she said. "The answer is that I like it here. It means that I can work alongside my husband and my brother-in-law, sharing in the excitement of each new case we take on."

"You're a brave woman," said David.

"I'm sure that you and Peter have a lot to discuss," said Paul, moving to the door, "so we'll leave you alone for a while."

"Please stay. I'd appreciate it. You were actually there when my father was shot dead. I'd like to hear exactly what happened."

"Then I'll be happy to oblige you."

"I, meanwhile," said Charlotte, "will leave you alone. Please excuse me."

She let herself silently out of the room. Peter looked at their visitor.

"What brought you all the way from Nottingham?" he asked. "We'd like to think that our fame is spreading, but we don't flatter ourselves that anyone outside London knows who we are."

"I know," said David, "and so does Seth Hooper. It was talking to him that made me decide to come here. He sends his regards, by the way."

313

"That's good to hear. Please give him mine in return."

"I will."

"I'd have thought the first person you'd wish to see would be your brother."

"Edmund can wait."

"I had a rather prickly conversation with him at his hotel," said Peter. "He took exception to one of the questions I put to him."

"What was it?"

"I asked him when he'd start mourning your father. He certainly hasn't done so yet. It's almost as if he has no capacity for grief. Incidentally, he treats Mr Oxley with unconscionable rudeness. The latter was abruptly excluded from our conversation. He was deeply offended. Sir Roger clearly treated him differently."

"My father befriended people. Edmund uses them then casts them aside."

"That was my impression," said Peter, "but you mentioned news from Seth Hooper. What is it?"

"As you know, my father was due to present a petition to the Prince Regent. The Hampden Club has selected someone else to do it."

"Who is it?"

"You are looking at him, Mr Skillen," said David, modestly. "I'm not a member of the club, of course, but it's the least I can do in memory of my father. If Hooper and the others organise a march to London, they'll be arrested before they get anywhere near it. I, however, have the power of the church to guard me," he went on, indicating his bands. "There's another advantage I can boast. Hampden Clubs have been spied on regularly. Somehow I don't think the Home Secretary's agents have been keeping *me* under surveillance."

Peter told him about his visit to the Home Office and how, much to his disappointment, he came away feeling that Sidmouth was getting reports of dissident activity sent directly to him so that any signs of rebellion could be choked off before they'd even begun.

"What else are you going to do while you're here?" he asked.

"In spite of the state he'll be in after a post-mortem, I'd like to see my father and attend the inquest. Before that, a talk with your brother, Paul, is essential. Until I know *everything* that happened that night, I won't fully understand how he lost his life."

"I have vivid memories of the occasion," said Paul, "and I might be able to help you in another way."

"I don't follow."

"If you have a petition to present, how do you plan to get access to the Prince Regent? Those around him still believe that *he* was the real target for the assassin. As a result, they'll have tightened the protective cordon around him. At present, he's being kept safe in Brighton Pavilion."

"I'd assumed that he'd be in London."

"I'm afraid not."

"As for actually meeting His Royal Highness, I'm not quite sure how to go about it. I thought of seeking help from the Archbishop of Canterbury. I know that he resides at Lambeth Palace."

315

Both Paul and Peter were struck by his innocence with regard to the political and ecclesiastical structures of the capital. An obscure clergyman from Nottingham stood no chance of getting close to the archbishop, still less of having an audience with the Prince Regent. The fact that he'd be delivering a document setting out demands for radical reform made it even less likely that he'd get sympathy from either source.

"There is a more unorthodox way of going about it," suggested Peter as an idea began to form. "By chance, Paul may be going to Brighton Pavilion very soon in order to escort Miss Hannah Granville, a famous actress, whom the Prince Regent has taken an interest in ever since he saw her onstage as Lady Macbeth. I don't think that he could smuggle you into the royal presence, but he might at least be able to pass on your petition."

"Would you consider doing so, Paul?"

"It's worth a try," replied the other.

"Really," said David, "you and your brother lead extraordinary lives. Peter is able to walk whenever you wish into the Home Office and Paul, I now discover, may actually get to meet the Prince Regent."

"It's a happy coincidence, that's all," said Peter.

He was careful not to mention his brother's relationship with Hannah. Tolerant as he was in many ways, David Mellanby would hardly approve of two people living together before wedlock. It was safer to let him believe that Paul's friendship with Hannah was confined to his work as her bodyguard.

"Where are you intending to stay?" asked Peter.

"Well, I was going to join my brother at the Clarendon Hotel."

"Do you really want to be under the same roof as him?"

"To be quite candid," said David, "I don't. I'm rather dreading it."

"Then why not stay in London as our guest?"

"Oh, I couldn't impose on you at such short notice."

"Charlotte and I would be happy to have you."

"That's extremely kind of you, Mr Skillen, especially as my family was singularly inhospitable towards you."

"You'll be welcomed with open arms."

"Then I accept your invitation with the utmost thanks. Edmund and I are not as close as you and your brother clearly are. Besides, if I stay at the hotel, I'd have to look at the granite face of Mr Oxley over every meal."

Peter grinned. "That would be a deterrent, I grant you."

"I wonder if I might ask you some questions now, Paul."

"Before you do that," said Paul, "I need to give you a warning. The man who killed your father is still at liberty. For reasons I can't go into, we've established that he was responsible for two or even three other deaths. His murderous spree may not have ended there. It behoves you — and your brother — to keep your wits about you. Having assassinated the head of your family, he may conceivably have orders to kill other members of it."

"Thank you for telling me," said David with a slight shudder.

Alone in his room, the assassin was bewildered. Having gone to the trouble of breaking into the house of one of his victims, all that he'd found was a name that meant nothing whatsoever to him. The person above all others he sought was as far out of reach as ever and so was the additional money he'd been promised for his work. He was desperate to know the truth and to do so quickly. Time was against him. He was the target of a manhunt now. He needed to commit one more murder before he disappeared.

CHAPTER
TWENTY

After explaining to David Mellanby precisely what happened on the night of Sir Roger's murder, Paul Skillen decided to ride back to his house. He wished to see how Hannah was coping with their guest. On the previous day, he'd come home to find the two of them singing together while Hannah played the piano. Such a harmonious welcome couldn't be relied upon. He knew that Dorothea Glenn was shuttling between hope and despair all the time, praying that the man stabbed in the alleyway was not Orsino Price, then realising that the victim must have been him and that he'd gone to his grave after deluding her with empty promises. He hoped that she hadn't lapsed back into desolation. In the event, Paul arrived to find Hannah alone in the drawing room. As soon as he entered, she leapt up and flung her arms around him.

"Thank goodness!" she exclaimed.

"What's wrong?"

"I just wish you could have been here to protect me."

He was alarmed. "Has someone threatened you?"

"It certainly felt like a threat," said Hannah. "I was reading alone in here when I had a visitor. It was a messenger sent from Brighton Palace with another invitation from the Prince Regent. This one was different."

"In what way?" he asked.

"The messenger had to take my reply back to Brighton. He more or less stood over me while I wrote it."

"That's intolerable."

"Don't take me literally, Paul. I made him wait outside while I agonised over what I was going to say."

"I thought we'd agreed that we'd go to Brighton Pavilion together?"

"My hand was shaking so much that I couldn't trust it to write properly."

"I'm not surprised, Hannah. You were being bullied."

"That's why I needed you here to shield me."

"What did the Prince Regent's invitation actually say?"

"I'll show you."

Hannah picked up the letter from the side table and handed it to him. Paul read it with an amalgam of interest and annoyance. The hand was flowery, the stationery perfumed and the sentiments expressed made him snort with repugnance.

"He doesn't leave much to the imagination, does he?"

"That's just his way of expressing his admiration."

"This is not an invitation," said Paul, "it's a demand couched in colourful language. If *I'd* been here, I'd have urged you to refuse to go anywhere near him."

"One can't spurn royalty, Paul."

"*I* can — without any effort at all."

320

"I'm afraid that I'd be made to pay."

"They stopped exiling people to desert islands years ago, Hannah. The simple fact is that you were coerced and that's not gentlemanly, to say the very least."

"Hold me tight."

He hugged her close for minutes, then eased her onto the sofa, sitting beside her in the process. Hannah was no longer shivering. His return had soothed her.

"Where is Dorothea?" he asked.

"She's having a rest."

"How is she?"

"Well, she's been remarkably calm today. I gave her a singing lesson and showed her the practice routine I go through when I'm rehearsing any songs I have in a play. Dorothea is a keen pupil."

"What did she think of your invitation?"

"She was enthralled by it. When I let her hold it, she couldn't believe that she had something of royal significance in her hands. Dorothea said that I ought to frame it and hang it on the wall."

"If you do," he said, "I'll smash the glass and burn the letter."

"There's no need to be quite so touchy about it, Paul."

"How else am I to react when the Prince Regent takes advantage of his privileged position to woo the woman I love?"

"I've had far more explicit offers in the past and you've laughed at them."

321

"They didn't have the force of royalty behind them." His anger suddenly vanished to be replaced by a broad smile. "I may have just the answer."

"What is it?"

"Something has just fallen into our laps, Hannah."

He told her about the unexpected arrival of David Mellanby and how Peter had offered him hospitality. Sir Roger's younger son, he explained, had been given a petition for the Prince Regent but was uncertain how to deliver it.

"Peter wondered if you could do it," said Paul.

"What sort of petition is it?"

"It's one that lists the grievances of the lower classes in Nottinghamshire. It's replaced the earlier petition and points out that Sir Roger Mellanby was murdered before he could present it. In essence, it's a plea for intervention, Hannah. There's a foolish idea abroad that the Prince Regent is somehow above the political fray and has the power to impose his will on Parliament whenever he chooses."

"Does that mean he'd take any notice of this new petition?"

"No, it doesn't. He'd probably fling it straight back at you."

"Then why are you advising me to give it to him?"

"Because it will engineer our escape," said Paul, mischievously. "You'll have *accepted* his invitation yet made yourself thoroughly unwelcome by thrusting the petition at him. With a bit of luck and a following wind, we'll be in and out of Brighton Pavilion in less than ten minutes."

322

David Mellanby felt that his family obligation came first. Before he was ready to stay in with Peter and Charlotte, therefore, he thought he should speak to his brother and went off in a cab. Peter arranged to pick him up from the Clarendon Hotel later on. Left alone with his wife, he took another look at her sketch of Harry Scattergood. It was very lifelike.

"You've sent Paul off on another search, my love," he said. "Now that he realises whom he saw outside the theatre, my brother is convinced that Harry is somehow involved in this case. As soon as he's been home to see that everything is well, Paul is going to dedicate himself to finding this man." He studied Scattergood's face. "It won't be easy. Harry is as cunning as a fox."

"Paul has caught a lot of foxes in his time."

"I know. He loves the chase."

Gully Ackford sauntered in, holding a letter.

"This has just been delivered by hand," he said. "It's addressed to 'Mr Skillen' but it doesn't say which one."

"Well, Paul's not here to read it," said Peter, "so I'll do so." He took the letter and opened it. "It's from Mrs Denley."

"Then it was intended for Paul's eyes," said Charlotte.

"They're both firmly fixed on the search for Harry Scattergood. There's a note of urgency in Mrs Denley's appeal. I don't think she can wait until Paul is free to attend to her. I'll go in his stead."

"Tell her that you *are* Paul," joked Ackford. "She won't know the difference."

"Mrs Denley might not but *I* will and I'm not going to deceive her. A call for help like this must be answered promptly."

"What does she say?" asked Charlotte.

"See for yourself."

Peter handed her the letter and she read it. She thrust it back at him.

"You're right," she said. "There's a whiff of desperation here. Something has really upset Mrs Denley. Go to her, Peter."

Oswald Ferriday was walking down a corridor in the House of Commons when he saw Sir Marcus Brough strolling towards him. They exchanged greetings and stopped for a friendly chat.

"I wasn't expecting to see you here today," said Sir Marcus.

"This is my bolt-hole," explained the other. "If I stay at home, I'm bearded by one or other of the Skillen brothers."

"Don't bank on being safe here, Oswald. I was accosted by Paul Skillen as I left the chamber yesterday. He's infernally persistent."

"So is his brother."

"Each is as bad as the other."

"Neither of them ever met the Radical Dandy," said Ferriday, "yet they're conducting an investigation into his death as if they were close relatives of his."

"How right you are, Oswald. Talking of relatives . . ."

"Yes?"

324

"Sir Roger has finally gone — thank heaven — but there's a rumour that he may be replaced by someone else from the Mellanby family."

"I don't like the sound of that."

"Don't worry. From what I hear, Edmund, his elder son, is cut from a very different cloth. There'll be no more blazing oratory about the need for reform."

"That's a relief."

"He's a much more amenable and, I fancy, a more malleable human being. My hope is that he won't pose anything like the threat that his father did."

"As usual, you're well informed, Sir Marcus."

"Intelligence somehow drifts into my ear."

"How sound is it?"

"Oh, I can guarantee its authenticity, Oswald. The Radical Dandy will soon become a distant memory."

"I can't wait for that to happen," said Ferriday. "His ferocious personal attack on me with regard to the Corn Laws went well beyond acceptable limits. It was vicious. I tell you this in confidence," he went on, lowering his voice. "If someone else hadn't killed him, I'd have been tempted to do it myself."

"A number of us felt the same way," said Sir Marcus, smugly.

"Does anyone *know* who shot him?"

"I fear not and that's a great pity."

"Why is that?"

"I'd like to have shaken the fellow's hand and told him what a great service he's done to his country. The rebellion that's been rumbling away far too long has now been crushed because the only man who could have led it — Mellanby — is no longer alive to do so."

Ferriday smirked. "Goodbye and good riddance to him!"

Edmund Mellanby was less than pleased when his brother walked into the hotel. He was torn between surprise and antagonism.

"What the devil are *you* doing here, David?" he demanded.

"I've as much right as you to be in London," said the other, resolutely "He was *my* father as well, you know. I felt that my place was here."

"You'll only be in the way."

"I wanted to be present at the inquest."

"I could have told you exactly what happened."

"You don't understand, do you, Edmund? I don't want to hear *your* version of events. I mean to experience them for myself. Is there any law against my doing so?"

"It's . . . damned inconvenient, that's all."

They adjourned to the hotel lobby and sat down. While he hadn't expected a welcome, David was slightly taken aback by his brother's truculence. Accustomed to being ignored by Edmund, he was now being glared at as if he'd committed some heinous crime.

"Besides," resumed David, "I had another reason to be here. I've been entrusted with the task of presenting a petition to the Prince Regent." Edmund gave a hollow laugh. "It's a version of the earlier one and it explains that Father was supposed to present it. Given the fact that you will embark on a political career, it should have fallen to you to hand it over, but Seth Hooper and the others felt that they couldn't trust you to do so."

"They were quite right in that assumption," said Edmund, simmering with anger. "It's a document to which I could never subscribe. Given the opportunity, I'd have torn it to bits."

"That's no way to behave towards the people of Nottingham."

"Don't you dare criticise me, David."

"I speak as I find and I won't be browbeaten."

"Unlike you, I don't believe in Father's radical ideals. They were wild, irresponsible and dangerous. Now let's stop bickering like this," said Edmund, trying to contain his ire, "and force ourselves to behave like brothers. First things first — why don't you go and see if the hotel has a room available for you?"

"It won't be needed."

"Why not?"

"I already have accommodation."

"But you said you've only just arrived here."

"I called on a friend before I came to the hotel," said David, "and he was kind enough to invite me to stay at his home."

Edmund was roused. "You went to him *before* you came here?"

"Yes, I knew that he'd give me the welcome that you couldn't."

"And who *is* this welcoming friend?"

"Mr Peter Skillen."

"You'd prefer *his* company over mine?" said Edmund. "That's so insulting. You know how much I loathe the man."

"Well, I admire him, and I'll be glad to stay at his house."

"He's an interfering busybody."

"Peter is a man who's prepared to go to any lengths to solve the murder of our father. Isn't that what we both want, Edmund? It's more than either of us can do. Peter Skillen has the courage to carry on the search even though he knows that the killer is still at large and may turn on him if he gets too close. What have *you* done, Edmund? What efforts have *you* made to track down the assassin who was hired to blow out our father's brains?"

Surprised by David's passion, his brother looked embarrassed.

While she was waiting, Kitty Denley paced up and down the drawing room, pausing from time to time to stare through the window at the street outside. The servant who'd delivered her letter to the shooting gallery assured her that it had been put into a safe pair of hands. Yet there was still no sign of Paul Skillen. What could possibly be delaying him? Didn't he realise that her plea was desperate? After more walking to and fro, Kitty had worked herself up into a state of high anxiety. It was then that she heard the approach of a horse. Rushing once more to the window, she saw the rider dismount and hand the reins to the servant who came out to greet him. Kitty ran to the front door and opened it.

"Thank goodness you've come, Mr Skillen!" she said, beckoning him in. "I was afraid that you'd let me down."

"I'd never knowingly do that, Mrs Denley," said Peter.

He was led along a passageway and into the drawing room. Kitty closed the door firmly behind them. When she tried to speak, her visitor motioned her into silence.

"Let me begin with an apology," he said. "I know that you summoned Paul Skillen but he is not available today. I've come here in his stead."

She was startled. "But you *are* Mr Skillen."

"Indeed, I am, Mrs Denley, but my name is Peter Skillen. I'm Paul's twin brother. Since your letter was addressed to 'Mr Skillen', I opened it in error and, realising that there was no possibility that Paul could come here, I took the liberty of doing so myself."

"Oh, I see," said Kitty, uneasily.

"My brother and I have been retained to solve this murder, so we have pooled all the information we've gathered in relation to it. I am therefore fully cognisant of the meetings you've had with Paul. You've been very helpful to him."

"I tried to be, Mr Skillen."

"Why were you so desperate to speak to him?"

"There's been a . . . development," she said, "and it has left me deeply upset."

"Why don't you sit down and tell me all about it?"

329

She took his advice. After waiting for her to sit on the sofa, Peter settled into a chair nearby. He saw how accurate Paul's description of the woman had been and could easily understand why she'd attracted Sir Roger Mellanby. As Peter was appraising her, Kitty was in turn looking closely at him, trying to decide if he was trustworthy. At length, she spoke softly and rapidly.

"Earlier today, my husband called on me. Though I had no wish to speak to him, I didn't feel that I could turn him away. He'd come to accuse me of setting you and your brother on to him, whereas I had nothing to do with it. Well, I'd never even met you so how could I have urged you to question him?"

"Was that the only reason that he called here?"

"No, it wasn't. He told me that he missed me."

"That's understandable, Mrs Denley."

"He even dared to suggest that I might move back in with him," she said, "but that's impossible. In fact, I'm planning to live in Dorset."

"That wouldn't have pleased him."

"It shocked and angered him, Mr Skillen. But that discussion came later. As your brother will have told you, I left the family home because I was wrongly accused of welcoming Sir Roger's advances. In point of fact," she stressed, "he never made any advances and, if he had, I would have ended our acquaintance on the spot."

"I see."

She took a few moments to compose herself, then held his gaze.

"Are you married, Mr Skillen?"

"Yes, I'm very happily married."

"I enjoyed that same state of bliss years ago," she recalled, "but it soon began to fade. We didn't so much as drift apart as let the wine trade come between us. Suffice it to say that I came to see how little we really had in common. However, married couples generally learn to read each other's behaviour."

"My wife certainly does that to me," he said, fondly.

"One sometimes knows exactly what a marital partner is thinking even if he or she is saying something quite different. That's what happened with Hugh. When the news of Sir Roger's death first became known, my immediate response was to fear that my husband had been involved."

"And what did you decide?"

"I felt that I had to challenge him on the subject," she said. "When he called here earlier on, I did just that. Hugh couldn't bring himself to say anything in praise of Sir Roger, of course, but he showed no sign of pleasure or satisfaction in what had occurred. It was as if he wanted to escape any discussion of it."

"What happened?"

"I sensed that he hadn't really come to accuse me of setting you and your brother on to him. He was unusually secretive. I could hear it in his voice and see it in his mannerisms, Hugh was concealing his feelings. So I accused him directly, Mr Skillen," she said. "I looked him straight in the eye and asked him if he had any connection whatsoever with the murder of Sir Roger."

"What was his answer?"

"He didn't reply. But his face gave him away."

"Do you think that he *was* in some way involved?"

"I've been brooding on it for hours, Mr Skillen, and I came to the conclusion that he was. That's why I dashed off that letter. It shook me," she said, seriously. "It shook me to the core. Without realising it, I had been living all that time with a man who is capable of stooping to murder."

Paul Skillen was so certain that Harry Scattergood was somehow involved in the death of Sir Roger Mellanby that he went back to the place in Covent Garden where the murder had occurred. What had Scattergood been doing there and who was his companion? If they had nothing to hide, why had the two of them rushed off? As he went through the possibilities in his head, Paul wondered if he might get help from someone nearby. He walked quickly to the Golden Crown and went in.

Simeon Howlett was in his allotted seat but appeared to be fast asleep. Paul immediately bought the old man his favourite drink and set it down on the table in front of him. Howlett's eyelids fluttered like the wings of a caged bird.

"How wonderful!" he cried. "I was just dreaming about a glass of wine and one has miraculously appeared." After a first sip, he looked up at Paul. "Thank you, kind sir. Have you come to talk about Orsino Price again?"

"No, it's another name that interests me now."

"What is it?"

"Harry Scattergood."

Howlett sniffed. "I've never heard of him. Is he an actor?"

"He's a thief but that often obliges him to take on a false name in order to lead his victims astray. In that sense, he is a kind of actor."

"Why do you seek him?"

"He might have been involved in a recent murder."

"You're not talking about Sir Roger Mellanby, by any chance?"

"Indeed, I am."

"Then you should have been here when Mr Ruddock called in."

"Would that be *Chevy* Ruddock," asked Paul, interest immediately kindled. "He's a tall, gangly man with a face like a large potato."

"That's him."

"He works with the Runners."

"Actually," confided Howlett, "he's working *against* them at the moment. He and I went to a great deal of trouble to obtain some information and it was rejected."

"What sort of information?"

"It concerns Mr Giles Clearwater."

"Tell me more," urged Paul, sitting beside him. "I've heard mention of the man. Who exactly is he?"

"He's a character in *The Provok'd Husband*, a dreadful play that tried to ape Sir John Vanbrugh's sublime comedy, *The Provok'd Wife*. The latter is solid gold while the former is base metal."

"Let me get this correct. Ruddock asked you about someone called Giles Clearwater and you remembered that he belonged in a play. What happened when you told that to Chevy Ruddock?"

"He was overjoyed at first."

"And then?"

"The Runners slapped him down. It's unfair on him. They still believe that Clearwater is a real person. In fact, he wants to claim the reward for telling them where Sir Roger's killer is. It doesn't make sense to me."

"It does to me," said Paul as he realised what had happened. "Chevy Ruddock used his intelligence and they're treating him as if he's a fool. I need to speak to him." He shook Howlett's hand. "Enjoy your drink. You deserve it."

Harry Scattergood went through his plan one more time. Alan Kinnaird repeated it line by line. They were in the hotel where the latter was due to be arrested shortly in the guise of Charles Mifflin. The event had to be choreographed so that it looked convincing. If the Runners simply raided the hotel and seized the man they believed to be the killer, it would be too easy. There had at least to be an attempt at escape and Scattergood had worked out exactly the route to take. Once they'd had a verbal rehearsal, the two of them walked through it, inch by inch. Scattergood's task was to leave the hotel and tell those surrounding it in which room they could surprise the assassin. By the time Yeomans and Hale got there, Kinnaird would have taken to his heels. The chase would then be on.

Pleased with their final practice, Scattergood slapped his friend on the back.

"Well done, Alan!"

"What if I get clear?"

"You won't — there are far too many of them."

"Do you want me to fight back?"

"Have you ever heard of a killer giving in easily?"

"No, Harry. I haven't."

"Then remember one last thing. My name is Giles Clearwater. If you call me 'Harry' in front of them, then our whole plan will fall apart. I'll probably end up in the same cell as you and we wouldn't have a sniff of that reward money."

"I'll do as you say, Mr Clearwater."

"That's better."

Kinnaird bit his lip. "Something still worries me."

"I've told you before. There's *no* chance that the Runners will catch the real killer. We're completely safe."

"But if they *did* arrest him, they'd know I was a fraud."

"It simply can't happen."

"How can you be so sure?"

"Trust me," said Scattergood, brimming with confidence. "The assassin thinks the way I think. When you commit a serious crime, you disappear quickly."

He had read the letter dozens of times and become increasingly agitated. What he was holding was his own death warrant. It had been sent to the man who'd hired him in the first place, and it contained a curt command. Now that he'd served his purpose, the assassin had to be killed. At the end of the letter was a scrawled signature impossible to decipher. Though he pored over it for hours, he couldn't decide exactly what it was. Instead, he came up with four versions of what it might be. Of the quartet, one name was vaguely familiar, but he couldn't remember why.

His gathering fury was matched by his utter frustration. He'd found the name he wanted in the letter, yet the person who wrote it remained tantalisingly out of reach. It was so exasperating that his head began to pound and veins stood out on his temples. Hoping that fresh air might help to clear his brain, he stepped out into the street and strode uncaringly along a busy thoroughfare. Pedestrians, riders and carts brushed past him time and again but he hardly felt them. His mind was elsewhere. Then a wagon rumbled past and hit him with a glancing blow that made him stumble. He started to berate the driver when he noticed the wooden cases stacked on the vehicle. A name was painted on the side of them.

Paul's brief return home had helped to calm Hannah down slightly, but she still remained bruised by the turn of events. A polite invitation from the Prince Regent was very acceptable; a demand that she reached a prompt decision was not. She was never at her best under pressure and, in this case, the pressure had been intense. When she told Dorothea Glenn what had happened, the latter was incensed.

336

"What a terrible thing to do to you, Miss Granville!" she said.

"He's getting impatient."

"That's no excuse. You were entitled to take your time before you made up your mind. Instead of waiting, the Prince Regent has forced you into making a decision that you might regret in time."

"I'm already regretting it, Dorothea."

"What did Mr Skillen say?"

"He was livid. He said I'd been treated disrespect-fully If it had been anyone else but the Prince Regent, he would have confronted him. Paul is very protective of me. Anyway," said Hannah, "that's enough about me and my worries. What have you been doing? When you go off to your room like that, I never know if you've been resting or brooding unnecessarily on what happened."

"I've finally stopped doing that," said Dorothea, determinedly. "After looking back at everything that happened between us, I finally accepted that Orsino was abusing my friendship. It took a huge effort for me to admit that I was so naive but, when I did finally do it, I felt a wonderful sense of relief. Orsino held me in thrall. I haven't lost *him* at all. Someone helped me to escape his clutches. I mourn his death, naturally. Nobody deserves to die so young and in such a brutal manner. But I refuse to let him exercise influence over me from the grave."

"That was a courageous decision to make, Dorothea."

"You were the one who helped me to make it. When I was still in the grip of the illusion that Orsino and I were meant for each other, you let me talk for hours on end, even though you must have had reservations about the friendship that had arisen between us."

"I strove to keep my thoughts to myself."

"I can't thank you enough for that, Miss Granville. All in all," said Dorothea with a weak smile, "it's been a painful experience. However, I feel that it's given me a new strength and a determination to be more careful in the choice of my friends."

"You'll have plenty of those," said Hannah. "Talent such as yours will bring admirers coming to you in droves. That's what happened to me. I had to learn very quickly how to separate true friends from those wishing to exploit me."

"I'm learning that same lesson now."

"Then something good has come out of all that sorrow and remorse you endured." Hannah took a deep breath. "*I'm* the one struggling with sorrow and remorse now. I was foolish to let myself be bullied into accepting that invitation from Brighton Pavilion. I simply don't wish to meet the Prince Regent again."

Chevy Ruddock and William Filbert were part of a group waiting in Bow Street for the summons to arrest the assassin. Ordinarily, the promise of action made Ruddock's blood race. He loved the idea of being involved in a significant event because it would help his chances of promotion. This time the excitement was missing. He felt cheated, ignored and belittled.

"It's wrong, Bill," he said to his friend. "I did what they told me to do and found out that this man is an impostor. They didn't believe me. Mr Yeomans was vicious. It was like being horsewhipped."

"Ignore him, Chevy."

"It was unkind."

"Yeomans and Hale are monsters. Look at today. While we're shivering out here in the cold, they're sitting in the warmth of the chief magistrate's office. It's one rule for them and one for us."

"It makes me feel as if I don't want to do this job any more. Have you ever had that urge to walk away and forget all about the foot patrol?"

"Yes," said Filbert, chortling. "I have it every day."

"I'm serious, Bill. I don't feel appreciated."

"That's the way it is for people like us."

"What do I have to do to make them take notice of me?"

"Don't ask me, Chevy. I take pains to make sure that they *don't* notice me. I keep my head down. It's the best way."

"Well, it wouldn't work for me. I need to have pride in what I do. Where is the pride in being rebuked by Mr Yeomans when I actually uncover evidence of a fraud? Why can't they see that I tried to save them from making a terrible mistake?"

Unable to mask his anger, Ruddock apologised to his friend and moved away from the group. He needed to be alone for a while.

★ ★ ★

Paul had ridden to Bow Street in the hope that he might find Ruddock there. After tethering his horse, he'd crept up to the group and was in time to hear the latter's complaints. As soon as Ruddock drifted away from the other members of the foot patrol, Paul moved in and took him by the arm.

"I need to speak to you in private," he whispered.

Ruddock was alarmed. "I can't talk to you, Mr Skillen. You're our rival. Mr Yeomans will kill me if he sees me with you."

"That's why we need to be out of sight," said Paul.

He took Ruddock around the corner, then tried to still his companion's fears.

"I'm on your side, Chevy," he said. "I've spoken to Simeon Howlett and I admire what you did. Giles Clearwater is an impostor."

Ruddock was thrilled. "*You* believe it as well?"

"I know it to be true."

"Oh, it's so kind of you to say so, Mr Skillen. After I was shouted at by Mr Yeomans and Mr Hale, I began to wonder if I'd made a mistake. But I haven't. You found out the truth as well."

"Why are you all waiting here?"

"We're supposed to be on our way to arrest the man who killed Sir Roger Mellanby. The assassin has been tracked by this so-called Giles Clearwater. But how can he do that when he's just a character in a bad play?"

"I think I know the explanation for that," said Paul. He heard the rasping voice of Micah Yeomans calling

340

his men together. "You'd better go, Chevy. Don't mention that you saw me and don't be downhearted."

"Why not?"

"I have a feeling that we're going to be proved right."

Standing outside the hotel, Harry Scattergood sent a message to Bow Street and awaited the response. He was confident that the Runners would come in force. Two floors above him, Alan Kinnaird was watching from a window so that he knew exactly when to attempt his escape. He'd put his trust in his friend and, despite the tremors he was feeling, he believed that everything would go as planned. At the end of it all was a large amount of money shared between him and Scattergood. Keeping his mind on that helped to drive away any niggling doubts.

Yeomans and Hale had hired two carriages to take five men apiece to the hotel. When they left Bow Street, it never occurred to any of them to look over their shoulders. Had they done so, they'd have seen Paul Skillen trailing them on his horse. After a dash through the streets, they clattered to a halt at the point where the man they knew as Giles Clearwater was waiting. Yeomans jumped out of the first carriage and ran over to him. Hale was with him.

"Is he still inside?" he asked.

"You have my word on it," replied Scattergood.

"Is he alone?"

"Oh, yes. I'm certain of that."

"Where exactly is he?"

"He's in room 29. It's on the second floor."

"Deploy the men, Alfred."

"I will," said Hale.

Watched by Paul from his vantage point nearby, Hale stationed the men in pairs around the four sides of the hotel, then rushed back to rejoin Yeomans. With Scattergood leading them, the Runners went into the hotel and rushed across to the counter. Yeomans wasted no time on explanations. He simply demanded a master key that would open the door of the relevant room. The manager handed it over without protest. The three of them headed for the staircase. They crept up the steps until they came to the second floor. A narrow passageway confronted them. Leading the way, Yeomans took out a pistol from his belt. Hale had his own weapon. The trio tried to move as silently as they could. When they reached the room they wanted, Yeomans inserted the master key gently into the lock.

After checking that Hale was ready, he suddenly turned the key, flung the door open and charged in with his gun at the ready. Hale followed suit. But it was all to no avail. There was nobody there. They searched under the bed and looked in the wardrobe, but it was evident that the place was empty.

"The bird has flown," said Scattergood. "Get after him!"

Chevy Ruddock, meanwhile, was lurking outside the rear entrance of the hotel with Filbert. After lighting his pipe, the latter inhaled the tobacco.

"It will be the same as usual, Chevy," he said, rancorously. "We do the work and they get all the bleeding credit. We're the ones who'll have to catch this devil and he'll be dangerous."

"No, he won't," said Ruddock.

"But he's an assassin. That means he kills people."

"He's working with a crook named Giles Clearwater. That means he's not an assassin at all. I don't really know what's going on, Bill, but one thing is certain. We're *not* going to arrest the man who shot Sir Roger Mellanby dead."

"Yes, we are."

"Mr Skillen agrees with me."

"Eh?"

"I spoke to him earlier."

Filbert frowned. "Do you think that was wise, Chevy?"

"He's the one person who believes I'm right. Peter or Paul Skillen — I don't know which one it was — is clever enough to work it out. We're being tricked, Bill."

"Let me ask you one question —"

But he had no time to do so. The back door of the hotel suddenly opened and Kinnaird hurtled out, colliding with the two men and forcing them apart. Ruddock immediately gave chase, but Filbert was winded by the power of the impact. A hue and cry developed with all the men stationed outside the hotel joining in the chase through the crowded streets. Eager to take part in the manhunt, Paul kicked his horse into action. He was soon well ahead of the chasing pack.

Kinnaird was fleet-footed but he couldn't outrun the pursuit for long. Now that Scattergood's plan had been activated, his friend was having qualms about it. Being arrested by a gang of men from the foot patrol meant that he would probably be pummelled until he lost consciousness. He might be seriously wounded and unable to make the escape from custody that Scattergood had promised. With the dangers starting to outweigh the rewards, Kinnaird opted for a change of decision. The plan had to be ditched. He was running to save his life.

Lungs bursting and legs starting to ache, he did everything he could to escape, twisting and turning, diving down lanes and plunging at one point into a market and causing mayhem amongst the stalls. It all served to put him well ahead of Ruddock and the others, but he sensed that he still wasn't safe.

Paul rode at a steady canter, keeping the fugitive in sight from his elevated position but giving him time to run until he was completely exhausted. As it was, the man was visibly slowing and beginning to stumble. When he saw his quarry turn into the courtyard of an inn, Paul slowed his horse to a trot. Caution was needed. The man would certainly be armed and was unlikely to surrender without a fight. The first thing that Paul did as he entered the courtyard was to peer through one of the windows. The bar was quite empty and there was no sign of a panting newcomer. After moving to a second window to see the room from a different angle, he accepted that the man had gone to ground elsewhere. The only possibility left was that he'd dived into the stables.

Dismounting from his horse, Paul led him by the bridle as if he were a patron of the inn wishing to leave the animal in a safe place. As he found him an empty stall, he talked affectionately to the horse and got a responsive whinny. In the gloomy interior, there was a compound of smells. The stink of sweat on horseflesh blended with the stench of manure and was tempered by the aroma of fresh hay. But there was something else that Paul's nostrils picked up. It was the odour of fear. The man was there. When he listened carefully, Paul could hear his laboured breathing. Pretending to leave, he tethered his horse and gave it a friendly slap on the rump before going out. Instead of walking to the inn, however, he waited outside the door.

The sound of movement inside the stables was almost instantaneous. Paul could hear the sound of feet descending a ladder followed by the rustle of straw. He guessed that the man was going to steal one of the horses to make his escape. First of all, he'd check to see that the coast was clear. It was the moment for which Paul was waiting. The second a head poked out from the stables, he came alive, hurling himself forward and dragging the man out into the courtyard. The element of surprise gave Paul an initial advantage but, even though he'd been fatigued by the chase, the man found reserves of strength and fought back. They grappled, punched, kicked and did everything possible to get the upper hand. Paul yelled in disgust when the man spat in his face. He reacted angrily, getting in a relay of punches to the body before stamping hard on the man's foot to send him off balance. Using his shoulder, Paul knocked him to the ground, then dived on top of him, letting his weight hold his adversary on his back. He was now able to get in a series of powerful hooks to the head. Blood was soon cascading down the fugitive's face, getting into his eyes and blurring his vision. Feeling the resistance weakening, Paul summoned up his strength for a decisive punch to the jaw. There was a grunt of pain and Kinnaird became too groggy to fight on.

Paul got to his feet and lifted his prisoner up by his hair.

"What are you and Harry Scattergood up to?" he demanded.

When he got to the warehouse, the assassin had the reassuring sensation that he'd found the man at last. He took out the letter again and looked at the signature. Of the four guesses he'd made at deciphering it, it was the first — Denley. The name was painted on the doors ahead of him in large letters. From inside the warehouse, he could hear the sounds of crates being loaded and bottles rattling. Judging by the size of the premises, the wine dealer was a very successful businessman. The assassin resolved to deprive him of more than his wealth. One last hurdle faced him. He had to find a way to get close to Hugh Denley.

Losing the man they'd chased so hard was a painful experience, but having to admit their failure to Yeomans

346

was even more agonising. As they dribbled back to the hotel in disgrace, he gave each and every one of them a roasting. The moment Yeomans finished, Hale took over to add more scorn and humiliation. One man had somehow managed to elude all eight of them. They'd never be allowed to forget it.

For his part, Harry Scattergood was mystified. He'd given strict instructions to Kinnaird to be taken prisoner after a scuffle with the posse. What had happened to him? Had he lost his nerve and bolted? Had he betrayed his friend and gone into hiding? One conclusion was unavoidable. The well-rehearsed plan had been summarily abandoned. There'd be no reward for the capture of the false assassin.

Having chastised his men, Yeomans now turned his fire on Scattergood, accusing him of calling them too late to arrest the man in his hotel room.

"This is *your* fault," he bellowed.

"It's the fault of your useless men," retorted Scattergood. "They let the rogue slip through their fingers. You should train them properly."

"Don't you tell me how to do my job."

"Somebody needs to, Mr Yeomans."

The row quickly accelerated with insults galore from both parties. It was not only entertaining for Yeomans' men, it was a salve for their wounded pride. They were so absorbed in watching the fiery debate that they didn't notice the two people approaching. One was Paul Skillen, leading his horse with one hand and pulling a blood-covered Alan Kinnaird with the other.

The prisoner's wrists were tied securely behind his back.

It was Chevy Ruddock who finally spotted them.

"He's been caught," he yelled. "Mr Skillen has apprehended him."

"What was *he* doing here?" cried Yeomans, breaking away from his argument. "The assassin was ours until we let him escape."

"That was your second mistake, Micah," teased Paul. "The first one was in assuming that this man I caught had anything whatsoever to do with Sir Roger's murder. He's no assassin," he went on. "He's a confederate of Mr Giles Clearwater."

"I've never laid eyes on this fellow before," said Scattergood, indignantly.

"Don't believe a word that he says."

"The credit for the arrest shouldn't go to me," confessed Paul. "The real hero is Chevy Ruddock." All eyes turned to their colleague. "He was the person who discovered the truth and he was cruelly ignored by those above him."

"Quite rightly," shouted Yeomans.

"I say the same," added Hale, defiantly.

"Then let me show you how easily you were tricked," said Paul, drawing his sword in a flash and holding it at Scattergood's throat. "Don't move an inch, Harry, or I'll cut your Adam's apple out and toss it to the dogs."

"You are very much mistaken, sir," said Scattergood, trying to brazen it out. "My name is Giles Clearwater and I'll be taking an action against you for this grotesque slander."

348

"He *can't* be Giles Clearwater," said Ruddock. "I proved it."

"Indeed, you did, Chevy," agreed Paul. "The one thing you didn't realise was that the man who purloined that name was no less a person than Harry Scattergood." There was general amazement. "He persuaded his friend, Kinnaird, to *pretend* to be the assassin so that they could claim the reward."

"This is absolute nonsense," said Scattergood, haughtily.

"It's no use, Harry," warned Kinnaird. "Skillen knows everything."

Scattergood tried to get away, but Paul was ready, sticking out a foot to trip him up then standing over him with the point of his sword at his captive's throat once more. Scattergood was hissing like a snake.

"Since you first found out that he was an impostor," said Paul, looking at Ruddock, "*you* should have the honour of arresting him." There was loud applause for Ruddock. "As for the rest of you, don't always respect your leaders. Next time they criticise you, remind them that they were completely taken in by Harry Scattergood, one of the wiliest criminals in the whole of London."

Yeomans and Hale cringed in the face of mocking laughter.

Before he accepted her judgement, Peter had questioned Kitty Denley at length. She was able to quote several instances of her husband vowing to kill Sir Roger Mellanby. After his embarrassing defeat in the duel, Hugh Denley had been even more determined to strike back at the politician. His wife knew for a fact that her husband had paid someone to gather information about the Radical Dandy's private life. What Kitty couldn't be certain about was whether or not Denley had been acting alone or in concert with one of the politician's many enemies in Parliament.

Armed with the evidence she'd given him, Peter went to the wine merchant's premises and asked to see him. Denley reluctantly agreed and soon wished that he hadn't done so because his visitor was asking unsettling questions.

"Do you admit that you had Sir Roger spied on?" asked Peter.

"That's a wild accusation, Mr Skillen."

"It was made by Mrs Denley."

"My wife would say anything to get me into trouble."

"She was able to give me a firm assurance that she overheard you giving instructions to someone to pry into Sir Roger's private life. Either you did or you didn't. Which one is it?"

"Kitty was mistaken in what she overheard."

"So you do admit that instructions were given?"

"I admit nothing."

"You went to see your wife earlier today."

"Yes, I did."

"Why was that?"

"My principal objective was to complain about you and your brother. I told Kitty that I resented the way that she'd unleashed the pair of you on to me without any reason to do so."

"I never even met your wife, Mr Denley I came at my brother's suggestion in the hope that I might get to the truth."

"Then the truth is that I had nothing whatsoever to do with the assassination, though I'm happy to confess that it brought me a great deal of satisfaction. I loathed everything that Mellanby stood for. Whoever silenced that dangerous voice is a public benefactor."

"Does that mean you condone the crime of murder?"

"No, of course I don't."

"You sound as if you want the killer to get away with it," said Peter. "How much did you pay him?"

Denley blushed. They were in his office, a large, well-appointed room with a selection of bottles of wine displayed on a table. A series of framed awards hung on the walls. The firm was clearly a leader in the market. Close to the window was an exquisite sofa for occasions when Denley needed to relax. In a corner was a sizeable safe on top of which were some wine goblets.

"I must ask you to leave, Mr Skillen," said Denley, pulling himself up to his full height. "If you refuse to do so, I'll have you removed."

"There was another reason why you visited your wife, wasn't there?"

"The door is behind you."

"You not only told Mrs Denley that you missed her, you were clearly hoping to effect some sort of reconciliation in due course."

"That's a private matter."

"Your wife was shocked that you should even have raised the issue. It was only after you'd left that she realised what you were trying to do. You were anxious to lure her back into the family home to restore the impression of normality. It would put to bed all those rumours about an attachment between your wife and Sir Roger Mellanby. Moreover, it would divert any suspicion of your involvement in Sir Roger's death away from you."

"This is insufferable," said Denley. "I want you out of here."

Before he could even walk towards the door, however, it opened to admit a man who locked the door behind him, then pulled out a pistol from under his coat. He moved it from one to the other.

"Which one of you is Hugh Denley?"

"I am," said the wine merchant, nervously

"Then I want the rest of my money."

"Who are you?"

"I'm the person you hired to kill Sir Roger Mellanby," said the other, "and I obeyed my instructions. Instead of paying me my full fee, you ordered someone to have me killed."

"I did nothing of the kind."

"That person is no longer alive, and neither is the one who tried to shoot me dead in St James's Park."

"Please believe me," cried Denley. "I don't know what you're talking about."

"Yes, you do," said Peter.

"Keep out of this," ordered the assassin.

"But I came here to accuse Mr Denley of having blood on his hands."

"He'll have it all over him by the time I've finished with him. Stand back," he added as Peter took a step towards him. "I can shoot just as well with either hand."

He produced a second pistol from inside his coat and pointed towards Peter who took a step backwards. Denley was trembling with fear but Peter remained calm and watchful. He was surprised how young and elegant the assassin was.

"Open that safe," demanded the newcomer.

"You're making a terrible mistake," said Denley. "Whoever told you that I was implicated in the murder was lying."

"The person who told me was *you*."

"That's impossible."

"I have your letter to prove it."

He tucked one of the pistols under his arm so that he could take the letter out of his pocket. When he'd slapped it down on the desk, he grabbed the other pistol again and kept it trained on Peter. Denley was frozen with horror. He couldn't even bear to look at the letter.

"Read it out," snarled the assassin. "Pick it up and read it out."

Shaking all over, Denley picked up the letter and forced himself to look at it. His manner suddenly changed completely. Relief flooded through him.

"I didn't write this," he said.

"Don't lie to me," warned the assassin. "It has your name on it — Denley."

"Yes," interjected Peter, realising what must have happened, "but it may not be *Mr* Denley. Unless I'm mistaken, that letter was signed by his wife."

"It was," confirmed Denley. He opened a drawer. "I'll show you. I have other letters from my wife." Pulling out a sheaf of correspondence, he picked out a letter. "Look at her signature. It's identical to the one in your letter."

Putting one pistol under his arm again, the man took the missive from him. It was the moment that Peter had been hoping for and he reacted quickly. While the assassin was momentarily distracted, he grabbed one of the bottles of wine and smashed it against the back of his head, causing the bottle to shatter and send wine and shards of glass everywhere. It also made the man drop the pistol under his arm and pull the trigger on the other one, firing into the sofa before releasing the weapon from his powerless fingers. Denley was aghast and shrunk back but Peter knew that the assassin was not finished yet. The man had been stunned but was still able to stagger. Ignoring the broken glass, Peter caught hold of him and flung him against a wall, taking all the breath out of him. Before the assassin could even begin to fight back, Peter felled him with an uppercut. He picked up the pistol that was still loaded and stood over him.

"I owe you an apology, Mr Denley," he said.

"No apology is needed. You just saved my life."

"After accusing you of something you didn't do, I made a terrible mess of your carpet and ruined a bottle of your best wine."

"I'll gladly give you a crate of that vintage, Mr Skillen."

"All that I crave is the chance to retrieve that bullet from your sofa. It's an unusual memento," said Peter, "but — along with the reward money for capturing the assassin — it's one that I'll treasure."

Paul, meanwhile, was back at the shooting gallery, regaling his friends with the story of how he'd arrested the man who'd been Scattergood's assistant and exposed their fraudulent plan. Charlotte was delighted, Huckvale was amused and Ackford shook with laughter.

"That's wonderful news, Paul," he said. "Yeomans and Hale will have red faces for weeks."

"They weren't the only dupes, Gully," said Paul. "The chief magistrate was also fooled. We have to take our hats off to Harry Scattergood. He made all three of them look stupid."

"But he makes his living as a thief," Huckvale pointed out. "Why did he turn himself into a gentleman?"

"He thought there'd be more profit in it, Jem."

"Wait a moment," said Charlotte, thinking of the consequences of the deception. "Harry might have claimed the reward but this friend of his, Kinnaird, would have finished up at the gallows."

"They would have worked out how to avoid that fate," said Paul. "We all know that Harry is a master at escaping. He'll have devised a way to whisk Kinnaird out of Newgate long before his appointment with the hangman. That's the beauty of this situation. The Runners may have the satisfaction of locking up the two of them but how long will they stay behind bars?"

"A couple of days at most," said Ackford. "Then Harry will get the pair of them out of their cells with those magic fingers of his. There'll be another reward offered for his capture. You and Peter will have to nab him yet again."

Kitty Denley was at first pleased when Peter arrived back at her house, then she saw the flecks of red on his face and the ugly wet patches on his clothing. She stared at him in disbelief.

"What happened, Mr Skillen?"

"A bottle of wine was smashed in your husband's office," he explained. "Some of it went over me and a few pieces of glass hit me in the face."

"You need to see a doctor."

"I'm quite unharmed, I assure you. I just wanted to tell you what happened."

"Did you challenge him?" she asked.

"Yes, I did."

"What did he say?"

"He wasn't really in a position to say anything, Mrs Denley, because I'd knocked him to the floor."

Kitty was astonished. "Did my husband attack you?"

356

"No, he was cowering behind his desk. The person I'm talking about is the one hired to kill Sir Roger Mellanby. He was the man I overpowered before he could add your husband's name to his list of victims. Don't look so worried," he added as she backed away in horror. "Your husband survived unhurt. As for the man determined to kill him, I made sure that he was in safe custody before I came here."

"Wasn't Hugh arrested as well?"

"There was no point. He had nothing to do with the murder — though I hardly need to tell you that, do I? You only sent me there to shift any suspicion away from yourself. Unfortunately, your plan failed."

"What plan?" she asked, desperately trying to regain her composure.

"The one you devised to blame someone else for your crime."

"I don't understand a word that you're saying, Mr Skillen."

"Then perhaps you should look at your *own* words instead."

Taking out the letter that the assassin had been carrying, he held it in front of her so that she could read her own writing. Kitty let out a cry of anguish and put her hands to her face. Peter waited until she'd got over the initial shock and slowly lowered her hands. She tried to muster some dignity.

"That letter was not written by me," she claimed.

"Your husband swore that it had been."

"Exactly — he knows my hand well enough to copy it."

"You've been found out, Mrs Denley. Blatant lies are no use to you any more. Your husband had good reason to despise Sir Roger, but you were the one with the real urge to have him killed."

"That's not true — I loved him!"

"Unfortunately, he didn't return that love."

"Yes, he did," she cried. There was a long pause before she spoke again. "For a while, anyway — then things changed."

"He promised to marry you, didn't he?" said Peter. "It's the only thing that could have made you leave your husband and face public censure as a result. You were counting on the fact that Sir Roger's wife would soon die and that — after you'd secured a divorce — you would eventually become the second Lady Mellanby." He saw her blanch. "I've been to the family home in Nottinghamshire. I don't mean this unkindly, Mrs Denley, but I don't think that Sir Roger felt for one second that you might belong there. It was a cruel promise. He lied to you."

"That's why he deserved to die," she cried, abandoning her vain attempt at innocence. "He deceived me and that was not the only example of it. Because I was married, it was not easy to arrange a rendezvous with him. What I didn't know at the time was that if *I* was unavailable, he'd find someone else to share his bed. His preference was for actresses, the younger the better. Sir Roger was an ogre."

"Is that why you had him killed outside the Covent Garden Theatre?"

"Yes, it is. He was besotted with someone named Hannah Granville," she said with distaste. "She was appearing in a play there. When he returned to London, I knew that the first place he'd go to was that theatre. After the performance, he'd rush around to the stage door with her other 'admirers' — for want of a better word — and offer her the blandishments he once whispered into *my* ear."

"You must have felt utterly wronged," said Peter.

"I was in pain, Mr Skillen, absolute agony."

"Having someone shot dead is not an acceptable way to deal with your suffering."

She bared her teeth. "I got what I wanted."

"Then you must now let the law take its course."

Kitty Denley sagged. When she realised what lay in store for her, she began to tremble. The deep satisfaction she'd felt at the death of her former lover had now been replaced by naked fear. Peter took a firm hold on her arm.

"You'll have to come with me," he said.

"Must I?" she pleaded. "Don't you have any pity for me?"

"None at all, I fear."

"But I was the *victim*."

"That thought should console you as you walk to the gallows."

Holding her tight, he marched her to the front door.

Paul rode back home to pass on the good news. When he entered the house, he noticed a difference but was unable to decide what it was. He was welcomed by Hannah with a warm embrace.

"What's happened?" he asked.

"Dorothea has gone. I was glad that we could help her but there is a sense of release now that she's departed."

"Why did she leave?"

"She's gone back home, Paul. She felt that the best thing for her was a break from acting and has withdrawn from the production of *Measure for Measure*. It was a bold decision — and a wise one, in my view."

"As long as she's in London, she'll be brooding about Orsino Price."

"He won't dominate her mind quite so much in Lincolnshire. When she feels ready to come back, I promised Dorothea that I'd speak to some theatre managers on her behalf. She's too good an actress to lose from the profession. But what's been happening?" she went on, appraising him. "You seem to be in a happy mood."

"I'm in an exultant mood, Hannah. I made an important arrest today."

He told her about the way that he'd been involved in the chase after Kinnaird and how he'd helped to expose Scattergood's fraudulent scheme. His major news, however, concerned his brother.

"Peter did even better than me," he freely acknowledged. "He not only met and overpowered the assassin, he also arrested the person who hired him."

"Was it one of those politicians?"

"No, it wasn't. In fact, it wasn't a man at all. It was Mrs Denley. She's very resourceful. Having been seduced by Sir Roger Mellanby with the promise of one day becoming his wife, she found out that she was not the only woman in London familiar with his bed. What galled her most, Peter said, was that her rivals were all much younger than her. You can imagine how she felt," he continued. "What are those lines from one of Congreve's plays? *Heav'n has no rage, like love to hatred turn'd/Nor Hell a fury, like a woman scorn'd* — I couldn't have put it better myself."

"So the Radical Dandy was simply a philanderer?"

"No, Hannah, give the man his due. What happened in his private life doesn't invalidate his achievements in the political sphere. He gave a voice to people who are unjustly denied one, and will always be remembered for that. When he stood up to speak, he was utterly fearless."

"I wish that I could be like that," she said.

"And so you shall."

"What do you mean?"

"You're the finest actress of your generation and you live with someone who adores you. I'm not letting you be at the beck and call of a fat, ugly, lascivious man who thinks that he can compel you to do anything he wants."

"But I've already accepted his invitation."

"You were forced into doing so, Hannah. That's deplorable."

"Well, I can't get out of it now."

"Oh yes, you can," insisted Paul. "Show your mettle. Dorothea may have pulled out of *Measure for Measure* but you haven't. When rehearsals start on Monday, you will be Isabella. Send a letter to Brighton Pavilion to explain that you're unable to go there. I'll deliver it by hand and offer that petition to the Prince Regent at the same time. Both documents will give him a profound shock."

She was baffled. "Why am *I* unable to be there in person?"

"I told you. You're Isabella now."

"So?"

"It would be improper. You are about to become a novice in a nunnery."

Hugging each other, the two of them laughed happily.